THE EMERALD TABLET

The Forgotten Worlds
Book 1

PJ Hoover

Children's Brains are Yummy Books
Dallas, Texas

The Emerald Tablet
The Forgotten Worlds
Book 1

Text Copyright © 2008 by PJ Hoover

Hardcover Edition 2008
First Paperback Edition 2012

CIP data available.

Children's Brains are Yummy Books
Dallas, Texas
www.cbaybooks.com

For CPSIA compliance, see our website
at www.cbaybooks.com.

Pinted in the United States of America.

ISBN: 978-1-933767-19-2
ISBN: 978-1-933767-16-1 (ebook)

For Riley, who always believes in me.

Table of Contents

1. The Mirror Comes to Life. 1
2. The Picture Is a Teleporter 7
3. The Kiosk Checks in Benjamin 12
4. The World According to Proteus. 22
5. The Fast, Green Thing on Benjamin's Shoulder 29
6. Andy Wants to Visit the Ruling Hall. 33
7. Jack Gets Them in Trouble. 39
8. Once Again, They Leave the Tour. 45
9. Hunters Don't Use Keys 58
10. Telekinetically Speaking 68
11. A Series of Unusual Classes 73
12. Guys and Telegnosis 80
13. Astronomy Doesn't Put Everyone to Sleep 86
14. The Sky Collapses. 92
15. The World Is a Ball. 103
16. Morpheus's Secret 114
17. They Plan to Break the Rules 123
18. One Day in Bangkok 130
19. An Agent from the Other Side. 142
20. The Teachers Play With a Toy 149
21. Heidi Drags Them to a Museum 157
22. The Records Department Is Really Boring 167
23. The Universal Travel Agent 176
24. Xanadu Is Not Just in a Poem 182

25. Inside the Fountain 193
26. The Forest Is Haunted 201
27. The Owner of the Universal Travel Agent 205
28. It's a Good Thing Benjamin Has the Keys 212
29. Benjamin Shows Off 220
30. Benjamin Breaks His Leg 229
31. Benjamin Loses the Keys 238
32. Practicing the Orb Pays Off 250
33. Hair Standing on End 261
34. Benjamin Faces the Truth 272
35. And as Always, Life Must Go On 281

The Mirror Comes to Life

When Benjamin Holt saw his mom disappear into a pin-prick of light, he shouldn't have been surprised; his life was already weird. What with him and his best friend Andy constantly arguing over what was better—telepathy or telekinesis—he knew he didn't lead a normal life. But vanishing into thin air—this hit the top of the freak-out scale.

Hidden behind his bedroom door, Benjamin stared at the spot where she'd been. And then he looked at the picture—the one she'd had her palm on as she disappeared. They'd had the velvet tiger picture forever, and, to the best of Benjamin's knowledge, it had never before sucked anyone else into nothingness.

Three minutes went by. Still no mom. Benjamin walked over and tapped the hideous tiger picture with his finger. Nothing. And so he dared to put his own palm on it.

This is when Benjamin decided he must've been dreaming, because when he looked down, his feet were still firmly planted on the ground. And so he decided since he was still sleeping to go back to bed.

No sooner had Benjamin gone back to his room and crawled into bed, his mirror started talking. "Benjamin Holt?" the unfamiliar voice asked. "Do I have the right house?"

Benjamin bolted upright. He hadn't had time to fall back asleep, so he knew the voice couldn't be a new dream. But he'd for sure dreamed the picture thing, so the mirror just must be more of the same. That made sense. He pinched himself—hard—to check, and it hurt. Not a dream.

"Benjamin Holt, get up!" the voice said.

Benjamin threw the covers off and walked to the mirror. If the thing didn't shut up, he'd toss it out the window—and then get some sleep. But then he actually looked at the mirror and jumped when he saw a man looking back at him.

"What in the world?" Benjamin asked, taking a few steps—maybe ten steps—backwards.

"Ah, there you are. Why are you still sleeping? Today is the big day," the man said, as if that explained everything.

"What big day?" Benjamin asked, pinching himself again. It still hurt.

"Why your first day of summer school!" the man announced, grinning from ear to ear.

"Summer school!" Benjamin exclaimed, now continuously pinching his arm. Not only did it hurt, it started turning red. But Benjamin didn't care. His mom had vanished into thin air. There was a strange man in his mirror. And to top it off, the man thought Benjamin was going to spend his summer in a classroom.

But the man kept smiling. "My name is Proteus Ajax, and I am here to invite you to summer school."

"I'm not going to summer school," Benjamin replied, crossing his arms over his chest.

The man crossed his own arms and stared back. His wide smile began to look less like a smile and more like clenched teeth. "It's not really a request. And please don't be tardy."

Benjamin stared but had no idea what to say.

"Now, if there's nothing else, I really must get on to the next student," Proteus Ajax said.

"What do you mean—the next student? Do you mean Andy?" Benjamin asked, feeling just the slightest glimmer of hope that his best friend might have to suffer too.

Proteus looked down, then back up. "I have already notified Andy Grow. I'll be seeing you shortly." And without another word, his face vanished.

The mirror once again reflected Benjamin's image, and he noticed his gaping mouth. Shutting it, he studied the mirror, touching it with his right hand and then with both hands. He lifted it away from the wall and looked behind it. Nothing unusual back there. But the velvet tiger picture which sucked his mom up had looked normal too.

Did his parents know about this summer school thing? Had they been the ones to sign him up? And did they know his mirror could talk? For the first day of summer break, things were not going at all like Benjamin had planned. He had no intention of wasting his entire break in summer school. And why had he and Andy been signed up in the first place? With a sigh, he opened his bedroom door; he needed to talk to his parents right away.

Benjamin headed downstairs, dodging toy cars flying through the air. As with any morning, chaos had erupted. Becca, his eight month old sister, was crying, and Derrick and Douglas, his twin five year old brothers, were doing what they always did. Telekinesis. They were always levitating something—Benjamin's homework or Becca's rattle. One time they even levitated eggs. Nobody liked to talk about that. Today it was toy cars—no less than five each—racing around the room. It still irked Benjamin how good they were at telekinesis. When he'd been their age, he'd hardly been able to lift one—and that was on a good day.

Benjamin grabbed one of the cars out of the air. "You guys know you're not supposed to levitate stuff when Mom's not around."

"Who's levitating stuff?"

Benjamin's spun around when his mom walked into the room, and all the other cars immediately hit the floor. So he must've imagined her vanishing.

His mom looked down at the pileup and then looked over at the twins. They shrank under her gaze. And then the excuses started.

"It wasn't our fault," Douglas said.

"Yeah. Not our fault," Derrick added. "We just started playing car chase, and Benji walked in and ruined everything."

"How many times do I have to tell you not to levitate things when I'm not around?" she said. "Telekinesis is not something normal five year old boys can do!"

4

"But..." Douglas began.

His mom put up her hand, stopping Douglas mid-excuse. She looked at the cars on the floor, and they lifted up, gliding over to the basket where a hundred more were kept and dropped in.

"*What am I going to do with them?*" Benjamin heard his mom think as she shook her head. "All right, Benjamin, into the kitchen. We don't have that long," she said aloud, pushing him from behind.

Benjamin's dad and Joey Duncan sat at the kitchen table, but when Benjamin and his mom walked in, Joey got up. The only things Benjamin knew about Joey Duncan were he worked with Benjamin's dad and he was the coolest person in the world. It wasn't just the ponytail and special powers just like Benjamin's; it was that he never minded when Benjamin used his powers around him.

"*All I'm saying is that if the escape rate doesn't go down, things are going to change.*" Benjamin heard Joey's telepathic comment clearly.

"What escape rate?" Benjamin replied audibly.

Benjamin felt a mind block go up in the room, and no one spoke. At least not aloud. Nor could he hear any more telepathic thoughts. He was almost thirteen now. Why did all the grownups still exclude him from conversations? He wasn't a baby anymore.

"What escape rate?" Benjamin repeated.

The mind block went down.

"Oh, it's nothing," Joey replied. "I came over to give you a going away present."

Before Benjamin could say that he had no intention of going away, Joey telekinetically tossed an object to him. It stopped in front of Benjamin and rotated in the air.

The sphere was multilayered and constantly changed colors. The pieces didn't look like they could even be turned by hand, and, just for kicks, Benjamin telekinetically reached out and flipped one.

"What is it?" Benjamin asked. He'd never seen anything like it before and was pretty sure Joey hadn't bought it at a Wal-Mart.

"It's a Kinetic Orb," Joey said. "Kind of like a Rubik's Cube, but for smart people."

"Wow, thanks," Benjamin replied. "But I'm not going anywhere." But even as he said it, Benjamin knew, deep in the pit of his stomach, he was. He knew there was no getting out of this summer school thing, whatever it was.

"Yeah, whatever," Joey replied. "Anyway, I thought you might like it. The trick is not only to solve all the phases, but to learn to do it with your eyes closed."

"How in the world do I do that?" Benjamin asked.

"If I told you, it would take all the fun away," Joey replied with a smile. "Anyway, have a great summer, and I'll see you when you get back."

The Picture Is a Teleporter

Benjamin looked over and saw his duffle bag packed and by the stairs.

"I'm assuming you've spoken with Proteus Ajax," his mom said.

Once again, he shouldn't have been, but Benjamin was surprised to hear her say the name. "How do you know Proteus Ajax? Was he in your mirror too?"

"No, I met him this morning in person."

The image of his mom disappearing into a pinprick of light filled his mind. "Where? In the picture?"

"You weren't supposed to see me," she said. "You were supposed to be asleep."

"So I wasn't dreaming!" he said. "I knew it. But why was Proteus Ajax in our ugly picture?"

"He wasn't," Benjamin's mom said. "Our picture is a teleporter."

"A what?"

"A teleporter," his dad said. "It transports an object from

one place to another."

"Our picture teleports stuff?" Benjamin asked. "Like what?"

"Well, it teleported me this morning." His mom laughed. "And it's going to teleport you in a few minutes."

Benjamin's jaw dropped open, and he wasn't sure if it was because he had a teleporter in his house or because he'd be using it in a few minutes. He decided it was a combination of the two.

"I thought you'd be surprised," she replied.

"So where will I teleport to?" he asked. "I'm not going to summer school." One last effort. Even though at this point he kind of wanted to use the teleporter, even if it did mean summer school.

"Yes, Benjamin, you are," his dad replied. "And you're going to another world."

"Another world!" Seriously. Maybe his parents were playing a trick on him. "Is that all?"

"Not quite," his mom said. "You're not really human. But that's all we're going to tell you."

Benjamin threw a few last minute items into his backpack, still waiting for the punch line of the joke. His parents had told him nothing else and sworn him to secrecy, but Derrick and Douglas had pestered him nonetheless. He hated to leave them and Becca, but, at the same time, some new world you could teleport to would have to be pretty cool, right?

Even with his excitement, when he reached the family room, Benjamin actually had to fight to keep tears from springing to his eyes. He squatted down to the twin's level. "You guys be good," he said. Derrick started to cry, and Douglas looked just on the verge.

"But we're gonna miss you," Derrick said, wiping tears from his eyes.

Douglas suddenly seemed to remember something. "We have a going away present for you." He pulled a wad of balled up paper towels from his pocket. It had the letter 'D' written on it twice. "Here you go," he said. "We wrapped it ourselves."

Benjamin took the small present. "I wonder what it is."

"It's a car," Derrick blurted out before Benjamin could open it.

"You're not supposed to tell him," Douglas said. "Now, it's not a surprise."

"It's still a surprise," Benjamin replied. "I don't know which car it is."

"It's our favorite black police car," Derrick told Benjamin.

Benjamin unwrapped the paper towels. "Wow! Thanks! But won't you guys miss it?" he asked, remembering the telekinetic car chase.

"Yeah, but we talked about it, and we want you to have it," Derrick said.

Benjamin stood up and put the car in his front pocket. Next he picked up Becca. She smiled and kicked her legs. "Go tell Mommy if the twins levitate stuff. And go tell mommy if they take your toys." He shot his best stern look at the boys. He then hugged Becca and kissed her, thinking about how much she'd grow in eight weeks.

"Well, we better get you going," Benjamin's mom said after his dad had gone out front with the kids.

"Won't you be teleporting with me?" Benjamin asked. He liked how the word sounded.

"No, you'll be on your own."

"What if I get lost?" Benjamin asked.

"You won't get lost."

They walked upstairs and stood in front of the tiger picture; it was velvet and ugly—just like always.

"This has to remain a secret from your brothers and sister. Do you understand?"

Benjamin nodded his head.

"I already have to keep it disabled. Otherwise, knowing the twins, they'd probably just stumble upon it." She reached out and put her palm on the picture; a holographic keypad appeared. His mom then entered a thirty-two number sequence on the keypad. Benjamin didn't dare blink as he watched, afraid if he did, he might miss something.

"Just put your palm on the picture, and you'll be gone," she said. She smiled as if she'd told him to do something normal like put away his laundry or unload the dishwasher.

Maybe his face betrayed how nervous he was, because she grabbed him and gave him a hug and a kiss on the cheek. "We love you so much. Be good, and don't get into any trouble," she advised him. "I don't want reports of any levitating frogs or tormented girls."

"I love you too," he said. "And I'll be good, I promise. What trouble could I get into anyway?"

His mom rolled her eyes.

"Is this how I do this?" Benjamin asked. He reached up and put his palm on the picture. Everything disappeared.

The Kiosk Checks in Benjamin

Benjamin wondered if his atoms had been scrambled. He hadn't felt like they had, but really he had nothing to compare it to. The teleportation was pretty much instantaneous, and when the world around him immediately returned, he found himself back in normal surroundings.

Well, sort of normal.

He stood on a platform in an atrium the size of a football field underneath a dome ceiling. Mammoth columns held up the dome, and people mobbed the place. Benjamin stared, but forced himself to blink once he felt his eyes get all dry and glassy.

A voice to his left snapped Benjamin out of his stupor. "Welcome, Benjamin Holt. Step off the platform to your left." Benjamin turned to look. An old man with ears the size of oversized monarch butterflies stared back.

"How do you know my name?" Benjamin asked, but wondered why he did. Maybe the better question to ask would be 'What world am I on?'

"We've been expecting you, of course. And you arrived exactly on time—which is quite an accomplishment. Not everyone does, you know, and then things really get messed up. We have to shut down the whole platform waiting for them. Once there was a student who was nearly five hours late. Can you imagine? And another time, three platforms stalled at once." The old man shook his head and his ears flapped back and forth. "But hurry down. The next student is scheduled to arrive any minute now."

"Where do I go?" Benjamin asked the man as he exited the platform.

The old man pointed to his ears. "Listen for instructions," he said. "And, goodbye." He turned his back on Benjamin and welcomed the next kid who'd just arrived where Benjamin had just been standing.

Benjamin has no idea if he should walk left or right, or if it really mattered.

"Welcome to summer school. Please report to a kiosk for your homeroom assignment," a female voice said over an intercom.

After standing frozen for the better part of a minute trying to figure out what was going on, Benjamin came to the conclusion that the kiosks were actually the columns. It was the lines of kids queued up to them that finally gave it away.

He made his way to the nearest column and stood there for close to fifteen minutes. Hopefully summer school wouldn't just be a lot of waiting in lines. Finally, though, his turn arrived.

"Name, please," a female voice said.

"Benjamin Holt," he replied, leaning his mouth close to the kiosk disk.

"Thank you, Benjamin Holt. Date of Birth please," the voice requested.

"June twenty-first."

"Thank you, Benjamin Holt," the voice said. "Please place your hand palm down on the disk in front of you."

Benjamin had barely placed his right hand palm down when the kiosk lit up, sending a small shock through his body as it did so. He jumped back and yanked his hand away.

"Thank you, Benjamin Holt. DNA match confirmed. Welcome to summer school. Your homeroom will be down Primary Hallway Number Zero, Secondary Hallway Number Seven, Tertiary Hallway Number One and will be in Classroom Number Three."

"DNA match? How do you know my DNA?" Benjamin asked, but the kiosk had already reset. "Name, please," it kept repeating.

"Where is Primary Hallway Number Zero?" Benjamin muttered. He walked around the atrium, looking for a sign. The first hallway he saw had a large number five above it. This was good. Benjamin kept going and passed hallways until they looped back around to zero.

As he passed through the threshold, the female voice he now recognized spoke. "If you wish to deposit your luggage into a luggage terminal, it will be delivered to your dormitory." Actually, that didn't sound too bad. As heavy as his duffle bag was, he figured maybe his parents had packed rocks in it. He moved to a terminal currently in use by a blond girl. The girl stared at her oversized suitcase on the floor which suddenly began to levitate, wobbling violently as it did so. Reaching the inside of the large recess, it fell with a resounding thud. She turned, saw Benjamin, flushed red, and then hurried away down the hall. Benjamin smoothly levitated his own bag inside the terminal and started down the long hallway ahead.

But apparently not everyone trusted the luggage terminal. Up ahead, a skinny, black kid walked down the hall dragging behind him a duffle bag even bigger than he was.

"I could help you if you want," Benjamin offered, walking over to him. "By the way, I'm Benjamin Holt." Maybe it wouldn't be so bad to make a friend here.

"Gary Goodweather." The boy extended his hand and Benjamin shook it.

"What homeroom are you headed to?" Benjamin asked.

"0713," Gary answered.

"Me too," Benjamin replied, easily picking up on the lingo. "We could take turns carrying your bag until we get there."

Gary shrugged. "As long as you don't mind."

"I don't mind." Benjamin hefted the bag onto his right shoulder. "Wow! What do you have in here anyway?"

"Oh, you know, just the basic stuff anyone would need—clothes, shoes, my chess set, books..."

"Books! No wonder it's so heavy. Why'd you pack books?" Benjamin asked.

"I haven't read them yet, and this summer school thing came along so fast, I barely had time to throw them into my bag before it was time to go," Gary answered. "Anyway, I really like to read and re-read the actual books. I always get more and more out of them each time I go through them. You know what I mean?"

"Not really," Benjamin answered. He'd have just memorized them and been done with it.

Out of the corner of his eye, something green caught Benjamin's attention. He turned to look, but all he saw was an empty bench. It must've been his imagination. After the morning he'd been having, everything could have been his imagination. Without hardly thinking about it, he pinched himself again. Still not a dream.

They turned left down Tertiary Hallway Number One. Again he caught sight of something green, but, when he looked, he saw another empty bench. Great. Now there was some fast, imaginary, green thing following him.

About halfway down the hall, there were four large doors stretching to the ceiling. Benjamin and Gary saw the one marked with the three and walked in.

As soon as they were in the classroom, Benjamin dropped Gary's duffle bag from his shoulder. It landed on the foot of the blond girl Benjamin had seen at the luggage terminal.

"Ouch! What'd you do that for?" For a second, Benjamin thought she was going to punch him, but instead she started rubbing her foot.

"Oh, I didn't even see..." Benjamin began.

"Hey, be careful with that. The chess set is my favorite, and it's kind of fragile," Gary said to Benjamin.

"Oh, sorry. It was just really getting heavy," Benjamin replied. He turned to the girl. "Sorry, I didn't see you standing there. I just couldn't carry that thing any more. He packed books in it," Benjamin said, motioning his head toward Gary.

"Well, you never know when they might come in handy," Gary said.

"Yeah, well just be careful next time you drop something," the girl said, still nursing her foot.

"You're one to talk about dropping stuff," Benjamin replied, referring to her suitcase at the luggage terminal.

The girl flushed red, obviously getting the reference. "I didn't see you using telekinesis on that duffle bag," she said. She whirled around, her blond hair turned bright, flaming red, and she stomped away.

"Did you see that?" Benjamin asked Gary. "Did you see her hair? It just changed color. I swear it did."

"Yeah, I saw it too," Gary said.

"That's a little weird, don't you think?" Benjamin said.

"Well, I don't think you should say anything. You already made a bad impression," Gary said.

"Hey, Benjamin!"

Benjamin grinned from ear to ear when he heard Andy's voice.

Andy hurried over. "I was wondering when you were gonna show up."

Nearly every head in the room turned to look when Andy called out to Benjamin. Apparently not everyone here had a best friend along. Benjamin noticed the blond—well, actually, now the red-headed girl—had also turned to look. Pretending she wasn't watching, she started talking to another girl nearby.

"Andy! What's up with this summer school thing? When I got the call this morning—or whatever it was—I couldn't believe it." Benjamin looked curious. "And do you have a teleporter in your hallway?"

"Unfortunately, ours is in my sister's closet," Andy said.

"How long have you been here?" Benjamin asked.

"For at least two hours. I was the second person here. It was just me and that girl over there for like a half hour." He motioned over to the brunette girl now engaged in conversation with the blond/red-headed girl. "But then more people started to filter in." Andy turned to Gary, seeing him for the first time. "I'm Andy Grow by the way."

"Gary Goodweather," Gary answered, extending his hand which Andy shook.

"Gary insisted on bringing his duffle bag with him rather than leaving it in the luggage terminal. He packed books in it." Benjamin laughed.

"Why didn't you just memorize them?" Andy asked.

"Well, I just really ..." Gary began.

The brunette girl had made her way over to Andy with the now blond again girl in tow. "Hi, Andy," she said.

"Oh, hi, Iva," Andy replied. Benjamin noticed Andy was staring at the girl. Not that he could really blame Andy. She was beautiful. Her dark hair was long and straight and reached well past her shoulders. Her light brown eyes lit up her face, and, apparently, Andy's also.

When Iva turned to Benjamin and Gary, Benjamin felt his face heat up.

"Hi," she said, "I'm Iva Marinina, and this is Heidi Dylan," she motioned to the blond girl. Benjamin glanced to Heidi, but felt his eyes being drawn back to Iva. He looked down at his shoes, then back at Heidi, hoping Andy hadn't noticed his reaction.

Heidi gave Andy a big smile though Andy's eyes were still glued on Iva. She then turned to Benjamin and Gary, barely smiling as she rubbed her foot.

"You're rubbing the wrong foot," Benjamin said.

Heidi smirked, but then put her foot down. "Sympathy pain," she said.

"Yeah, whatever," he said. "I'm Benjamin Holt." And then he put on his best smile. No need to make enemies the first day. Even if she was making more of the foot thing than was necessary.

"Gary Goodweather," Gary put out his hand to greet them. They both giggled when they shook his hand in return.

"Did your hair change color a minute ago, or was that my imagination?" Benjamin asked Heidi.

Gary elbowed Benjamin in the side.

"Well, I know it did," Benjamin defended himself.

Heidi reached up and smoothed her hair. "Oh, yeah, it does that sometimes when my emotions flare up."

"That's pretty cool," Iva said. "You mean you can have any hair color you want?"

"Well, not really," Heidi answered. "It's changed color like that ever since I was about five, but I still haven't figured out how to control it. I always have to wear a hat in public." She shrugged.

"So you and Benjamin know each other?" Iva asked Andy.

"Yeah, we've lived next door to each other our whole lives," Andy replied.

It was at that moment the large entryway door closed with a suctioning sound. Everyone turned to look.

"Welcome to summer school!" the voice of Proteus Ajax sounded from the front of the room. Everyone's eyes locked on the man who had just appeared behind the teacher's desk. "My name is Proteus Ajax, and I believe I've had the pleasure of already meeting all of you wonderful Year One Denarians."

"What's a Denarian?" Andy whispered.

"A person between ten and twenty," Gary replied. "Haven't you read the dictionary?"

"Are you kidding?" Andy answered.

"Please take a seat. We'll get our business out of the way and then break for the day," Proteus Ajax instructed.

There wasn't a great rush for the desks, but eventually, everyone sat down. Heidi and Iva sat in the front row, and Benjamin, Andy, and Gary went to sit in the three seats just behind them. Just as Benjamin was about to sit down, the green thing returned. And vanished. But this time he was sure of it. There had been something there. But what in the world is green and fast and can disappear into thin air? He looked under the desk and chair, but saw nothing. As he stood back up, he realized he was the only student still standing. Every face in the room stared back at him.

"Oh, uh, I just thought I saw something, um, green on my chair, and then it wasn't there, and, uh, I thought maybe it was under the desk, or something," Benjamin's face heated up as Heidi and Iva looked at him like he was a total idiot.

"Yes, well, please go ahead and sit down, Benjamin Holt, is it?" Proteus Ajax said. Benjamin nodded and quickly sat down.

"You thought you saw something green?" Andy whispered. "Do you realize how stupid that sounds?"

"I think I have an idea," Benjamin muttered under his breath.

"Nothing like drawing attention to yourself on the first day," Andy replied.

The World According to Proteus

"Who would like to guess where we are?" Proteus looked around the classroom. A fast hand went up.

"Yes, Ryan Jordan?"

"Are we on Mars?" Ryan asked. Several students laughed out loud. "My older brother told me I was going to Mars."

"I'm afraid your brother played a bit of a practical joke on you," Proteus said. "And everyone can refrain from asking about the other major planets you know of."

Iva raised her hand.

"Yes, Iva Marinina?"

"Are we in Atlantis?" she asked.

"Good guess," Proteus said.

Iva smiled.

"But no, not Atlantis."

Her face fell.

"You're close though," Proteus said. A standard map of the world appeared behind him, with all the major land masses illuminated. However, on the far left and the far right were two connecting sides of another large land mass, one Benjamin had never seen before. The map slowly shifted right, until the two halves joined.

Proteus Ajax pointed to the land. "Ladies and gentlemen: the continent of Lemuria."

So this was the new world his parents had hinted about?

"Let me give you a brief history of the Earth and Lemuria." Proteus said, leaning back on his desk. The map in the background turned into an image of mostly water. Large land masses started moving.

"When the Earth was young, millions of years ago, it was nearly all water. Land masses began to form and move around. I am sure many of you have heard of these large land masses—Pangaea, Gondwanaland, and many others. These land plates form the theory of Plate-tectonics." The map kept shifting as Proteus spoke. "The jigsaw puzzle of taking all of the continents known to humans and fitting them together is well-known but not exact. There are holes when the land masses are placed together. One of these missing land masses is known as Lemuria and is located in the middle of the Pacific Ocean."

Okay, so Benjamin was in the middle of the Pacific Ocean on a continent called Lemuria. Given his morning with the talking mirror and the ugly picture teleporter, that seemed reasonable.

"It is on this continent that telegens developed 900,000 years ago," Proteus said.

"What are telegens?" Benjamin asked.

Proteus waved his arms around. "We're all telegens. People

from Lemuria are called telegens."

Benjamin nodded. Okay, so his parents had been telling the truth about him not being human. Maybe.

Proteus continued. "Telegens developed rapidly, both physically and mentally. For thousands of years, they lived on Lemuria, and then 400,000 years ago they expanded out to Atlantis." The map shifted to show a second large oceanic continent.

Benjamin looked at Iva. She sat up a little straighter in her seat and smiled.

"When humans first appeared on Earth 200,000 years ago, they had no idea about Lemuria or Atlantis," Proteus said. "And they looked just like us—at least on the outside. But their brains were like infants compared to ours."

"They did advance though; think of ancient civilizations you know—Greek, Egyptian, Indian." He rubbed his hands together. "And that's when the problems began. Lemurian telegens thought humans should never know about us; Atlantis did not agree. And so a shield went up around Lemuria, and 25,000 years ago, a mighty cataclysm was caused. The continent of Lemuria sank into the Pacific Ocean, and an advanced lookout system disguised as a ring of volcanoes was placed around it, known as the Ring of Fire.

"But then the telegens of Atlantis started to cause trouble. They mixed with humans and gave them knowledge. And all they asked for in return was worship and sacrifice. They came to be known as the ancient gods and goddesses of these civilizations.

"Gaea was the first and many others followed. If their wishes were not granted, they were fierce in their punishment."

Gary raised his hand. "So you're telling us that all the Greek and Egyptian gods and goddesses were actually just normal people from Atlantis."

"If telegens are normal. And actually, it wasn't just Greece and Egypt. It extended to all ancient civilizations—Norse, Indian, Sumerian, Chinese. Most of the mythological stories you hear are based on fact."

"So what happened to Atlantis?" Benjamin asked, raising his hand as he spoke.

"Well, through the Ring of Fire and the use of highly trained agents, Lemuria kept watch over the events on the Earth. Humans were almost totally enslaved, and Lemuria was helpless to prevent it.

"Finally, 10,000 years ago, Lemuria devised a plan to stop the telegens of Atlantis once and for all. A protective barrier similar to the one around Lemuria was erected around Atlantis. A mighty flood was caused, and the continent of Atlantis plunged to the bottom of the Atlantic Ocean. However, in this case, the barrier was designed not only to keep humans out but also to keep the telegens of Atlantis from escaping. The civilizations the false gods had come so close to destroying were restored and repaired. Telegen agents were placed among the humans to keep watch. And, for humans, recorded history began." The map behind Proteus adjusted to no longer show either Lemuria or Atlantis.

Proteus Ajax rested his hands on his desk. "Any questions?"

"So, are telegens and humans genetically identical?" Gary asked. "I mean, will humans eventually become as advanced as we are?"

"Doubtful," Proteus began. "Is anyone familiar with DNA?"

Gary nodded his head so hard it made Benjamin dizzy.

"Excellent. Then you understand minor DNA differences can account for major differences in cerebral abilities."

Gary again nodded his head so hard Benjamin wondered if it would come off. Andy elbowed Benjamin who tried not to laugh.

"Why haven't humans discovered the sunken continents?" Heidi asked. "I mean, they're huge. Wouldn't it be kind of hard to hide those?"

"The barrier around Lemuria creates the illusion to an outsider of looking deep onto the ocean floor. The illusion will withstand any sensory test given to it by humans. From an insider's point of view, it's just as if you are outside, above the depths of the ocean. The weather we have here perfectly reflects the weather conditions above the surface. The night stars and sky are exactly the same. The wind blows; the seasons change. There is essentially no difference," Proteus Ajax finished.

"Yes, but how long will the barriers last?" Benjamin asked.

The smile fell of Proteus's face. "Someone always has to ask that. And the official answer is forever."

"And the unofficial answer?" Andy asked.

Proteus sighed. "Here's what I can tell you. The barrier

around Lemuria is fine."

"And Atlantis?" Benjamin pressed on.

"Is failing," Proteus said. "Telegens are already getting out. And if the barrier's not fixed, it probably won't last longer than another decade."

As Proteus said it, Benjamin realized this must have been what his dad and Joey had been talking about this morning. People escaping from Atlantis.

A girl in the front row raised her hand.

"Yes, Suneeta Manvar."

"Who rules Lemuria?" she asked.

"A future leader in training." Proteus smiled at Suneeta.

Andy groaned and rolled his eyes at Benjamin. "*Teacher's pet,*" he thought to Benjamin.

Benjamin stifled his laughter.

"The people and continent of Lemuria are overseen by two rulers—twins—a brother and a sister. The supreme rulers are chosen based not only on their mental abilities, but also on their compassion and tolerance. The rulers are not always twins—it's not a requirement—but twins are always more powerful together."

Benjamin immediately thought of his twin brothers, Derrick and Douglas, and their unusual, strong telekinetic abilities at such a young age. Well, that explained that.

"One last question?" Proteus Ajax announced.

Benjamin cleared his throat. "Why do we all live somewhere besides Lemuria, and why has all this been kept secret until now?"

"Each agent family is placed somewhere on Earth for a specific purpose. As to exactly what that purpose is, you would have to talk with your parents. But I have to warn you—they may not be able to tell you."

"You mean our parents are spies?" Andy asked, not bothering to raise his hand.

"We prefer to use the term 'agent' instead of spy. Anyway, to address the second part of the question, you have never been told who you really are as it has been determined that under the age of thirteen, the information cannot be trusted to be kept secret," Proteus explained.

"Ah, Benjamin Holt, I see you have made a new friend." Proteus smiled at Benjamin just as Benjamin felt something settle down upon his left shoulder.

The Fast, Green Thing on Benjamin's Shoulder

Benjamin jumped up, out of his seat, trying to swat at the thing on his shoulder.

"Oh, there's no need to do that, now, is there?" the small kind-of human-looking thing said to Benjamin as it grabbed hold of his collar and held on for dear life.

Benjamin looked to Proteus Ajax. "What is this thing?"

"This thing?" the green thing asked. "Since when am I referred to as a thing?" The thing put its little hands on its little hips. "I happen to be a Nogical, and I have a full name, though you don't need to know it. So, instead, you may call me Jack."

Benjamin hesitated, but sat back down, and the little Nogical, Jack, sat upon his shoulder. Benjamin tried not to flinch.

"What exactly is a Nogical, and why is there one on my shoulder?" Benjamin asked. The Nogical rested back on his hands and crossed his legs.

"A Nogical is kind of like a really small telegen, but different," Proteus Ajax said. "As to why this one has chosen to sit on your shoulder, you'll have to ask him. It's not often that a Nogical chooses to associate with telegens, so you should consider yourself fortunate. Nogicals make valuable friends."

"Yeah, so you'll be stuck with me for a while." Jack smiled. "Oh, I won't bother you much. Just pretend I'm not here if you have to."

"Yes, but where did he come from?" Benjamin asked.

"A genetic engineering experiment, I'm afraid," Proteus said.

"You're afraid?" Jack said. "What's that supposed to mean?"

Proteus smirked. "Don't play dumb. You know as well as I do that the Nogicals were created after the big genetic engineering crackdown."

"You mean they were never supposed to have been created?" Ryan Jordan, the same boy who thought they were on Mars, asked.

"There are always exceptions to the rules," Jack, the Nogical, said. "And Nogicals just happen to be the perfect exception."

"Right," Proteus agreed. "Perfect and illegal."

Benjamin looked sideways at Jack. Perfect? He figured maybe the light green skin color of the little man served some purpose. But the blue hair and bright yellow eyes? That had to be some kind of experiment gone wrong. Maybe it took some getting used to.

"Are there other species like Jack?" Gary asked. By the way Gary's mouth had been hanging open, Benjamin was surprised he'd actually been able to close it to form words.

"Nope," Jack said, sitting up a little straighter.

"No is right," Proteus said. "After the Nogical fiasco, telegnostics were put in place to make sure no more telegens were genetically engineered."

Benjamin noticed Iva had raised her hand to ask a question when the boy sitting next to Ryan Jordan beat her to it. "What's a telegnostic?" he asked. Iva looked over and glared at him.

"Someone who can sense thoughts and events from far away, across distance or time," Proteus said. "When a telegnostic is honed in on one type of idea—in this case genetic engineering—they are perfect watchdogs. You'll be learning much more about telegnosis along with other cerebral abilities in your classes," Proteus said, trying to get the class's attention back from Jack.

Benjamin looked at Jack. Jack smiled back at Benjamin. "You won't even know I'm around," Jack said. Benjamin tried to relax, but found it hard to pretend the small man wasn't on his shoulder. Would Jack be around all the time? Would he have to shower with the Nogical on his shoulder? That didn't sound too good. And on cue, the Nogical disappeared.

"What a treat! I haven't seen a Nogical in years." Proteus clapped his hands together. "Anyway, enough about that. We have some logistical issues to go over now." He raised a gold piece of metal, about the size of his palm, into the air. He touched two fingers to the top of it, and it tripled in size. "Please pull this item out of your backpack."

Everyone in the class reached down underneath their

desks into the school-provided backpacks to retrieve the object. "This is your personal sheaf," Proteus began. "It has been coded to match only your DNA signature."

"What does it do?" Ryan Jordan asked, looking at the back of the piece of metal, then the front, hoping to see something. He tried prodding at it with his fingers with no success.

"Your sheaf does everything. You may think of it as your Internet connection to the world—well, not quite the world; it doesn't connect to the human Internet, but you'll hardly find that a limitation."

Proteus explained how to operate the thing. With little effort, Benjamin accessed his class schedule just by thinking about it. His schedule had boring, normal subjects like science and homeroom, but telepathy, telekinesis, telegnosis, and teleportation sounded promising.

Then Proteus went over the rules. They were pretty basic. Year One Denarians couldn't leave the city. Judging by the map, Benjamin thought this shouldn't be a problem; there ought to be plenty to keep them busy just in the capital city of Mu.

"Are there any final questions before we break for the day?"

With the apparent information overload, no one, not even Ryan Jordan asked another question.

Andy Wants to Visit
the Ruling Hall

Benjamin, Andy, and Gary got their things settled in their dorm room and then tried to figure out what to do with the rest of the day. Here it was only lunch time, and classes didn't start until tomorrow.

"I think we should go to the Ruling Hall," Gary said. "I was checking my sheaf, and it's supposed to have the biggest library in all of Lemuria."

"I'm not wasting my first day here in some boring government building," Andy said. "That's like the last thing in the world I'd want to do."

"So what do you suggest?" Gary asked in return.

"We could sneak around the city spying on people," Andy said.

"We don't know anyone to spy on," Benjamin said.

"Anyway, spying on people isn't polite," Jack said, appearing directly in front of Benjamin's face.

Benjamin had to admit it—it would be handy to learn to

teleport like Jack.

"So why are you doing it then?" Andy asked.

"I'm not spying on you guys," Jack said. "I just thought I'd come along to the Ruling Hall with you."

"We're not going to the Ruling Hall," Benjamin replied.

"Right," Andy added. "No libraries."

Jack laughed a tiny little laugh. "There's more to the Ruling Hall than just libraries."

"Like what?" Andy asked.

"Like it's the most important structure in all of the known, and unknown, world," Jack replied.

"Boring," Andy answered.

"I have an idea," Benjamin said as his stomach growled. "Why don't we just head out into the city and get some lunch?"

"And then go to the Ruling Hall," Gary added.

"Lunch—fine. Ruling Hall—no way," Andy replied.

As they left the school, the wind started blowing dark clouds into the sky; it figured that Lemuria wouldn't be spared even a thunderstorm. They picked a restaurant on Mu Way, the main thoroughfare of the capital city, called The Deimos Diner. The three boys walked in and immediately spotted Iva and Heidi at a circular booth in the corner. When they smiled and waved, Benjamin felt his stomach clench up, though he couldn't imagine why.

"*I guess we should go join them,*" Andy telepathically said, already starting over to the table.

"*Yeah, probably,*" Benjamin replied. "*They might get their feelings hurt if we don't."*

"You know I can hear every word you're saying."

Benjamin stopped walking as he heard Heidi's voice in his head. Was she really that good at telepathy? Could she hear everything he was thinking?

"You guys are welcome to join us for lunch, but don't feel like you have to do us any favors," Heidi said audibly once they reached the table.

Not bothering to reply, Andy slid onto the bench next to Iva. Benjamin tried not to smile and sat down.

"So what are you guys doing for the rest of the day?" Benjamin asked.

"We're going to the Ruling Hall," Iva replied.

"That's where I wanted to go also," Gary replied. "But..."

"And since Gary wanted to go there, that's where we're going too," Andy quickly finished.

"We are?" Gary asked.

"Of course we are," Andy replied. "I was just kidding before."

Benjamin stared at his friend, then glanced at Heidi. She smiled back but didn't say a word.

"So, what's so special about the Ruling Hall anyway?" Benjamin asked.

"It's supposed to have more rooms than you could explore in your life. Endless stairways, secret passages, hidden doors," Iva said. "And the inventions housed in the Hall are more brilliant than we could ever imagine."

"How do you know that?" Andy asked.

"Well, that's what Kyri the Telegnosis teacher told me," Iva replied.

"You met with a teacher already?" Andy asked.

"I was really interested in telegnosis when Proteus Ajax mentioned it, so I went and found our teacher and introduced myself," Iva replied.

"That seems like such a…a teacher's pet thing to do," Andy said.

Iva ignored the remark. "She said I had the strongest telegnostic pathways she'd ever seen. And she told me some history of telegnosis on the Earth. Did you know the Oracles at Delphi were actually telegnostics?"

"What's Delphi?" Andy asked.

Iva opened her mouth to reply but stopped when she noticed Benjamin and Andy weren't listening anymore; they were staring at the man walking through the open door.

"Mr. Burton?" Benjamin and Andy called out in unison. The man smiled at the greeting and strode over to their booth.

"Hi, boys. It's great to see you," he said. "I was hoping I'd run into you."

"But…but Mr. Burton, are you…are you a telegen?" Benjamin asked. Nothing their seventh grade science teacher from back in Virginia had ever done had even remotely suggested he had super brain powers. Nothing.

"Well, yes, come to think of it, I am." He smiled. "I guess I've done a decent job of hiding it," he said.

"So that explains how you always knew it was us," Benjamin said.

"What was always us?" Heidi asked.

Mr. Burton smiled at the girls. "It seems that Benjamin and Andy here like to play practical jokes on some of the other students in class. If I'm not mistaken, their most recent prank involved a dead frog jumping on a young lady's head."

"You made a frog jump on some girl's head?" Gary said with admiration.

"You use telekinesis in your science class back home?" Iva asked in amazement.

"They aren't supposed to," Mr. Burton replied, but laughed anyway. "But I can't say that I blame them. Life among the humans does get rather tedious."

"So I guess you knew we were telegens all along," Benjamin said.

"Of course, but I wasn't allowed to say anything. Not even your parents know about me." Mr. Burton smiled at the other students. "I'm Kennias Burton by the way. I teach science at their middle school in Virginia."

"I can't believe you have a telegen for a science teacher," Gary said. "Man, I'm jealous. My science teacher doesn't even know what a meniscus is. I constantly have to bite my tongue to keep from correcting him."

"What is a meniscus?" Heidi asked.

Gary rolled his eyes. "Doesn't anybody read anymore?"

"A meniscus has something to do with monkeys, right?" Andy asked.

Gary shook his head and sighed. "It's a phase boundary curved due to surface tension."

Andy, and even Heidi, looked back at him like he was nuts. Heidi shrugged.

"So what are you kids doing today?" Mr. Burton asked.

"We're going to the Ruling Hall," Benjamin answered.

"Oh, wonderful. You'll love it," Mr. Burton replied.

Benjamin and Andy looked at each other with doubt.

"I felt the same way when I was younger, but I was wrong. If I didn't have pressing matters to attend to, I'd join you. I don't get many days away from Virginia, so, when I make it to Lemuria, I'm stuck with boring, administrative tasks." He gave them a conspiratorial smile. "But do enjoy yourself. I hear there are some hidden passageways on the lower floors. There's one I've heard about in particular on floor i4. They say that nobody has ever found it, and that whoever does will never return." He winked.

"Floor i4?" Andy asked. "What's floor i4?"

"Didn't you check your class schedule?" Gary asked. "That's how they label the lower levels."

"Why?" Andy said.

"Because i^2 is negative one, so the negative floors are denoted with an i," Gary explained. "Duh. Imaginary numbers."

"Oh, yeah," Andy said. "Duh. I can't believe I didn't realize that myself."

Benjamin couldn't help but laugh. Andy and imaginary numbers.

"Well I'm glad somebody's interested in learning," Mr. Burton said. "Anyway, have fun. And try not to get in any trouble."

Jack Gets Them in Trouble

They walked down Mu Way toward the Ruling Hall. Even without a map, it would've been pretty hard to miss, what with the shining, golden onion dome on top.

Jack popped into existence. "Breathtaking, isn't it?" he said, seeing the looks on their faces.

"That's putting it mildly," Iva said. Her mouth hung open as if she were trying to find just the right words to describe it. "Why does it look so Indian?"

"Oh, the architecture of Lemuria has influenced architecture all over the world, in nearly every country on the globe," Jack answered. "Skyscrapers are even a fad in some parts of Lemuria."

"Are they as tall as Taipei 101?" Heidi asked.

"What's Taipei 101?" Andy asked.

"You really need to get out more, Andy," Iva scolded. "Taipei 101 is only the tallest building in the world." Andy turned redder than a tomato.

"Well, that's not quite true. Taipei 101 looks like a toy

model compared to some of the buildings in Wondersky City. But you won't find any skyscrapers in Mu; they have restrictions on height here," Jack said.

The sky let out a loud rumble of thunder. Lightning flashed, and then the rain started coming down in sheets. Heidi and Iva immediately tried to cover their heads with their hands.

"Can we go in now?" Iva asked. "I'm getting soaked out here."

As they ran into the building, they passed through some sort of chamber, entering soaked from the rain and emerging completely dry.

"Hey, what just happened?" Heidi asked, running her hand through her now dry, but brown, hair.

"I don't know about the color change, but we did just pass through a dehydrating chamber," Jack said. "They're automatically turned on when it rains or snows."

Heidi held out a lock of her hair so she could see it.

"You don't look bad as a brunette," Benjamin said.

"Yes, but I'm a blond." She sighed.

They exited the dehydrating chamber into a long wide hallway with scales as tall as the ceiling on either side. The scale on the right sat in perfect balance, the sign above it reading 'Lemuria'. The scale on the left tilted slightly, but was still stable in its unbalanced position. The sign above it read 'Atlantis'.

"They show the strength of the shields around the sunken continents," Jack said.

Benjamin moved closer to get a better look. "What keeps them balanced?"

"Well the outward pressure from the barriers presses down on the left, and the inward pressure presses down on the right." He waved his small hand at the Atlantis scale. "Atlantis won't last more than ten years."

"And then what happens?" Heidi asked.

"Well, then the continent rises, and the people of Atlantis are free to roam about on Earth, where they'll no doubt seize control and enslave the human race again," Jack answered with a shrug.

"So, what are we doing to stop it?" Iva asked.

"Lemuria is trying everything it can, but not much seems to help," Jack replied. "If you have any ideas, I'm sure the Deimos twins would love to hear them."

Jack gave them a tour of everything. It was true; the Ruling Hall was endless. He obviously been here before—many times—so when they turned a corner and found nothing but a closed door, Benjamin figured maybe the Nogical was just playing a trick on them.

But Jack leaned in close. "It's the Ruling Chamber," he said. "You know, we can go inside as long as no one sees us."

"Sounds great," Andy replied, already walking toward the door. He leaned against it, waiting until no one was around, and then opened it. "Quick, hurry." He motioned the rest of them inside.

Iva looked torn, but hurried after Heidi once she realized she was the only one still outside. Andy quickly shut the door behind her.

"The ruling chamber of Lemuria," Jack announced, levitating over to one of the two thrones and settling upon the large velvet cushion. "Yep. Here's where all the big decisions are made."

"Really?" Iva asked, her large brown eyes taking in the surroundings.

"Well, probably not," Jack admitted. "But it's still a cool place to visit. They only open it up once a year."

Suddenly Jack's eyebrows creased. He sat still, as if in deep thought. Finally he spoke. "I just found out I have to leave to attend to some other stuff."

"You're leaving? Will you be back to finish the tour?" Iva asked.

"No, I don't think so. But you'll be fine," Jack said and vanished without another word.

"I think we should go too," Iva said.

"Iva's right," Gary said. "We shouldn't be here. Let's go."

"But I was just getting comfortable," Andy said, sitting down on one of the thrones.

"I can see that," a voice said.

Five heads turned to look in the direction the voice came from. Two figures stood, side by side, and very nearly identical in appearance except one was a man and the other was a woman.

"We were just going," Benjamin said, hurrying toward the door. A sick feeling in his gut told him who these two people were.

"Without introducing yourselves?" the female asked. "Isn't that a bit rude?"

Benjamin froze, unsure what to do. Did he dare just walk over and say hello? He looked at Andy who was still sitting on the throne, a horrified look upon his face.

Thankfully it was Gary who took control of the awkward moment. "My name's Gary Goodweather," Gary said, walking over and extending his hand for the couple to shake.

"Gary Goodweather," the man repeated. "It is a pleasure to meet you." They shook his hand in return. "My name is Helios Deimos, and this is my sister, Selene."

"So you two rule this whole world?" Heidi asked, walking over also.

"I thought so," Selene Deimos replied, "until I saw your friend over there on my throne."

Andy bolted upright off of the throne. "Yeah, I'm really sorry about that." He walked over and introduced himself. "We kind of ended up in this room somehow, and I was just taking a break."

"I didn't want to come in here in the first place," Iva announced as she walked over. "But Benjamin's friend Jack made us come in."

Helios and Selene turned and focused their attention on Benjamin. "Is that so?"

"Yeah, I guess so," Benjamin replied. "But he's a Nogical." Now why had he gone and said that? What did it matter whether a Nogical led them into the ruling chamber or not?

"So you have a friend who's a Nogical?" Helios asked. "Quite unusual. But as coincidences go, I know Jack the Nogical also. So any friend of Jack's is a friend of mine."

Benjamin felt relief wash through him. So it had paid off to mention the Nogical connection. He'd have to remember that in the future. "I'm Benjamin Holt by the way."

"It's a pleasure to meet you, Benjamin Holt," Selene Deimos replied. "Now please, continue your visit of the Ruling Hall. But in the future you may want to avoid areas not on the main tour."

Once Again, They
Leave the Tour

The official tour guide wasn't half as good as Jack; before long, all of them were bored stiff.

"Who's ready to head down to i4 to look for the hidden passageway Mr. Burton told us about?" Andy asked with a devilish grin. Benjamin looked at Andy and grinned back.

"You heard what Selene Deimos just said," Gary said. "Avoid areas not on the main tour. Those levels are off limits."

"Let's just try," Heidi said, moving over to join Andy and Benjamin.

"I think Gary's right," Iva said. "The sign said the lower levels are closed to the public."

"Well, then maybe we won't be able to get down there," Andy said. "And if not, we can just turn around and leave." Andy smiled again, and when Benjamin looked, he was sure the smile was directed toward Iva. Was it his imagination, or was Andy acting a bit odd? Heidi glanced at Benjamin and smiled knowingly, like she'd just read his thoughts. Which she probably had.

Still, Iva and Gary didn't budge.

"Do you always break the rules?" Iva asked Andy.

"Do you always stick to them?" Andy asked. "Come on. Have a little fun, will you?"

Iva glared at him, but she and Gary joined them.

When they reached floor i3, the main staircase they'd been on ended. "See. We can't go any farther," Iva said. She glanced around, looking to see if anyone was watching. "Let's go back."

But already Heidi was looking around for another set of stairs and coming up empty. The level was vacant, just a big, empty circle with nowhere to go but back up. In the center of the floor, a fancy mosaic decorated the white marble tile. It caught Benjamin's eye, so he walked over to it. It was a large circle, about ten feet in diameter, with a smaller concentric circle inside it. Connecting the large and small circles were a series of lines spaced about ten inches apart. Benjamin stared at it. Gary, Andy, Heidi, and Iva walked over to join him.

"What are you looking at?" Andy asked.

"I don't know. There's something strange about this mosaic, like the light isn't reflecting off it right," Benjamin said.

Gary looked at it. "I see what you mean." He squatted down, looking at it from a different angle. "It looks flat to me," he said. He placed his foot on the design, and then walked straight across it. "I think it's just for decoration."

"I'm not so sure," Benjamin said. He stared at it a while longer, then decided to try something. Nothing ventured, nothing gained. Like he was stepping on thin ice, Benjamin placed his right foot on one of the line divisions. Without a word, he placed his left foot on the next division. His left foot disappeared. After a few more steps, he vanished from his thighs down.

"It's a staircase," he said to his friends.

"But how could that be?" Gary asked. "I just walked across it, and I didn't fall in."

Benjamin shrugged. "I don't know," he said. He took a few more steps, now up to his chest in the floor. With five more steps, he was gone. Heidi was next, and Andy, Iva, and Gary quickly followed.

"Wow, where are we?" Heidi asked once they all reached the bottom. Unlike the rest of the ornate Ruling Hall, floor i4 reminded Benjamin of a hospital—utilitarian and white.

"Somewhere we're not supposed to be," Gary said. He looked up the staircase like he wished they were still back on i3.

"So, which way do we go?" Benjamin asked.

"I think we should go this way," Iva said, pointing to the third hallway on the left.

"Why?" Benjamin asked. "They all look the same."

Iva shrugged. "It just feels right."

"Well, I guess it's as good as any of them," Andy said. He began walking in the direction Iva had suggested. With a shrug, Benjamin and Heidi followed, Gary trailing behind.

The farther they walked, the more sub-hallways sprouted off the main one. At Iva's suggestions, they chose a path, first turning left, then right, then right again. Pretty soon, the turns and whiteness made Benjamin's head spin.

"These all look alike," Gary said.

"And isn't it kind of weird that there's no one else around?" Heidi said.

"Well, it is off limits," Iva said.

"Did you guys just hear that?" Gary asked.

"I didn't hear anything," Andy replied.

"Me neither," Heidi agreed.

"Sure you did. It sounded like someone slamming a door," Gary said. His friends just stared at him. "What, you really didn't hear anything?" He listened. "See, there it is again, except it was a different door, closer this time."

"I think you're hearing things," Andy said. "We're the only ones making noise down here."

"No, I think I heard something that time." Benjamin nodded at Gary.

"How good is your hearing, Gary?" Andy asked.

"I can hear a pin drop at the distance of a football field," Gary replied. "I tried some experiments to test it one time."

"*Crazy,*" Andy thought to Benjamin. "*He's tested his hearing?*"

Benjamin laughed out loud in response.

"What's so funny?" Gary asked.

Years of telepathic conversations prepared Benjamin for his answer. "Just nervous I guess," he replied.

"*You know, as weak as your mind blocks are, he'll probably be able to read your thoughts soon.*"

Benjamin felt the blood drain out of his face when Heidi's

48

mind sounded in his head. He looked at her, and she scowled back.

At Iva's bidding, they turned right and ran straight into a wall.

"I think you need to work on your woman's intuition a little bit, Iva," Andy said. "This is a dead end."

"Yes, I can see that," Iva said, biting her lip. "But I really had the feeling this was the way to go. I would have sworn to it."

"But there's nowhere to go," Andy said. "Maybe the right way was really the left way," he laughed.

"There has to be a secret passageway or something," Iva said, ignoring him.

"Well, technically, there doesn't have to be," Gary said.

But then Benjamin began to walk forward, toward the wall.

"Hey, what are you doing, Benjamin?" Andy asked.

Benjamin didn't answer because he didn't know. He stopped in front of the wall and, without saying a word, placed both palms flat on the surface in front of him. From the white wall sprang green light, emanating from under his palms. Brighter and brighter the light glowed, until suddenly, the white wall vanished. Benjamin lowered his arms back to his sides.

"Whoa, what just happened?" Gary asked.

"Yeah, what just happened?" Andy echoed.

Benjamin turned to them. "I don't know. I just knew the wall was a door, and I'd be able to open it."

"How in the world would you know that?" Andy asked.

Benjamin looked down at his palms. "No idea. It just came to me." He turned back to look at the double doors in front of him.

"So, do we knock?" Andy asked.

"Well, I don't think we should just walk right in," Gary said.

"I can read some thoughts behind the doors," Heidi said. "Whoever's in there knows we're out here."

On cue, the doors began to swing outward. Benjamin jumped back to move out of their way. When they finished opening, he peeked inside, and then started to walk forward.

"Oh, come in, come in," a voice said. "I've been expecting you. It's a pleasure to see you again after all this time." The students looked in the direction of the voice. There was a low table with some sort of strange chess game sitting on it. Two chairs were placed on opposite sides of the table. The two figures in the chairs looked up at exactly the same moment. They were identical. Each was an old man, with long gray hair and an unkempt beard, dressed in matching white pants and shirts.

"How could you have been expecting us?" Benjamin asked both men.

"Well, you've been making plenty of noise for one thing," the man on the left replied, standing up. He looked around at each of them, and Benjamin noticed his face fell. "You didn't bring him with you."

"Who?" Benjamin asked.

"Nobody," the man on the right said, standing up. "It doesn't matter."

"Who are you?" Gary asked neither man in particular.

They both stood a little taller. "I am Hexer, the keeper of the Tablet," the man on the right replied. "The companion of the One Mind."

"What does that mean?" Andy asked.

"I guard the most sacred of relics. In me is entrusted the secrets of all that is possible," the man on the left replied.

"Is that supposed to be a riddle or something?" Andy asked.

"I am the watcher of riddles, the master of the truth," the old man on the right said.

"And what is your name?" Gary asked the other man.

"I am Hexer," the man on the left said.

"But I thought he said he was Hexer," Heidi said.

"Well, I did," the Hexer on the right said.

"She was asking me," the Hexer on the left said.

"No, she was asking me," the Hexer on the right said. "Weren't you?"

"No, actually, I was asking him," Heidi said, motioning to the Hexer on the left.

"So, which one of you is really Hexer?" Andy asked.

"I am," the two Hexers said in unison.

Gary narrowed his eyes and looked at them. "I don't get it. How can you both be the same person?"

"There haven't always been two of us," the Hexer on the left said.

"So, why are there two of you now?" Andy asked.

The Hexer on the left opened his mouth to speak, but the

Hexer on the right shot him a silencing look. "We don't talk about it," the Hexer on the right said.

"So what is it that you guard?" Benjamin asked, changing the subject back. He wasn't too interested in identically named twins; but they had mentioned secrets. "I mean, what's the most sacred of relics?"

"It's good you don't know. We do our best to keep secret the existence and location of The Emerald Tablet," the Hexer on the left replied.

"The Emerald Tablet?" Benjamin asked, looking to the others for some sign of recognition, but even Gary shook his head.

"A tablet which contains the sum of all knowledge. It contains the very recipe for the creation of the world and for the survival of telegens in the future," the Hexer on the right said. "It must never fall into the wrong hands or be used for ill purposes."

"So, can we see it?" Gary asked. His eyes had grown huge at the words 'sum of all knowledge'.

"Of course. Any who make it this far are allowed to enter the chamber of the Tablet." The Hexers stepped apart and extended their hands in the direction of a small door.

Benjamin didn't wait; he started walking forward. His friends followed, close on his heels. "Okay," he said. "I guess we'll go check it out now."

"Help yourself." Both Hexers settled back in their chairs, returning to their game.

Benjamin reached the door and placed his hand on the palm pad. It lit up, and the door slid sideways. The room ahead stretched like a passageway into the underworld. The darkness enveloped them as they walked in, and the door closed behind them, sealing off every last bit of light around.

"It's kind of dark in here," Heidi said, and if Benjamin hadn't known better, he would have sworn she took a step closer to him.

But soon enough his eyes adjusted. "There's a light down there." He pointed, but had no idea if anyone could see him. So he started walking.

The ceiling light turned out to be no bigger than a pizza. But in the center stood a pulpit with a green crystal object. It was engraved with markings that Benjamin figured were either letters or chicken scratch.

"It looks similar to the ancient Phoenician alphabet, though it's not exact," Gary said, squinting to get a better look.

"How could you possibly know that?" Andy asked. He stared at Gary like he'd just explained the theory of relativity.

"I studied it one summer," Gary replied.

"You studied Ancient Phoenician?" Andy said. He looked to Benjamin who rolled his eyes in response, avoiding Heidi's glare.

"Yeah, it's really a quite remarkable language," Gary said. "Many English sounds and letter combinations come from Ancient Phoenician."

"So, what does the tablet say?" Benjamin asked.

Gary leaned over the tablet, trying to make out the strange letters. "I think it says:

Step close and you will see
The truth which all agree
Gives knowledge and sets you free
And strengthens with the power of three.

Draw near and you will find
The hidden truth told by the blind
Given out for all mankind
But use with care, I must remind.

Take always the path of love
For it is the one which is above
But not for one unworthy of
With no one left to belove.

Seize the moment and prevail
And drink from the flowing grail.
Step carefully the final trail
And balance the broken scale."

"So how is that the sum of all knowledge?" Andy asked. "It's a poem."

"Maybe we have to get one of the Hexers out there to help us," Iva said. "Isn't he, I mean, aren't they, the keepers of the Tablet?"

"Maybe there's more on the other side," Benjamin said. He reached out and grabbed the Tablet, preparing to turn it over, but when he touched it, it sprang to life. Green light shot through the room.

"Welcome, Benjamin Holt. We have been expecting you."
The voice came from the Tablet, but reverberated throughout
the entire chamber.

Benjamin let go of the Tablet and jumped back. "What was
that?" he said.

"It sounded like it was greeting you," Heidi said in a whisper, taking a step back to join him.

Benjamin took a deep breath, then stepped forward again.
He knew he was crazy to do it, but he placed a hand back on
the Tablet.

"I have awaited your arrival for many ages, Benjamin Holt,"
the voice said again.

"How do you know who I am?" Benjamin asked.

"I am the source of all knowledge," the Tablet replied.

"How could you have been expecting me?" Benjamin asked.

"I have chosen you as my champion, and you have chosen wisely in your companions to assist you in your task," the
Tablet said.

"What task? What champion?" Benjamin said.

"The task of restoring the balance to the world, for telegens and humans alike," the Tablet said. "The task of allowing
all of Earth to live in peace."

"Restoring the balance? Peace on Earth?" Benjamin said.
"Are you kidding? I hadn't even heard of Lemuria until this
morning. I think you made a mistake. I'm the wrong guy."

"No, Benjamin Holt. Only you will be able to perform this
task," the Tablet replied.

"But, why?" Benjamin said.

"A formal alliance must be formed before I can speak aloud the pathway to walk. All must be bonded together, devoted to the search for the truth," the Tablet said.

"What kind of alliance?" Heidi asked, and Benjamin was sure he saw a sparkle in her eye.

"An alliance of friendship. An alliance of trust. An alliance of minds. An alliance of power. Once formed, this alliance can never be broken. Place your right hands on the words you see before you," the Tablet instructed.

They looked at each other. Benjamin already had his right hand on the Emerald Tablet. Heidi looked at Benjamin then placed her hand next to his. Slowly the rest placed their hands on the Tablet—first Andy, then Iva, then finally Gary. The moment all five hands made contact, the brilliant green light began to pulse, first gradually, then quickly. Benjamin tried to lift his hand, but found he couldn't move it; it felt as though his hand had been melded to the Tablet. And then he felt it—the thoughts of his companions in his mind. He felt their strengths and weaknesses, felt their emotions. And then he could feel his own mind spread out, flowing through the minds of those around him. It was as though they had become one mind, one entity. But no sooner than the bond had started, it stopped, and the green light held steady.

"*Was that kind of weird, or was it just me?*" Benjamin heard Andy's thoughts.

Andy was right. It was kind of weird. Kind of really weird.

"The formation of the Alliance is complete," the Tablet spoke. "You are given the task of restoring the balance of

Lemuria and Atlantis. If you do not succeed, then no one shall."

"But how?" Benjamin asked. Talk about receiving an impossible homework assignment. This one had to beat all known records.

"You must find the three keys of the hunter and bring them together. When the keys are joined, the answers to all your questions will be given." The light from the Tablet blinked out.

"Wait," Benjamin said, grabbing the side of the tablet. "What do you mean? What am I supposed to do?"

Nothing happened. The Tablet was still, and the green light was gone. Benjamin stepped back in despair.

"Well, that wasn't very helpful," Andy said. "What keys? What hunter? Don't you think it could have been a little more specific?"

"Maybe you should try to see if you can get it to talk some more," Heidi suggested to Benjamin. He felt her thought before she said it. Weird.

He leaned back over the Tablet, and once again gently rested his hands on the green crystal, but it remained lifeless. Why wouldn't it talk anymore? He felt like picking it up and throwing it against the wall, but managed to hold his frustration back. They stared at it for a while longer, and then Benjamin turned and began to walk away.

"Where are you going?" Iva asked.

"You heard the Tablet," Benjamin said. "Obviously there's some sort of cryptic treasure hunt we have to go on. I guess we better start looking for some keys."

Hunters Don't Use Keys

When they left the ruling hall, the rain was coming down like a monsoon. They ran up Mu Way to the school, no one even bothering to try to say anything about the Emerald Tablet, or about the treasure hunt, or about the newly formed alliance. It wasn't until they returned to school, found a dehydrating chamber, and decided to grab dinner that anyone mentioned it.

"Benjamin, what was that thing talking about?" Andy asked once they all sat down. They huddled close, and Andy lowered his voice. "I mean, you've been my best friend for like forever, not some champion who's going to save the world."

"Yeah, I'm not sure I quite understand how you're going to single handedly protect all of mankind," Gary agreed.

"Trust me, you guys, I'm as confused as the rest of you," Benjamin said. "But I know one thing the tablet was very specific about. It's not just me. We're all in this together. Remember the Alliance? It said we were all bonded together to search for the truth, and I believe it. When we had our hands on the Tablet, I swear I felt like all of our minds were joined together. It felt like we were all one person."

"It wasn't just you," Iva said. "I felt the same way. I can still feel it a little bit now."

"There was some really special type of telepathy going on," Heidi said. "It was totally different than how I normally feel. I can pretty much read people's thoughts and emotions, but with the Alliance, I felt like our minds were actually meshed together. And even now I can sense each of you in the back of my mind, even when I try to block you out."

"I bet you can't read my mind."

Heidi's head whipped over as Ryan Jordan, the kid who thought they were on Mars, butted into the conversation. He sat down next to them with Jonathan Sheehan, the same kid who'd beat Iva to the telegnostic question, in tow. Benjamin noticed Iva glared at him again.

"Of course I can read your mind," Heidi replied.

"And stop listening to our conversation," Benjamin snapped. Now was not the right time for an interruption.

"What are you guys talking about that's so secretive?" Ryan asked.

"Yeah, really," Jonathan added. "We haven't even been here a whole day yet. What could you possibly be whispering about?"

"It's actually none of your business," Benjamin replied.

"No need to get so touchy about it," Ryan said. "Keep your secrets if you want to. All I was saying is that there's no way she could read my mind. My parents can't even break though my mind shields."

"They can too," Heidi replied. "I can read your mind enough to know you're lying about that."

"I am not," Ryan said.

"Whatever. Anyway, all you're thinking about is that Iva is pretty and you're trying to impress her because you want to ask her out," Heidi continued.

Benjamin and Andy busted out laughing as Ryan's face changed from white to pink to red.

"I was not!" he exclaimed. "I so totally was not thinking that. You're just making things up to act like you can read minds."

"I just read 'em as I see 'em," Heidi replied.

"Yeah, well just stay out of my mind," Ryan said and turned away.

"Yeah, well just stop eavesdropping on our conversations," Benjamin replied, still laughing.

Heidi shrugged and turned back to the others. "He's the one who challenged me in the first place."

"So does he really think I'm pretty?" Iva asked.

"Of course," Heidi replied. "Every guy in here thinks you're pretty. Especially Andy."

Andy immediately stopped laughing, flushing down to his neck. But Benjamin laughed all the harder.

"So how are we supposed to get food?" Andy asked. "I'm starving."

Benjamin noticed the abrupt change in conversation and shared a quick, conspiratorial smile with Heidi.

"Did somebody request food?" A thin sheet of metal appeared on the table in front of each of them, listing a variety of food choices.

Andy blinked and looked down at the menu. "Did you just talk?"

"Yes, I will be taking your order for your meal," the menu answered.

"Are there any vegetarian options?" Iva asked. "I'm a strict vegetarian."

Her menu shimmered and changed.

"A vegetarian—like you don't eat meat?" Andy asked.

"Is there any other kind?" Iva asked.

"Do you eat fish?" Andy asked.

"No. No animal flesh," Iva replied.

"Chicken. What about chicken?" Andy persisted.

Iva didn't reply.

"I'll just have a hamburger," Benjamin announced.

"Make that two," Andy said.

"Three," Gary added.

Heidi shrugged. "I think I'll go ahead and get the hamburger too."

Iva scowled. "I'll take the tofu."

Within a minute, steaming food appeared in front of them.

"That's pretty cool," Andy said in awe. "Where'd it come from?"

"It must be teleported here from elsewhere," Gary replied. "There's really no other logical explanation."

"So why did that doorman...or doormen...or whatever,

Hexer, say it was a pleasure to meet you again?" Andy asked, steering the conversation back to the incident with the Emerald Tablet.

"Actually what he said was that it was a pleasure to see you again," Iva corrected.

"Either way, what's that supposed to mean?" Gary asked.

"Maybe he saw us arriving at school this morning," Benjamin said.

"No," Gary said. "I don't think that guy, or guys, have left that room in a very long time."

"Must get kind of boring with only yourself to keep you company," Andy said.

"Maybe for you," Heidi said, "but I think anybody would be delighted to be in my company for an extended period of time. Even myself."

Andy laughed. "I'm sure that's true, but I mean, come on. How many games of chess can someone really play? Especially if you know what the other person is thinking."

"It wasn't chess," Gary said quickly. "It was Chaturanga, the oldest ancestor of chess known to man."

"Whatever, Gary," Andy said.

"Well anyway, I'm sure he didn't mean anything by the comment," Benjamin said. "It was probably just a passing remark."

Andy shrugged, but let the subject drop.

"So what do we do next?" Heidi asked.

"Well, I guess we need to figure out what these keys are that we're supposed to find," Benjamin replied. "And that's where I'm hoping for suggestions."

"Are you guys trying to figure out what to do for the rest of the night?" Ryan asked, leaning over again in an attempt to rejoin the conversation.

"Seriously, how many hints do you need?" Andy asked. "Whatever we decide to do, it's not gonna include you."

Ryan's face hardened, but he and Jonathan apparently got the hint because they stood up.

"Well maybe we can get together some other time," Ryan replied, looking directly at Iva and not at Andy.

"Yeah, maybe," Iva replied, and her face reddened the smallest amount.

"And stop eavesdropping," Benjamin added as they walked away.

"Man, those guys don't take a hint," Andy said. "Couldn't they see we were busy?"

"I think you made that pretty clear," Heidi said, shaking her head. "Could you have been any ruder?"

"Whatever," Benjamin said. "What's our plan?"

Gary spoke first. "We should probably look in the library to see if we can find any information about the keys there."

"I was thinking we could do a search on our classroom sheaves," Heidi said. "Proteus did say they were like our Internet connection to the world."

"Maybe we could ask around," Andy suggested, "You know, like spies."

"Who would we ask?" Benjamin said. "The only person we know is Proteus Ajax."

"That's not a bad idea," Andy said, looking upward as he thought. "Proteus Ajax may know something."

"I was just kidding," Benjamin said. "We don't need to ask anybody anything."

"I bet Proteus knows a lot of what goes on around this school," Heidi said.

"Don't ask Proteus anything," Benjamin replied again. He didn't think Proteus—or anyone for that matter—should be told about what the Emerald Tablet had said.

"Do you think our parents would know anything?" Gary suggested. "We could ask them."

"I don't think we should involve our parents in this just yet," Andy said. "They'd think we should tell a teacher and not mess in matters of good versus evil. You know how parents can be."

"Yeah, you're probably right," Benjamin replied. "Okay, why doesn't Gary start looking around in the library, Heidi and I can work on the sheaves, and Andy, why don't you and Iva ask around and see if you can find out anything." He tried not to smile as he suggested it. "But be casual. I don't want anyone knowing what we're up to."

"Casual is my middle name," Andy said. "No one will have any idea."

They quickly ate and headed off for their assigned tasks. Gary headed to the main library on the fifth floor. Benjamin and Heidi decided to stay in the dining hall. And Andy announced he and Iva were going to start by spying on Proteus Ajax.

Benjamin and Heidi pulled out their classroom sheaves and expanded them.

"What should we search on?" Heidi asked.

"I don't know. Why don't we just keep trying different things? Maybe we'll get a hit eventually," Benjamin suggested.

Heidi thought for a moment. "Maybe there's some sort of gate hunters have to open or something. You know, to get to some sort of hunting ground."

"That doesn't seem right," Benjamin replied. "How about keys that open a safe where weapons are kept?"

"My idea sounded better than that," Heidi said.

"Heidi, do you need help with something?"

Benjamin looked up to see a scary, wrinkled face leaning over the table.

"Oh, hi, Leena." Heidi smiled at her. "Yeah, we were just doing some research."

"But we don't need any help," Benjamin added quickly.

"*Wait a minute Benjamin,*" Heidi told him inaudibly.

"Have you heard about anything strange going on, Leena?" Heidi asked.

"*Who in the world is this woman, Heidi?*" Benjamin irritably thought back. What was she thinking? Hadn't they just agreed not to tell anyone about anything?

"*She's just a woman who works in the girl's dorms,*" Heidi replied.

"Strange?" Leena creased her forehead. "Like what?"

"Anything about keys or hunters?" Heidi asked.

"Heidi!" Benjamin had heard enough. "We need to get

back to work, and we don't need anyone's help."

The scary woman, Leena, glared at him in response. "Heidi and I were having a conversation." She then turned back to Heidi. "If you have anything you want to talk about, come by. I'm always around." She cast a final look at Benjamin, and then walked away.

"Why did you do that?" Benjamin asked Heidi. "I can't believe you did that."

"Benjamin, she's just a cleaning lady. It's no big deal. And since she works here, she probably hears a lot," Heidi replied.

"Just don't say anything else to her," Benjamin replied.

They sat there for close to two hours, testing ideas out on each other, using their sheaves to try to find any information they could on keys or a hunter. But nothing the sheaves returned made any sense. Benjamin began to wonder if the whole thing had been a joke. Keys of the Hunter. What kind of stupid riddle was that anyway?

"So, did you guys have any luck?" Benjamin asked Iva, Gary, and Andy when they got back.

"Nothing," Gary said. "I found absolutely nothing." He thought for a moment, and his eyes sort of glazed over. "But you should have seen all the books they have. And that was just the main library. There are a bunch of other specialized libraries, and that's not even counting the library connected to the Ruling Hall."

"Sounds exciting." Andy grimaced as he said it.

"It was," Gary said. "I can't wait to go back. So how about

you guys? Did you find anything?"

"Not on the hunter and key thing, but we did find out that Proteus Ajax has a girlfriend who actually happens to be our teleportation teacher," Andy said. *"And she's totally hot,"* he added secretly to Benjamin.

Benjamin smiled but then realized by the way Heidi rolled her eyes that she'd overheard also. Did she always listen in?

"How do you know that?" Gary asked.

"Well, we saw them together, talking," Andy replied. "They were in a teacher's lounge, and they were holding hands. Her name's Asia Philippa."

"And did I mention she's totally hot?" he added silently.

"So you got nothing on the keys?" Heidi asked.

Andy shook his head. "No. Nothing."

"Good detective work," Heidi smirked in reply.

10

Telekinetically Speaking

Benjamin probably should have felt more nervous walking into Telekinesis, his first class of summer school. But years of making frog legs wiggle in science class gave him confidence. But then a balding, black man teleported into the classroom, and telekinesis as Benjamin knew it was gone forever. The teacher looked them over, his eyes narrowing more with every second which went by.

"My name is Pantheros Pavlos, and one thing I will not tolerate is goofing around. You may overhear some of the older students calling me 'The Panther' behind my back. That is not a behavior I would encourage you to mimic. You may refer to me as Pantheros if you would like, or Mr. Pavlos if you feel you must."

Benjamin tried not to squirm in his seat. He dared to shoot a sideways glance over to Andy, but Andy's eyes were glued to The Panther.

"As this is beginner Telekinesis, I do not expect much of you," The Panther continued. "If you're too good, you'll be stuck with me in years to come. That is not a recommendation to hide your abilities; I will know if you are, and you will be sorry." The Panther laced his fingers, and turned his palms outward, cracking his knuckles. "Now, where should we begin?"

Ryan Jordan raised his hand. "How about with a demonstration?"

"That was a rhetorical question, Mr. Jordan," The Panther said. "I certainly do not need suggestions on how to teach. But since you asked..."

The Panther looked at the students, and their frozen faces looked back. And then every chair in the room lifted into the air. Benjamin looked at Andy, and couldn't hold back the wide smile that broke onto his face; Andy grinned back. Benjamin looked over to Gary and saw his hands clenching the sides of his chair. Gary gave a nervous laugh. The chairs kept lifting, higher and higher, until they all hovered near the ceiling.

"Is this the kind of demonstration you were looking for, Mr. Jordan?" The Panther asked. Ryan, pale faced and shaking, held onto his chair for dear life.

"Um, yes, this is fine, Mr. Pavlos," Ryan called down.

"Okay, then." The chairs and students descended to the floor, settling down with barely a sound. Benjamin jumped up and started applauding, followed quickly by Andy, and then the remainder of the class.

"Thank you, thank you," The Panther said. "I'm glad you liked my little 'demonstration.'" He cleared his throat. "I'll be spending the next hour getting an idea of your ability. You'll be competing with each other all summer, and I need to know how best to pair you up. Who's first?"

Ryan quickly raised his hand.

"Fine. Mr. Jordan will be first. Front of the room."

Ryan immediately walked up next to The Panther who turned to face him. He pointed to a large display of stones, varying from about the size of a fist to larger than a man. "Pick a stone and lift it and hold it there for thirty seconds."

Ryan glanced at the stones and bit his lip, before settling on one of medium weight, about the size of a small pumpkin. The stone wobbled, and then rose off the ground. At twenty-five seconds, the stone started to shake and by the end of the thirty second period, it wobbled so violently Benjamin was afraid it might fly over out of control and hit him.

"Should I be wearing a helmet?" Andy asked.

Benjamin and Heidi busted out laughing, but Ryan glared at Andy in return.

"A bad display perhaps, but a strong natural ability," The Panther said. "Who's next?"

Gary went next. He chose the lightest stone he could find, and just barely held it in the air for five seconds. Heidi chose a stone about the size of brick, though after ten seconds, it fell to the floor with a loud crash.

Iva picked a stone, about the size of a dinner plate. She lifted her arms as she held it in the air for the full thirty seconds, guiding it with her arms back down to the ground. Her face retained its usual calm composure the entire time.

"This isn't ballet class," Jonathan Sheehan called out. Benjamin looked over as he said it and noticed Ryan punched him on the shoulder in response.

"Well done, Ms. Marinina. An elegant display of grace under pressure," The Panther commended her.

Iva's eyes lit up, and she smiled.

Andy selected a stone just bigger than Ryan's, glaring at Ryan as he did so. Ryan pretended to look the other way. Andy easily lifted the stone high in the air and held it there, spinning it for effect. The class applauded as the stone spun faster and faster. Andy smiled and bowed, forgetting to watch what he was doing. The stone immediately fell toward the floor, being stopped mid-fall by The Panther who set it upon the ground.

Ryan Jordan and Jonathan Sheehan fell over laughing. "So who needs the helmet now?" Ryan called out.

The Panther pointed his finger at Andy. "Mind the object of your telekinesis, Mr. Grow. Irresponsible telekinesis is just one of the many ways to get kicked out of school."

Andy's face turned beet red, and he quickly returned to his seat, avoiding looking at Iva as he sat down. Benjamin felt Andy's intense embarrassment through the Alliance bond; he'd have to be sure to make fun of Andy later.

Finally, only Benjamin remained. He got up and made his way to the center of the classroom. "Pick the biggest one," Jack said, suddenly appearing on his shoulder. Benjamin jumped in surprise. He hadn't seen the small man since the day before. Jack smiled and waved to him.

"What? Are you nuts? It must weigh five hundred pounds," Benjamin replied in his mind.

"*So what if you can't lift it? At least you'll have tried,*" Jack answered.

"Hey, no fair if the Nogical helps him," Ryan said.

"I'm not going to help," Jack answered Ryan. "He doesn't need any help." Without another word, Jack vanished.

"So which one will it be?" The Panther asked Benjamin as the class watched.

Benjamin looked at the largest stone. It was huge. How could he ever lift that? It must be impossible. He didn't want to embarrass himself in front of everyone like Andy had. But he also didn't want it to look like Andy was better at telekinesis. Okay, so not the heaviest one, but definitely something bigger than Ryan or Andy; he'd show them who was the best at telekinesis.

Levitating the beach ball sized rock was hard at first—much harder than he actually would have thought. But come to think of it, the only things he'd really spent much time levitating in the past were frogs and dinner plates. But though it was hard, he did lift it, and hold it, for the entire thirty seconds. The class applauded—not as loudly as they had for Andy—but they did applaud. Through the Alliance bond, he felt Andy's presence and a slight bit of jealously to go along with it. Benjamin smiled. He was better.

A Series of Unusual Classes

The day continued with Telepathy and Teleportation. Although Benjamin shouldn't have been surprised after the little he'd experienced of Heidi's telepathy skills, the class turned into nothing but the teacher testing Heidi's abilities.

Mrs. Zen, the telepathy teacher, was more of a nerd than Gary. With black rimmed glasses and baggy clothes, she stumbled into the room, catching her oversized shirt on the doorknob before regaining her composure. She kicked the door shut with her foot and proceeded to the large desk at the front of the room.

"Good afternoon. I am Mrs. Zen, and I will be your Telepathy teacher." She looked out upon the mass of students in the class.

"Can anyone tell me what I am thinking about, right now, at this very moment?" She studied the students.

Heidi threw up her hand.

"Yes, Ms. Dylan?" Mrs. Zen asked.

"You're thinking about the third volcano starting from the

northeast in the Ring of Fire," Heidi stated.

Mrs. Zen cocked her head, just a little. "Exactly right. Interesting. There's never been a Year One Denarian who's been able to break through my first day mind shield. There must have been some weakness I wasn't aware of." She settled herself. "Let's try again, shall we?" She directed an challenging smile toward Heidi. "What am I thinking about, right now, at this very moment?"

Heidi's hand again shot up.

"Yes, Ms. Dylan?" Mrs. Zen asked, raising an eyebrow.

"You're thinking about a row of five volcanic statues on Easter Island." Heidi said.

Mrs. Zen's mouth dropped open. "I...um...uh... um... I'm completely astounded. That is amazing. Truly amazing. I would like to try one more time. Now, please get up and go to the back of the classroom." Heidi stood up and walked all the way to the back part of the room. "Please turn around and face the back wall." Heidi turned around toward the wall. Mrs. Zen also turned around such that her back now faced the class. "What am I thinking about, right now, at this very moment?" she asked.

Heidi did not hesitate. "You are thinking about a secret chamber under the paw of the Sphinx."

"How in the world is she doing that?" Benjamin said to Andy and Gary, not even trying to whisper.

"Could she possibly be cheating somehow?" Gary asked.

"Completely impossible to cheat," Mrs. Zen snapped, overhearing the question. "Ms. Dylan, you may return to your seat." Heidi did so. Mrs. Zen shook her head. "Well, I believe you have found a strength. Clearly this summer may be more interesting than I previously had thought."

"Wait until you guys see Asia Philippa," Andy said as he, Benjamin, and Gary walked up the fifteen flights of stairs to teleportation. "She's totally hot."

"That's what you said yesterday, but you're kidding, right?" Benjamin asked. "A hot teacher?"

"Just wait," Andy replied.

They hurried up the stairs and got to the room just as the chime sounded; the door swung shut, nearly hitting Benjamin in the back. Just as they sat down a woman materialized at the front of the room. She had long brown hair, worn in tight curls and wore perfectly fitted black pants and a black shirt. Her face took a break from its no nonsense composure to flash a brief smile at the students.

"My name is Athanasia Philippa, but you may call me Asia. I will be your instructor for Teleportation, the most difficult of subjects in this school. The study of Teleportation is a gradual one. If you master the theories of Teleportation, you should have no problem teleporting yourself to just about anywhere you may like. If you do not properly learn these theories, then I am sorry to say your success rate will be low even when teleporting inanimate objects."

"*Wow, you weren't kidding,*" Benjamin thought to Andy. "*She is hot.*" Heidi turned around and gave him a dirty look which he chose to ignore.

"*Tell me about it,*" Andy replied.

"Teleportation is the act of dematerializing an object from one location and rematerializing it to another location."

"*Are you sure she's dating Proteus?*" Benjamin asked.

"*Completely sure. Can you believe it?*" Andy replied.

"In the weeks to come, we will be focusing on natural teleportation—the teleportation of objects without using machines. We will study complex formulas and theorems to determine proper end points, and we will practice on inanimate objects only. Depending on your skill levels, you may have the opportunity to practice on animate objects in succeeding years."

A long brown curl had fallen into her face as she talked. She brushed it behind her ear.

"*She's all business though, isn't she?*" Gary thought to Benjamin and Andy.

She pointed to the desk behind her at a large basket of wooden cubes. "For the remainder of class today, we will practice teleporting these cubes." The cubes began to dematerialize one by one and rematerialize on the desks in front of each student.

"In accordance with Bailey's theorem on dematerialization, when a telegen aspires to teleport an object, a transient path must be chosen through the cerebral cortex without distressing other compulsory life sustaining functions. Now please go ahead and begin." She turned away.

"Do you have any idea what she's talking about?" Andy asked Gary.

Gary shook his head. "I think she said when we teleport stuff we have to remember to breathe."

"Great," Andy replied. "That should be enough to get us started."

Benjamin, Andy, and Gary sat staring at their cubes. And they sat. And they stared. They stared harder. As they continued staring, Andy finally burst out laughing. "Well, I don't think my cube's going to run away from me."

Gary laughed too. "I think it would be a lot faster to just move the cube with my hand, don't you?"

It was pretty funny. Benjamin grinned, but kept staring at the cube. "Maybe there's some sort of secret."

"Well, of course there's a secret," Jack said, appearing out of thin air right on top of the cube. "The secret is that you're going about it all wrong. I mean, what are you trying to do—stare the cube to death?" He laughed. Benjamin, Andy, and Gary looked at one another, and Benjamin felt his face redden.

"So, how do I do it then?" Benjamin asked.

"It's easy," Jack said. "It's just fancy telekinesis. I don't know what Asia was talking about, but here's how I do it. You have to picture in your mind where the cube is starting, and where you want the cube to end up. Once you have a firm grasp on these pictures, you simply move the cube from the starting point into your mind. You then shift the cube in your mind a little bit. Finally, you move the cube from your mind to the ending point." Jack smiled. "Simple, huh?"

"Yeah. That really clears thing up," Andy replied with a smirk. "I'll just go ahead and get started."

Benjamin, however, gave Jack his full attention. "You mean when the object moves, I actually have it inside my mind?"

"Exactly."

"But what if it doesn't fit?" Benjamin asked.

"That's where a powerful mind comes in handy," Jack answered.

"But, how about when people teleport themselves?" Gary began. "How can you put yourself into your own mind, when your mind isn't really there, it's inside yourself?"

"That's a paradox; just don't think about it," Jack answered. He leaned closer and started to whisper, "Now, don't tell Asia over there I said this, but in my opinion, teleportation works better if you just don't give it too much thought. She always tries to make it way more complicated than it really is. Sure, the theory is interesting and all, but all we really want to do is materialize right in front of our friends to try to scare them, right?" He disappeared from on top of the block and rematerialized right in front of Gary's face. "Boo!" Gary jumped. The boys started laughing, and Asia looked over. Jack disappeared.

"Please continue with your practice," she instructed and looked back to the students she was helping.

Jack reappeared. "So, let's see you try it again," he encouraged Benjamin.

Benjamin focused on the cube. He tried to create a point inside his mind. That was easy enough. But, how did he move the object into his mind? Pop. There it was. Before he knew what happened, the cube was in his mind, and not on the desk. But he hadn't done anything. Just as quickly, it left his mind, reappearing on the desk.

"I thought I should help you that time, just so you could see how it feels," Jack said.

Benjamin shook his head. "You could have warned me," he said. "But, thanks, I guess. That felt pretty cool."

"Just wait until you teleport yourself," Jack replied.

Guys and Telegnosis

Benjamin, Gary, and Andy entered the dining hall and walked over to the table where Heidi and Iva already sat. The cleaning lady, Leena Teasag, was sitting down talking to them. She looked at the boys, then got up from the table and walked away. Benjamin decided not to say anything. It had been a long day of classes, and he didn't feel like arguing with Heidi about private conversations with Leena.

"I'm starving," Heidi exclaimed once the boys reached the table. "Is anybody else super hungry tonight?"

"I sure am," Gary agreed. "I think it was all that telekinesis we were doing."

"Well, I don't know how much doing I was doing," Heidi said, "but at least I still tried. But, obviously, some of us are pretty good at telekinesis, huh?"

"I'm just glad I beat Ryan in The Panther's class," Benjamin laughed. "Can you imagine losing a Kinesis Combat to him?" He glanced over to the next table where Ryan and Jonathan sat. Ryan immediately looked up and glared back. Benjamin

80

looked away.

"*You think he can read my mind?*" he quietly asked Heidi.

"*I don't think so,*" she replied. "*I can sense his thoughts though, and right now, he's not even thinking about Iva. All he's thinking about is telekinesis.*"

"So what's up with you and Telepathy anyway?" he audibly asked her.

"I don't know," Heidi said. "I always just thought my telepathic abilities were normal. Well, I mean normal for people like us."

"It's definitely not normal to be able to see five statues on some island I've never even heard of," Andy said. "Easter Island? What's that? Does the Easter Bunny live there or something?"

"Well, I'd never heard of Easter Island before either," she said. "But there it was in her mind, plain as day."

"So can you read all of our minds, right now?" Andy asked.

"Without the Alliance bond?" Benjamin added.

"Well, I guess I could if I wanted to," Heidi replied. "But over the years, I've gotten pretty good at filtering out and ignoring most everything unimportant. I still have a hard time blocking really strong thoughts or emotions, though."

"So, what am I thinking about?" Andy tested her.

"Well, duh," Heidi replied. "You're thinking about how you were showing off in Telekinesis when you were spinning the rock around and around."

"I was not showing off," Andy protested. "I was just testing my skill level. Okay, how about now?"

"You're thinking about teleportation, and how you think

81

Asia Philippa is hot," Heidi replied.

"I am not," Andy exclaimed.

"Oh, really," Heidi said. "I think you are."

"Okay, maybe the thought crossed my mind, but it wasn't my main thought."

"Do you want me to tell you who is?" Heidi asked sweetly.

Andy turned bright red, looked down at his menu, and then quickly said, "No, that's okay. I believe you can read our minds, so you can go ahead and start filtering again, okay?"

Gary picked up the Kinetic Orb Benjamin had brought in with him. "Hey, this is cool." Amazingly, Gary levitated it in front of him and began to solve it, starting with the blue phase.

"You have to start with the center pieces of each phase," Andy told him. "That's the way to solve it."

Gary ignored Andy, instead concentrating on the sphere. At first, it looked like nothing, but then it began to take shape. One phase, then the next. As Gary continued solving it, his pace quickened. Before long, the Orb was complete. Gary levitated it down on the desk once again.

"Wow, that was great," Benjamin said. "Have you done it before?"

"Are you kidding? I don't even know what it is," Gary said. "I'm just pretty good with games and riddles and stuff like that." He looked at Andy. "And you don't have to start with the center pieces."

"That's how Benjamin said you have to solve it," Andy replied.

"No, what I say is that's the way you should solve it,"

Benjamin replied.

"Yeah, that's right. The way I chose is not the minimum number of moves, but it's the most mathematically straightforward algorithm," Gary explained.

Classes the next day consisted of Telegnosis and Science. True to her word, Iva had already met the Telegnosis teacher, Kyriake Eleni, and was already calling her just Kyri. And as Andy had predicted, Iva was definitely the teacher's pet. What Iva hadn't bargained on was anyone else being as good as she was at the subject.

"Jonathan Sheehan?" Iva said at lunch. "I can't believe he has such strong telegnostic powers."

"I'm sure yours are better," Heidi replied.

"But he's a guy," Iva replied.

"So?" Gary asked.

"So, you all heard Kyri. It's pretty unusual for a guy to be any good at telegnosis," Iva replied.

"I have a little bit of skill," Benjamin said.

"Nowhere near my skill level," Iva replied. "But for her to single him out in class! I just can't believe that." She looked down at the menu. "I'll take the fish sandwich."

"Fish!" Andy said. "But I thought you were a vegetarian."

"It's only fish, Andy. It's not real meat," Iva snapped. "And if I want to eat a fish sandwich I will, and I don't need you saying anything about it."

Andy opened his mouth to reply but quickly shut it. Anyone looking at Iva could tell she wasn't in the mood for teasing.

"Hey, Iva," Jonathan Sheehan called out from the next table where he was sitting with Ryan and two girls from their homeroom: Julie Macfarlane, and Suneeta Manvar.

Benjamin felt Iva tense up through the bond, but she pretended she didn't hear him.

"Hey, Iva," Jonathan called out again.

Iva finally turned to look.

"So how does it feel to have a guy be better than you at telegnosis?" Jonathan asked.

Iva's face flushed red, and Benjamin felt her anger through the Alliance bond.

"Hey, Jonathan," Andy called back. "How does it feel to have to cheat at telekinesis?"

"I don't cheat at telekinesis, and you know it," Jonathan called back.

"That's not what I heard," Andy replied.

"Yeah, well, you just wait until the next Kinesis Combat," Jonathan replied. "I'll stomp you."

After science class that afternoon, Benjamin couldn't believe Mr. Burton, his science teacher from back in Virginia, was really a telegen. "Okay, I've never seen Mr. Burton grow an extra set of arms like Mr. Hermes did today," Benjamin said.

"Well of course he wouldn't," Heidi said. "Not around humans."

"Not all telegens can grow and re-grow limbs you know," Gary said. "But I can. I had to re-grow my pinkie finger when I was little."

"You're kidding, right?" Andy asked.

Gary stuck out his hand in proof.

"It looks normal to me," Heidi said.

"Trust me, it's not. I remember I just had my seventh birthday, and my parents took me to the aquarium to celebrate. I knew I wasn't supposed to, but I stuck my hand in a small shark tank when no one was looking. You know, just to see what would happen," Gary explained.

"You stuck your hand in a shark tank just to see what would happen? What? Are you nuts?" Andy asked. He looked at Gary like maybe it was his brain he needed to re-grow.

"I guess so, because, before I knew it, the smallest shark of the bunch swam over and bit off my little finger. My parents totally freaked out. They quickly wrapped it up and hurried me out of there. They never said anything to anyone. I mean, don't people get sued over stuff like that? But then, after a month or so, it started to grow back. Once it started, it happened pretty fast—only took about a week. And here it is." Gary wiggled his pinkie.

"It was pretty cool when Mr. Hermes grew his hair," Iva said. "Not as cool as when Heidi changes her hair color though."

Heidi smoothed her now brown curly hair down. "Yeah, Julie Macfarlane keeps asking me if I can teach her how to do it. Frankly, I'd like to know how. It's been stuck this brown color for two days now, and I can't get it to change back."

Astronomy Doesn't Put
Everyone to Sleep

Out of more than sheer habit, although that was a big part of it, Benjamin resisted going to the first lecture of the summer. The whole evening would be wasted, and though it had only been a couple of days since the incident with the Emerald Tablet, it was starting to weigh on him. Some ancient relic had told him the fate of the world rested on his shoulders, and he was supposed to waste time going to lectures? He had to find more time to research the keys of the hunter—whatever they were. Yet, he didn't see any way he could really avoid the lecture; it was required coursework, and attendance was recorded.

Inside the main lecture hall, a man materialized on the platform in front of them. It was Mr. Hermes, their science teacher.

"In case you didn't get enough of me in science, you get me for lecture too," Mr. Hermes said. "At least for most of the lectures, so I hope you don't find me too boring."

"What are the lectures going to be about?" Jonathan asked the question everyone was wondering.

"Oh, we have a wonderful range of subjects lined up for the summer. It's always so difficult settling on the subjects for the lectures," Mr. Hermes said. "One of our more interesting lecture topics is Genetic Engineering."

"Well, won't that be something to hear?" Jack said. He appeared on the arm rest between Benjamin and Heidi. "I'll have to make sure I don't miss that one. I've been wanting to genetically engineer a telegen."

Mr. Hermes didn't notice the Nogical. "But what we're going to talk about tonight is astronomy."

"Oh, good," Jack said. "I was hoping that was tonight's lecture. Nothing like a quiet evening under the stars." He leaned back and closed his eyes.

"Please sit back and relax," Mr. Hermes said. The lights turned off in the lecture hall, and the domed ceiling became the nighttime sky. "But don't relax too much. I don't want anyone's snoring to disturb my lecture." On cue, Jack began to snore. For being so small, he could sure make plenty of noise.

Mr. Hermes started with the movement of the sun and the moon. Under the domed ceiling, Benjamin actually felt like he was outside. The ceiling really couldn't still be there. But he knew it was—and above it a giant dome keeping out the ocean.

Mr. Hermes covered eclipses, tides, and black holes. He then talked about constellations, most of which Benjamin recognized from family camping trips. Though he would never admit it, Benjamin loved astronomy. The sky was endless and filled with unexplained mysteries. Of course now that he was in Lemuria, his own life had plenty of mystery all on its own.

Benjamin loved the winter constellations, especially the ones surrounding the Orion myth—Taurus, Lepus, Canis Major and Minor, and of course Orion himself. In one myth, Gaea, the goddess of the Earth, ordered Orion killed by the giant scorpion Scorpius due to his boasting. Scorpius and Orion were placed at opposite ends of the sky where they would never battle again.

Benjamin remembered what Proteus Ajax had said about Gaea being one of the first of the telegens of Atlantis to declare herself a goddess to the humans of ancient Earth. Was Orion from Atlantis also?

Benjamin pressed the small holographic messenger near the side of his chair.

"Yes, Benjamin Holt?" Mr. Hermes said.

"I was wondering, was Orion from Atlantis? Proteus Ajax told us some of the Greek mythological figures were actually people of Atlantis trying to control the population of Earth," Benjamin said.

"Oh, good question, good question," Jack whispered to Benjamin, waking up fresh from his sleep.

"That's partially correct," Mr. Hermes said. "However, not all mythological figures were from Atlantis. Orion was actually from Lemuria, a highly skilled agent placed among the humans. Yet, Orion made one fatal mistake which led to his downfall. One day, he visited the court of King Oenopion where he fell deeply in love with one of the king's seven daughters, Merope. Like so many young men in love, Orion forgot his main duty, his service to Lemuria, and spent all his time persuading the king to allow him to marry Merope. Yet, nothing seemed to help; King Oenopion would not give his consent for the marriage. Enraged, Orion tried to kidnap Merope and marry her. The king blinded Orion and cast him far away. Orion visited the Oracle at Delphi who told him that the only way for his vision to be repaired would be to visit the false god from Atlantis, Apollo.

"Orion sought out Apollo and his twin sister Artemis. Apollo restored Orion's eyesight, but it seemed love had again sealed Orion's fate. He fell deeply in love with Artemis, a false goddess herself. Just when it seemed she might marry him, Apollo tricked her. Orion was swimming far from the shore. Apollo, knowing this, dared Artemis to shoot an arrow at the tiny speck on the top of the water, far, far away. Artemis easily loosed an arrow and hit the speck, which was in fact Orion. Orion was killed instantly," Mr. Hermes finished. "So, what lesson can we learn from the story of Orion?" he asked.

Andy spoke up. "Don't fall in love," he suggested. The entire class burst out laughing, even the girls.

"Well, maybe that too, but what I was thinking is that the story of Orion tells us that even the most gifted of us can be tricked by those who are evil," Mr. Hermes said. "Orion was a fantastic secret agent and was considered the most skilled hunter of his time. Nobody could even come close to competing with him. But Orion let down his guard against the enemy, and the jealous heart of Apollo caused his downfall."

A giant bell went off inside Benjamin's head. Orion. The hunter. Of course. Orion was known as a warrior, but he was better known as the biggest and best hunter in the whole world. Mythology across the whole of Earth, not just Greece, was sprinkled with the famous stories of Orion and his prowess over animals of all kinds. Taurus the Bull and Lepus the Hare were two of his favorite prey. His hunting dogs, Canis Major and Canis Minor were placed right up there in the sky with him. Could Orion be the hunter the Emerald Tablet had made reference to?

Benjamin didn't even try to focus on the rest of the lecture, most of it having to do with neighboring stars and their solar systems. Mr. Hermes then touched briefly on comets, meteors, and meteorites, talking about some of the more famous ones. All Benjamin thought about was expanding his search, including Orion, to see if anything would come up having to do with keys they were looking for. He'd never heard of any stories of Orion using keys, but then, he'd never heard of hidden continents under the ocean before this week.

It was ten o'clock when they left the lecture hall. Benjamin purposely fell behind, Andy, Gary, Heidi, and Iva joining him. Jack had left toward the end of the lecture, making excuses about how tired he was though he'd slept the entire time. Once no one else was around, Benjamin spoke.

"Did you guys pick up on that?" he asked.

"Pick up on what?" Iva said.

"Orion, the hunter," Benjamin accentuated the word. Their tired eyes looked back at him. He rolled his eyes. "Aren't we looking for information about a hunter?" he asked.

"Oh. Oh yeah, I get it," Gary said, covering his mouth as he yawned. "Maybe the hunter is Orion. Is that what you're thinking?"

"Yeah, that's what I'm thinking. At least I'm thinking its worth searching on." Benjamin frowned. "I mean, we don't have anything else to go on right now."

"But when are we going to have another chance to search?" Heidi asked. "They've got stuff planned for us like every night."

"Well, we can try to do some between classes," Gary suggested. "I don't mind going back to the library."

"And Andy and I can snoop around again," Iva said.

Andy quickly glanced at Iva and then looked away. Benjamin watched but didn't think Iva had noticed.

"Okay, why don't we just try to do what we can before the weekend? I don't think another couple days will matter that much," Benjamin said. But though none of his friends seemed to agree, he hated to wait any longer. He just wanted to get this whole matter resolved and behind him—find the keys and be done with it.

14

The Sky Collapses

Though the clue with Orion hadn't turned anything up yet, at least it gave Benjamin hope he would solve the riddle of the keys of the hunter—the hunter he knew just had to be Orion.

When the first Saturday rolled around, Benjamin could hardly believe it and almost regretted not having classes for the next two days. "What am I thinking?" he asked himself. "Who, besides Gary, gets upset that there aren't classes on the weekend?"

"Hey, happy birthday!" Andy said to Benjamin, slapping him on the back.

Benjamin stopped dead in his tracks. "My birthday?"

"Uh, yeah," Andy said. "Remember—comes once a year. You didn't forget, did you?"

"Kind of," Benjamin said. "But it's been a pretty busy week."

"Your birthday's the longest day of the year?" Gary asked. "How cool is that? Did you get anything?"

Benjamin held up the card he'd just opened. He read it and looked up. "My mom says they set up a DNA credit account for me. She says I can buy whatever I want."

"I wonder if my mom set one up for me," Andy replied. "Maybe I can buy myself something for your birthday. Or better yet, you can buy me something for your birthday."

"Don't count on it," Benjamin replied, laughing.

Jack appeared in front of Benjamin's face just as he exited the massive double doors of the school. In an impressive display of self control, Benjamin only jumped a little. Having the Nogical appear and disappear without warning was becoming more…normal.

"Mind if I tag along?" Jack didn't wait for an answer. "No, of course you don't. I mean why would you? So, we're headed for the Abilities Trials, right? I love the Abilities Trials. I never miss them. At least I haven't in over three hundred years." He smiled at the five students, then settled on Benjamin's left shoulder.

"You've been alive for three hundred years?" Heidi asked.

"Four hundred and twelve to be exact," Jack said. "In fact today is my birthday."

"Hey, it's my birthday too," Benjamin said.

"Tell me something I don't know," Jack said.

"You didn't tell us it was your birthday," Heidi said before Benjamin could ask Jack how he knew.

"I kind of forgot," Benjamin said. "Andy had to remind me."

"How can you forget your birthday?" Heidi asked.

"It's been a busy week," Benjamin defended. "And I've been a little bit preoccupied with the keys we're supposed to find."

"Why are you so worried about them?" Andy asked. "We

still have seven weeks of summer school left."

"That's why," Benjamin replied. "Because we only have seven weeks of summer school left. Somehow we have to find these three keys and bring peace on Earth in seven weeks." Yet he could tell through the Alliance bond that none of his friends, with the slight, possible exception of Iva, felt any urgency to find the hunter's keys.

"So, what are the trials like?" Gary asked Jack.

"It's like a bunch of people getting up and showing off in front of each other," Jack said. "But I'll admit it. I've seen it three hundred and five times, and each year I'm amazed by something."

"So, it's a competition, like we had in telekinesis class, right?" Heidi asked.

"I don't think you really competed with Jonathan Sheehan," Benjamin said. "I mean, it was more like a slaughter if you ask me." He, Andy, and Gary all started laughing.

Iva scowled at them. "Yes, well nobody did ask you, so why don't you just shut up next time."

Heidi smiled at Iva.

"Anyway, what are you laughing at, Gary?" Iva continued. "You let Suneeta beat you, and we all know she isn't very good at anything except brown-nosing. She has a hard time lifting her napkin in the dining hall."

Jack cleared his tiny little throat. "Anyway, to answer your question, it's not really a competition. It's more like a show. Telegens with all sorts of talents get up in front of the crowd and show off. But we better hurry if we want to get good seats."

The main arena was at the end of Mu Way, about a mile from the school. Spaced every so often were public teleporters with lines queued up to access them.

"Why don't more people teleport on their own?" Benjamin asked Jack.

"Most people can hardly even teleport a block anymore," Jack said.

Benjamin flushed. Though no one in the class had been successful yet, it still irked Benjamin that he hadn't been able to move the block. In fact, he'd even been spending some of his free time trying. Just when he felt like the block was about to move to his mind, his concentration would break.

"How common is it?" Heidi asked.

"Well, for you 'regular' telegens, only about one out of every sixty-four people is able to teleport themselves," Jack replied. "Of course, almost all Nogicals can teleport, so we hardly ever have to rely on machines."

As they walked, Benjamin squinted up at the passing shops and restaurants. Just as he opened his mouth, Iva beat him to it.

"Why are all the shop signs in Russian?" she asked. "I would have expected them to be in English, or something."

"They aren't in Russian," Andy said. "Of course they're in English."

"Yeah, it looks like English to me," Benjamin agreed.

"They're in any language you want," Jack answered. "In truth, they're in ancient Lemurian. The symbols interact with your mind and create an illusion. Which is good since hardly anyone bothers to learn ancient Lemurian anymore."

Benjamin was so focused on trying to break the illusion of the signs, when he finally looked forward again, a huge arena loomed above him. They found seats midway up the bleachers with the grassy field area far, far below. In fact it was so far below, Benjamin figured only maybe a super-telegen could hear or see anything. But before he could ask Jack about it, a hush fell over the crowd. A large holographic image appeared high in the air. Clear as day, it showed the rulers of Lemuria, Helios and Selene Deimos, larger than life, walking to their seats. They turned and faced the crowd, smiling and waving. As they sat down, applause broke out. Benjamin and his friends joined in with the crowd.

"Welcome to the Summer Solstice Ability Trials," Selene Deimos said. She might as well have been speaking a couple yards away from Benjamin she was so loud and clear. "I'm pleased everybody could join us."

"We have taken the privilege of altering the weather slightly to provide for a more enjoyable day," Helios said.

"It's raining today," Jack said in Benjamin's ear. "In fact, it's supposed to rain all week."

"No it's not. It's beautiful. I've never seen such a perfect day," Benjamin replied.

"That's because we live in a giant dome," Jack said. "Normally they don't mess with the weather, but on special occasions, it's permissible."

"They can do that?" Benjamin asked. "They can change the weather?"

"Of course they can do that. They're the rulers," Jack said. "Selene's especially good at it."

"And now, let the Ability Trials begin," Selene said. Applause erupted.

"Are the Deimos twins going to do anything special?" Andy asked over the cheering crowd.

"You mean other than changing the weather?" Jack said. "No, they normally don't expend their energy showing off for the population, just in case some kind of emergency comes up or something."

The telecaster had two heads, but that was only the start of the excitement. The first few acts of the Lemurian Summer Solstice Ability Trials were mostly for entertainment. A three-eyed juggler warmed up the audience by juggling sixteen balls. As he juggled, new balls teleported into the mix, but the rhythm continued, until there were a total of fifty. Done with the balls, he blindfolded all three of his eyes and began juggling flaming rings. The act ended when one of the rings landed on his head, burning his hair completely off. He quickly walked off the stage, re-growing his hair as he went.

A group of identically dressed, synchronized levitating females went next. They rose into the air and began a series of elaborate dance type movements, just like synchronized swimmers. Benjamin found himself yawning and wondering how long the routine could possibly go on. He joined the crowd's cheering at the end, because he was so happy the act was finally over.

Two large men introduced as Nori-san and Goro-san

walked out into the center of the arena next. They looked alike and were dressed as sumo wrestlers. The holographic image disappeared, and the two men seemed tiny at the bottom of the field. Benjamin and his friends joined as the crowd booed, thinking the holographic display had broken. Three rows in front of them, Ryan and Jonathan were throwing popcorn at the field. Although Benjamin was tempted to take the opportunity to toss the rest of Heidi's hotdog at them, he didn't.

Benjamin squinted down at the two men instead. Ignoring the booing from the crowd, Nori-san picked up a water bottle and took a long drink. He passed the water bottle to the other man, Goro-san, who also took a huge gulp, and then tossed the water bottle away.

The men walked five paces apart and squared off. It was going to be a sumo match. Suddenly, both men began to grow; they grew and grew and grew, until before long, they stood as tall as the seats where Benjamin and his friends sat.

"How in the world can anybody grow that big?" Benjamin asked.

"It's the water they drank," Jack answered. "It hydrates their pores and allows them to soak in all sorts of things from the air around them in order to grow."

"Amazing," Gary said. "That makes total sense. By keeping their pores moist, they're able to drink in the air, and thus, sort of inflate their bodies."

"Exactly," Jack said.

Benjamin and Andy looked at each other and shrugged. At least someone understood.

The sumo match ended with Nori-san nearly smashing into the crowded stands, freezing in midair just yards away from Benjamin and his friends.

"And that's how we do Sumo wrestling here in Lemuria," Jack quipped to Benjamin.

"I was sure he was gonna hit us," Gary said.

"I knew he'd stop," Andy said.

"Oh, really," Iva said. "Then why did you spill your soda down the front of your pants?"

Andy looked down at his pants; the front of them was soaked. "Benjamin must have bumped into me when he was trying to crawl under the seat."

Benjamin shot Andy a wry look but didn't respond. The next act was getting ready to start.

The holographic projector restarted and a small woman walked to the center of the arena. She almost whispered to the crowd, but the projector magnified her voice so all could hear.

"My name is Liro. This is my first time in the ability trials. It is an honor to be here. I will be giving a small telekinesis demonstration. Please do not be frightened." She cleared her throat and was silent.

"Why would I possibly be frightened of her?" Andy said.

"Let's just watch and see." Iva replied.

"What do you think she's gonna move?" Heidi asked.

"Can't you read her mind?" Benjamin asked.

"No, there's a lot of crowd interference, and she has it mostly blocked off," Heidi replied. "I think the better per-formers can shield their minds pretty well to avoid losing their concentration."

Liro held her place in the center of the arena. She took several deep breaths, inhaling and exhaling slowly. She closed her eyes, and raised her arms up above her head. All at once, every muscle in her arms tightened, her fingers outstretched toward the sky.

The wind began to howl. People's hair began to whip around. The sky slowly started to darken.

"I don't believe it," Jack said as his little eyes grew triple size. "Nobody has ever tried this before."

"Is she trying to change the weather?" Heidi asked, shouting to be heard over the whipping wind.

"No," Jack replied. "I think that's only a side effect. Look at that." He pointed straight upward.

"I don't believe it!" Andy said. "The sky is collapsing!"

It looked exactly like that. Where before there had been a beautiful light blue sky, a midnight blue blanket now pressed downward.

"It's not the sky," Jack said. "It's the dome. She's collapsing the dome down on us." He had to yell now to be heard over the wind and the crowd.

The dome continued on its downward course, collapsing like a giant had pressed down on it from the outside. Just as the point of the dome depression reached the top of the arena, it stopped. Here it held for a moment, then, at the same speed as its descent, it began to climb back up.

"That must be some dome to be able to withstand that kind of structural displacement," Gary said.

"Yeah. And I was beginning to think nothing could surprise me," Jack said.

The sky returned to its full brightness, and Liro lowered her arms and walked off the arena floor with her head down amid a mass of cheering.

The acts continued. Funny. Scary. Boring. The ability trials had it all. As the sun moved farther across the sky, the final performer in the Summer Solstice Trials came onto the stage.

"And now," the two-headed telecaster said with one of his heads. "The man of the hour."

"The ten time unofficial winner of the trials," the other head said.

A hush fell over the crowd.

"It is with my greatest pleasure that I introduce to you," the first head said.

"Andreas Matthias," the second head said.

The hush that had fallen over the crowd exploded into cheering.

"He always has something edgy planned," Jack leaned over and whispered in Benjamin's ear.

Andreas Matthias walked to the center of the arena, and, again, the crowd quieted down. Whispers broke out in the crowd as Andreas Matthias simply stood on the stage, watching the audience, not saying a word. He stood there for a full three minutes doing nothing. Not much edgy about that, Benjamin thought.

And then, everything around Benjamin disappeared. The world became a dullish gray. The sounds of the crowd vanished.

He was no longer with his friends at the trials. He was in a hallway, near a closed door with a light emitting from the bottom. Benjamin felt weightless, like he was being carried. He turned his head away from the door and saw an enormous man approaching. Just a silhouette, but there was something familiar about it. Quickly he turned his face back to the door as he heard a sound. Sobbing. There was someone behind the door crying. A woman. Something deep inside Benjamin ached as he heard the sound. He longed to go through the door. To be with the crying woman.

"I came as fast as I could," the silhouetted man said, distracting Benjamin from the crying. Benjamin turned toward the man, away from the door.

And then, without warning, Benjamin was back at the trials, in his seat, his friends around him. Their faces mirrored what Benjamin was sure his own looked like. What was that?

It took about half a minute, but resounding applause finally did break out. Benjamin realized that the entire episode must have been some sort of mind control trick. How could one person control the minds of the entire crowd at the same time? He noticed Andy and Gary had joined in with the crowd, clapping as hard as their hands would let them. But Benjamin didn't feel like clapping and noticed Iva didn't either. And Heidi just looked angry. Really angry.

All Benjamin felt was sick to his stomach. Like there was an empty hole there now and nothing to fill it. What did it mean? Was it a vision of the future? The past? A dream? And who was the woman who had been crying?

The World Is a Ball

No one tried to talk until they reached the main level and were back on Mu Way. There was too much going on. Too many people.

"Was that the coolest thing you've ever seen, or what?" Gary finally asked.

"It didn't feel so cool to me," Benjamin said. "I found it disturbing."

"Disturbing?" Andy asked. "Are you kidding? I felt like I was reliving the best experience in my life."

"Which was what?" Iva asked.

"Disney World! What else?" Andy exclaimed.

"So what just happened?" Iva asked. "Because I have to agree with Benjamin. The whole thing creeped me out."

"It was really weird," Heidi said. "I knew what he was gonna do before he even started, and I knew what he was doing when it was happening, but I still couldn't stop it. It was like I was standing back and watching him come in and control my mind." She shuddered. "I think he was picking memories out of our minds and replaying them."

"That's impossible," Iva said. "I never had that experience before."

"What was it?" Andy asked.

"I don't want to talk about it," Iva said. "But I know I've never had it."

"I can't explain it," Heidi said as her brow crinkled. "Maybe it was thoughts also."

Benjamin relaxed. At least he wasn't the only one who'd had a negative experience. "It must've been. Mine wasn't a memory either," he said.

"I felt so happy," Andy said. "It was kind of a bummer when I realized I was back at the trials."

"I think our friend Andreas Matthias is getting a little carried away with himself," Jack said. "I'm actually surprised the Deimos twins put up with that kind of display."

"Why wouldn't they?" Andy asked.

"Well, that trick Andreas just pulled borders closely on mind control, like Heidi just said," Jack replied. "Mind control is one of those restricted things—only used when absolutely necessary."

"So, why was it allowed then?" Heidi asked.

"I guess it wasn't true mind control," Jack answered. "Andreas placed an illusion field around each person in the stadium. Everyone was in total control of their own mind. But, still, it's walking the line if you ask me." Jack shook his head. "Anyway, it's been fun, but I really must run." And Jack, the Nogical, teleported away.

"So what did you guys relive?" Ryan Jordan asked, interrupting their conversation.

Heidi whipped her head around, her brown hair turning bright red. "Do you mind? Can't you see we're having a private conversation here?" Even if Benjamin hadn't felt her anger, the hair-changing-color thing would have given it away.

"Hey," Jonathan said. "We're just trying to be friendly. Why are you always so rude?"

"Because you guys are always butting into stuff that's none of your business," Andy replied. Benjamin glanced into Andy's mind and swore he felt jealousy hidden somewhere behind the anger. This Alliance thing seriously gave an inside perspective into almost everything.

"You know, I'll butt in whenever and wherever I want," Ryan replied. "And frankly, I'm a little sick of your attitude. But just go ahead and keep your little secrets."

He and Jonathan turned and walked away.

"They were trying to read our minds," Heidi said. "I mean Ryan was. I don't think Jonathan would have even stood a chance. And Ryan's still trying now."

"Can you hold him out?" Gary asked.

"Of course," Heidi laughed. "They're both pretty pathetic at telepathy."

"Still, we need to be a little more careful around them," Benjamin said. "I don't trust them."

"Yeah, me neither," Andy said. "So what are you gonna get for your birthday?" he asked, shifting the conversation. Benjamin could still sense the jealously and anger, but figured maybe saying something about it wouldn't be the coolest thing in the world to do.

"I don't know. Maybe we can find something cool in one of these shops." Benjamin gestured toward the countless stores lining the street.

"Let's try this one," Heidi said, nodding at a shop on the left. It had a variety of things—for lack of a better word—displayed in the front windows. A three dimensional sign above it read 'The Silver Touch' and showed a holographic silver cube floating in the air. As they entered the shop, a bell rang.

Immediately off to the right sat a large chess set; Gary made a beeline for it. "Whoa. This is beautiful. I've never seen anything like it," he said. And Gary wasn't understating. Each piece was made of a gem which changed color depending on the angle it was being viewed from.

"And you never will again," a voice said, coming from the back. "Each piece is a solitary piece of Ammolite—the rarest gem on Earth. It's so rare because each piece is a fossil of the ancient Cretaceous creature the Ammonite."

"It's amazing," Gary said.

"Well, go ahead. You can pick up a piece and feel it," the shopkeeper said.

Gary carefully picked up a rook standing on a white base. The piece was light and smooth and reflected a rainbow of colors.

"I've had this set for a long time," the shopkeeper said. "Nobody wants to spend the money to buy it. But I don't mind. I've come to look forward to seeing it here each day. I think I would miss it if it sold." Benjamin, Andy, Heidi, and Iva walked over to join Gary. The shopkeeper looked the students over. "Year One Denarians, I would guess. Summer school students, if I'm not mistaken."

The students nodded their heads.

"My name's Morpheus Midas." He extended his right hand. "Welcome to the Silver Touch."

Gary carefully placed the rook back on the chessboard, and shook the extended hand. "Gary Goodweather."

"Pleased to meet you, Gary. Are you a fan of chess?" Morpheus asked.

"Oh, I love to play, but I have a hard time finding anyone who puts up much of a challenge," Gary answered.

"Have you tried your telekinesis teacher?" Morpheus asked.

"You mean Pantheros Pavlos?" Iva said.

"Well, I called him The Panther when I was in school, but yes. Whenever I'm looking for some real competition, I still look him up." He smiled at Gary. "Of course, if you really are that good, you could come by any time you like for a game. I'm not bad." Morpheus Midas nodded to a poster hanging on the wall behind him. It had a close up picture of a checkmate.

"Bangkok Chess Open?" Gary said. "You mean you've played there?"

"What's the Bangkok Chess Open?" Andy asked.

"Only the biggest and most important chess tournament in the entire world," Gary replied. He looked back at Morpheus. "But it wouldn't really even be a challenge, would it? I mean, wouldn't you be able to read everybody's minds?"

"Well, I would if I let myself, but that wouldn't be very sportsmanlike," Morpheus answered. "No, I let it be solely a game of wit. In fact, there've been years that I've lost. Of course, sometimes that's been on purpose. We're not supposed to compete in events with humans, you know. So the whole thing has to be incognito, if you know what I mean." He winked.

"'The Silver Touch'? Morpheus Midas, you said?" Benjamin asked.

"The one and only," Morpheus said. "Have you heard of me?"

"Well, I've heard of King Midas," Benjamin replied, "but he turned things into gold, not silver. Right?" If the Greek gods were for real, then why not a mythological king?

Morpheus cleared his throat. "My notorious alchemist ancestor. Yes, he was a distant relative on my father's side, and yes, he did turn objects into gold. Much more common in my family, however, is transmuting objects into silver."

"You can change things into silver?" Heidi asked.

"Well, no, I can't, but the store has been in my family for generations," Morpheus said. "We may even still have some of the stuff that got changed over the ages around here." He glanced around the store.

The beauty of the Ammolite seemed to mesmerize Iva. "Do you have anything else made of Ammolite?" she asked. "You know, maybe something small, like jewelry?"

"Beautiful jewelry for a beautiful young lady," Morpheus

replied. Iva smiled. Andy scowled. "I have just the thing for you," Morpheus said, leading her over to a jewelry display case near what looked like an antique cash register. He reached into the case and picked up an elliptical shaped pendant suspended on a long silver chain and held it out to Iva.

"Oh, it's beautiful," she said, placing it over her head. "It's hard to tell exactly what colors are in it. It keeps changing," she said, admiring it.

"Ammolite is said to have special powers too," Morpheus said. "Have you learned anything about telemagnifiers yet in any of your classes?" he asked.

"Telemagnifiers?" Andy repeated.

"They're objects which can be used to increase the power of one's mind. Simply put, when the strength of the mind is not enough, the telemagnifiers amplify the mind's abilities," Morpheus said.

"You mean by wearing this pendant, I'll be able to lift heavier objects?" Iva asked.

"Oh, no, that's not quite right. You see, different telemagnifiers work with different abilities. In the case of Ammolite, telegnostic powers may be increased," Morpheus said.

"Telegnosis is my favorite subject," Iva said. "I feel like I was born for it."

"And so you may have been," Morpheus suggested.

"Well either you're the perfect salesman, or I was meant to find this pendant," Iva said, "but whichever it is, I'll take it."

"Perhaps it's both," Morpheus replied to Iva, chuckling, as he stamped her thumb down on a scanner pad to get her DNA credit account information.

The mention of the telemagnifiers gave Benjamin a great idea. Could the keys of the hunter—of Orion, if that really was a valid connection—be telemagnifiers? And if so, would Morpheus know where they could buy them?

"So what other kinds of telemagnifiers do you sell?" Benjamin asked. No need to be too direct.

"What kind are you looking for?" Morpheus asked. "I have big ones, small ones, yellow ones, ones you eat."

"Any that look like keys?" Benjamin asked. "Maybe that are pretty old?"

"Or that a hunter might use," Heidi added.

Benjamin wondered if she was reading his mind or had just figured out what he was getting at.

"Telemagnifiers that are keys, used by a hunter." Morpheus thought for a moment. "Can't say that I've seen any key tele-magnifiers. But I have multitudes of other items. I'm sure there's something to please everyone."

Okay, so it didn't sound like Morpheus knew anything about the keys of Orion.

"*It was a good idea though.*" Benjamin's head turned when he heard Heidi's voice in his head. He smiled at her, and she smiled back. It was still just weird getting used to so many people with telepathic skills.

"What do you have that would make a good birthday gift?" Benjamin asked.

"Who's the present for? Mother? Father? Brother? A young lady?" He winked.

Benjamin felt his face heat up. "Oh, no, it's for me. Today's my birthday, and my parents told me I could get myself something." Benjamin looked around the store. "But to tell you the truth, I really don't know what most of this stuff is. I'm pretty sure I don't want any jewelry," he said looking down at the case where Iva's pendant had come from.

Morpheus studied Benjamin. "I have the perfect thing." He walked over to a large display case in the center of the room. From it he pulled a small globe of the Earth, about the size of a golf ball.

"Oh, I don't need a globe," Benjamin said, hoping not to hurt the man's feelings.

"A globe! I hardly think so. This, young man, is a Geodine. Invented by one of my ancestors as a matter of fact." He held the object out to Benjamin.

"It looks like a globe to me," Andy agreed with Benjamin. "What's a Geodine? Does it mean really small globe or something?"

"I'll dim the lights and show you." Morpheus said. While he spoke, the lights in the room grew dark, and the door and windows shaded over. Benjamin held the Geodine on his right palm. "Activate it with your mind." Morpheus said. "It will understand the commands of whoever holds it."

In his mind, Benjamin willed the object to do something, but what, he had no idea. Regardless, the Geodine began to glow, blue and green, the colors of the earth. It cast out a three dimensional image of the earth, starting from what appeared to be the creation of the planet. The image shifted and swirled while a voice narrated the origin of the earth. Land masses could be seen forming, oceans growing.

"You can make the narration audible or telepathic, or turn if off completely," Morpheus said.

Benjamin willed off the sound. He found that he could control the speed of the events on Earth, could zoom in to any location he wanted for any time. He could see the creation of plants and animals, could see the Ice Age, could see the sinking of Lemuria. It was an entire history of the earth contained in a globe the size of a golf ball.

And then something really weird happened. Benjamin held the Geodine in his fist and closed his eyes. He wasn't sure why. He just did it. And an image flashed into his brain. Three hearts, intertwined. Yet as soon as the image appeared in his mind, it vanished, and Benjamin was left with a deep feeling of disappointment. Like he wanted to have a connection with whatever had caused the image to come to him, but he didn't.

Opening his eyes, he turned off the Geodine, looked up at Morpheus Midas. He knew he wasn't leaving the store without the thing, no matter what it cost. For whatever reason, he was meant to have this Geodine.

"It's perfect. I'll take it," he said. He tossed it up in the air to catch it, but missed, and he felt his heart stop beating—just for a second. The Geodine dropped to the floor, but landed softly, making barely a sound, and rolled a few feet away.

"Did I mention that it is virtually indestructible?" Morpheus said.

Benjamin's heart started beating again. "I'm glad to hear

that," he said, retrieving the Geodine from under the nearby table. He wrapped his fingers around it again and this time put it in his pocket.

16

Morpheus's Secret

As if the weight of saving the world wasn't enough, school was too busy. In the following week, Benjamin found little to no time to search for more clues about the keys. And what brief time he did have turned up nothing. But he and Heidi continued working on their sheaves when they could, and Gary spent every spare second he had in the library.

So when Saturday morning finally rolled around, everyone was ready for a break. With five differing opinions, trying to agree on something to do was just about impossible. Finally, they just decided to head into the city. Passing The Silver Touch, Heidi suggested they stop in to look at a ring she'd seen the week before.

When he walked into the shop, the first thing Benjamin saw was a chess game in play—with Morpheus Midas and The Panther on opposite sides of the Ammolite chess board.

Morpheus greeted them as they entered. "Hello, my friends. Are you back so soon?" he called.

Benjamin smiled and waved, but Gary didn't even pause as

he walked over to the chess board. "So, how's the game going?" he asked, studying the board and pieces.

"Well, you got me re-interested in chess, so I called my old teacher, The Panther, here to come play me a few games." Morpheus winked at the students. "I'm even going to play in the Bangkok Chess Open next weekend. How exciting. How exciting."

"He's going to play as long as nobody knows where he's going," The Panther replied. "You know you're not supposed to compete against the humans," he said. "It's completely and totally inappropriate, not to mention illegal. But since you insist upon going, I consider it my obligation to go with you."

Gary's eyes became wide and unblinking. "Oh, I'd love to go. Can I come along?"

The Panther slammed his fist down on the table, and Morpheus cringed as the chess pieces shook. "Even if you weren't one of my students, I would have to say no," The Panther said, "Absolutely not! It would be appalling for a Year One Denarian to leave the city of Mu. That kind of thing would get you kicked out of the school."

"Are you sure?" Gary asked.

Hadn't Gary heard The Panther? Or did he just want to get kicked out of school?

The Panther stared Gary down before scooting his chair out from the table.

"So, what may I help you with today?" Morpheus asked, the shopkeeper in him taking over.

"I saw a ring here last weekend that I think is Moonstone."

Heidi pointed to a gold ring with a spherical orange stone.

"Ah, yes, a beautiful piece," Morpheus said. "Let's try it on your finger, shall we?" He placed the large ring on her right hand.

"I've heard moonstone helps increase telepathic abilities," Heidi said. "Is that true?"

"Moonstone is indeed a powerful telemagnifier in the area of telepathy," Morpheus replied. "The wearer of this ring will see increased range in her telepathic powers."

"How much more do you want to increase your telepathic powers?" Benjamin asked. "You're already better than the rest of us put together."

Heidi giggled. "Oh, that's not quite true. I mean, I'm probably close, but there's always room for improvement," she replied.

"What kind of stone is that?" Iva asked, pointing to a teardrop shaped green stone. She didn't have to voice the similarity the glossy green stone had to the Emerald Tablet they'd seen in the Ruling Hall.

"A Moldavite," Morpheus said. "A strong telemagnifier. That particular one came from a meteor which landed in Australia. The Moldavite is a highly valued stone due to its extraterrestrial origins. It comes to Earth from space."

"It's color is unique," Iva said. "Are there many stones like it?"

Morpheus shook his head and sighed. "No, unfortunately they're extremely rare, especially here in Lemuria. We can track the meteors landing on Earth, but most of the time humans reach the Moldavites first."

After Heidi purchased the Moonstone ring, they left the store and headed back out to the city.

They weren't five steps out of the store when Iva stopped and spun around. "Do you guys remember what Mr. Hermes was talking about last week in the Astronomy lecture?" she asked.

"Sure," Andy said. "That was the night he was talking about Orion. We already know that."

"No, not about Orion. Don't you remember what else he talked about after that?" she said.

"I stopped listening after I figured out the hunter must be Orion," Benjamin said.

"And I stopped listening way before that," Andy added.

Iva rolled her eyes. "You guys really should pay better attention."

"Hey, don't generalize," Gary said. "I remember. He started talking about comets and other solar systems."

"He started talking about famous meteorites that had landed on Earth, many of them coming from some of the closest solar systems," Iva said.

"And...," Andy said impatiently. Apparently, even Iva's good looks couldn't keep Andy interested in Astronomy.

"And, he said that there was one famous meteorite from the solar system of Betelgeuse which allegedly landed in the hidden city of Shambhala," Iva said.

"And...," Andy said.

"Betelgeuse is in the solar system of Orion," Iva said.

"So you think maybe this has something to do with the

keys?" Benjamin asked.

"Well, don't you think it's a little bit of a coincidence that the Emerald Tablet is made of the stone of a meteorite and that there was a famous meteorite that came from a solar system in the great hunter?" she said.

"I see what you're saying," Benjamin said.

"It doesn't mean anything," Andy said.

Iva glared at him.

"I mean, I guess it could mean something," he amended.

"Well, it's at least worth investigating," Benjamin said. "We haven't got anything else."

They stayed out in the city for the rest of the day, but after dinner it was back to work. In one of the less crowded study rooms, Benjamin pulled out his sheaf, activated it, and began to perform some searches on meteorites and hunters, vocalizing his thoughts so everyone could hear. But it wasn't long before any hope he had of finding useful information was squashed.

Yes, there was a meteorite that had come from the solar system of Betelgeuse. Yes, Betelgeuse was in the constellation of Orion. Yes, the meteorite had allegedly landed in the mysterious and mythical city of Shambhala. No, the meteorite had never been found. But nothing alluded to keys associated with any of this. Benjamin felt like his head was going to explode from all the useless information they were finding.

"There's nothing here," he said, tossing the sheaf onto the table in front of him. "I think we're heading down a dead end." He looked at Iva. "It was a good idea though."

"What about this one?" Gary asked, picking up the sheaf.

"That's just gibberish," Andy said.

"No it's not," Gary replied. "It's the same language that was on the Emerald Tablet."

"You're kidding, right?" Benjamin grabbed the sheaf from Gary and looked down at it. "I've been staring at that the whole time and thought it was nothing. What does it say?"

"If you give it back, I'll translate it," Gary replied.

Benjamin handed the sheaf back to Gary who studied it. A smile crept onto his face. "Oh, that's clever," he said.

"What's clever?" Andy asked.

"It's a poem," Gary said.

"What's so clever about a poem?" Andy asked.

"It's written in the same verse style as the writing on The Emerald Tablet," Gary replied. "Listen.

> *"Shambhala is always near*
> *Though hidden beneath our sphere.*
> *The keys will there again appear*
> *And all the world will quake in fear."*

Benjamin leaned forward. "Did that say keys and Shambhala?" he asked.

Heidi grabbed the sheaf from Gary. "Yes," she said, and she didn't even notice as her hair turned white blond. "And there's more." She scanned the sheaf. "According to this, there was a meteorite that landed in Shambhala years ago. It was called the Stone of Shambhala, or the Chintamani Stone. The meteorite was divided by the leaders of Shambhala into three pieces, which were then referred to as the keys of Shambhala. The keys were placed in secret locations around the world, to be discovered when the Seeker of Justice had the need to enter the kingdom of Shambhala." She looked at Benjamin. "You must be the Seeker of Justice."

"But where is Shambhala? Does it really exist?" Andy asked. "How would Benjamin get there anyway?"

"It says here that Shambhala is actually under the protection of Lemuria. Its location is alleged to be somewhere in Tibet, and it's often referred to as an underground city." She looked up. "So, I'm guessing that it does exist."

"But, where would the meteorite, I mean the keys, have gone?" Benjamin asked. "How do we find them?"

"Well, it doesn't say that," Heidi answered. "I mean, they wouldn't be in very good hidden locations if this article said where they were, now would they?"

"No, I guess not, but I just thought maybe there would be a hint or something," Benjamin said.

Only six weeks left. Benjamin felt like pulling his hair out as he sat up late at night thinking about it. He'd gone to bed the same time as Gary and Andy, but couldn't sleep; in fact, the only thing he could do was think about the keys. If the keys really were from the Stone of Shambhala, then how would he find them?

Looking for something to do, he took out his Geodine, tossing it up in the air and catching it. He then put it in super fast forward mode. This mode showed the earth being created in the past and then destroyed in the future when the Sun expanded into a red giant. The entire process for the Geodine took about fifteen seconds. He slowed it down, focusing first on the destruction of the Earth, and then concentrating on the creation of the Earth. How could so much information be stored in such a tiny object?

As he watched the creation of the Earth, and the early years of the planet, he noticed the Earth being pummeled with lots of meteors, large craters being formed by the impact. And then it suddenly occurred to Benjamin. Would he be able to see the Shambhala meteorite hitting the Earth? He rewound the Geodine, focusing on the area of Earth known as Tibet.

Tibet didn't get nearly the hits that some places did. Only one meteorite had landed there in the last one hundred years. Benjamin focused his search on the period of time many thousands of years ago. Even then, Tibet didn't appear to be a meteorite hot bed. But finally, one particular meteorite did catch Benjamin's attention. The stone was green. He watched as it hit the Earth, near a large mountain. And then, it was as if the earth itself swallowed up the stone, hiding if from view. Could this be the meteorite they searched for?

With patience, Benjamin watched the area around where the meteorite had fallen, but no activity occurred there. Then, suddenly, he saw a stir of something. Benjamin zoomed in on the area. He could see a stone, green, and about a third the size of the meteorite, being taken away from Tibet. He watched the path of the stone, looking for its destination. It traveled south, heading by boat down the River Ping into Thailand. It continued traveling, until the river emptied into the Gulf of Thailand. And then the movement of the stone stopped. It was in Bangkok.

They Plan to Break the Rules

Benjamin ran back into the bedroom. "Hey, get up, get up. I know where the first key is," he said.

Andy rolled over and rubbed his eyes. "What time is it?" he asked.

"It's two in the morning, but that doesn't matter. I know where the first key is," Benjamin repeated.

"Well, where?" Andy asked. Both he and Gary were now sitting up.

"It's in Bangkok," Benjamin said.

"How could you know that?" Gary asked.

"Did you dream it?" Andy said, yawning.

"The Geodine showed me," Benjamin said. He pulled it out of his pocket and held it out in his hand. "I watched the meteorite land in Tibet, and then watched the stone, or at least part of it, being taken to Bangkok."

"That little globe showed that to you?" Andy asked.

"This little globe is amazing. It shows you everything. The key traveled by boat down the River Ping. It's in Thailand,"

Benjamin said. "We have to go get it."

"I hate to tell you this, but Bangkok's a pretty big place," Gary said. "How do we go about knowing where to look?"

"Maybe the Geodine can shown us more detail. Maybe it can show us where to look in Bangkok," Benjamin said.

"Yeah, but even if we do find out where it is," Gary said, "we can't leave Lemuria. We can't even leave the capital city. That's against the rules."

"Well, there must be some way to get there," Benjamin said.

"How? Just sneak off to Thailand?" Andy said. "Maybe we could go up to the nearest teleporter and say 'Send me to Thailand', or something like that." He let out a deep breath and sank back into his pillow.

"You think the teleporters won't let us go?" Benjamin said.

"Of course they won't let us!" Andy said. "I mean, they're school teleporters and everything around here seems to know our DNA code. Heck, I don't even know my DNA code. I'd be willing to bet they have travel out of the city totally blocked for Year One Denarians."

"You may be right," Benjamin said, sinking into a chair.

"And, I don't think any of us can teleport ourselves there," Andy continued. "I mean, I know you're showing promise, Benjamin, but you have a long way to go."

"Not that long," Benjamin replied.

"Face it, it's gonna be impossible to get there while we're still at summer school," Andy said. "We may just have to wait until we get back home and have our parents take us or something."

"There may be another way," Gary said suddenly.

Both Benjamin and Andy turned. What in the world would Gary be willing to break the rules for?

"Here's what I'm thinking," Gary said. "What's going on in Bangkok next weekend?"

"Chinese New Year?" Andy guessed.

Gary frowned at him. "Don't you ever listen to anything? You'll never be an agent if you don't start being more observant."

"Okay, so what's going on?" Benjamin asked.

"The Bangkok Chess Open," Gary stated.

"And..." Andy said.

"And, who do we know that's going to Bangkok, secretly, to play in the Bangkok Chess Open?" Gary asked.

And then Benjamin realized it. Gary would break the school rules for chess. "Morpheus Midas," Benjamin answered.

"And The Panther," Gary said. "They're going to the tournament, and they don't want anyone to know. So how do you think they're going to get there? The odds are that at least one of them has to rely on a teleporter machine."

"And so, if we found out which teleporter they were using, and used the same one, we could get to Bangkok," Benjamin said.

"Right," Gary said, smiling.

Benjamin smiled back. "I think we need to come up with a plan."

They spent the first half of Sunday devising a plan for the journey to Bangkok. Benjamin and Heidi studied the Geodine, zooming in on the arrival of the key to Bangkok. It was taken into a temple under construction at the time. By cross referencing the location of the temple and the year of the arrival on their sheaves, Benjamin and Heidi were able to determine the first key of Shambhala was inside the Temple of the Emerald Buddha.

The Emerald Buddha had been discovered accidentally in the fifteenth century. Because it was so valuable, it had been plastered over to hide its beauty from invaders. However, fate had different plans for the Emerald Buddha; lightning struck the statue, exposing the shiny green beneath. Nobody was certain when it had been created, and everyone assumed it was made of green jade or jasper. But now, Benjamin wondered if the actual stone was in fact Moldavite, the same as the Emerald Tablet and the keys they were after. After being discovered, the Buddha was lost to marauders, won back in war, moved from one capital city to another, but always worshiped. It was finally taken to Bangkok when the city was first forming, and a temple adjoining the Grand Palace of Siam was constructed for its worship—the Temple of the Emerald Buddha.

"So, why don't we just ask Morpheus again if we can go with him to the tournament?" Iva said. "He seems like a pretty nice guy. I bet he'd take us."

"Even if Morpheus said yes, The Panther would never let us go," Benjamin said. "You heard what he said."

"He said he'd kick us out of school," Heidi replied.

"I think he was just bluffing," Gary said.

"I could see it in his mind," Heidi replied. "It was no bluff."

"So, how are we going to sneak onto a public teleporter and walk around the temple looking for the key?" Heidi asked.

"Well, I doubt they'll use a public teleporter, and I don't think all of us should go," Benjamin said. "Here's my idea."

During the week, Andy and Iva would follow The Panther around, gathering what information they could about him. What teleporter did he use? Could he teleport without the assistance of a machine? If both he and Morpheus could, they'd need a new plan—fast.

At the same time, Gary and Heidi would go back to Morpheus Midas's store for more information. Under the false pretext that Heidi was looking for another telemagnifier, Gary would get more details on the events of the coming weekend. When was the tournament? What time were he and The Panther planning on leaving? When would they be coming back? Where was the tournament being held? And, could Morpheus himself teleport?

Benjamin would spend his free time mapping out the Grand Palace grounds and the layout of the Temple of the Emerald Buddha. He needed to know the security in place around the temple, to look for possible secret rooms inside the temple, and to calculate how long it would take him to get in and out.

They decided that only three of them could actually travel to Bangkok. Gary would go to watch over Morpheus and The Panther at the tournament, and Benjamin and Iva would go into the temple to look for the first key of Shambhala. Benjamin picked Iva over Heidi in case they needed her telegnostic abilities to find the key. Heidi pouted, but couldn't argue with the logic.

Andy and Heidi would stand guard back in Lemuria. They would remain near whatever teleporter was used and try to use telepathy to contact the others if something went wrong.

At the end of the week, Benjamin felt they had all the information they needed. The Panther could teleport, but Morpheus Midas could not. Morpheus had a private teleporter in the back of his store. By asking him about the tournament, Heidi easily picked the teleporter access code from his mind for Bangkok. The tournament started at nine o'clock on Saturday morning, and he and The Panther would leave around eight to get there. The teleporter in Bangkok was hidden about a fifteen minute walk from the Bangkok Chess Open. Benjamin figured the longest walk to the Palace grounds would be around twenty-three minutes.

To make sure communication wouldn't be an issue, they'd been practicing their telepathy all week. The telepathy practice areas were equipped with telepathy chambers, which came in extremely useful. The telepathy chambers were paired pods which two telegens could use to practice communicating over distances.

Gary easily communicated with Iva and Benjamin up to a five mile separation, which more than accounted for the one mile between the arena where the Chess Open was held and the Temple of the Emerald Buddha. He wouldn't have any problems letting them know when Morpheus and The Panther started to leave the tournament.

Communicating with Heidi and Andy back in Lemuria would have posed a problem for anyone other than Heidi Dylan, even with the bonding of the Alliance. The telepathy chambers showed that Heidi could send her thoughts into specific minds for distances upwards of six thousand miles. Using her moonstone ring telemagnifier, the separation increased to over ten thousand miles. And not only was she able to place thoughts into minds that far away, she could receive thoughts sent from that distance, at least from Benjamin.

And so they were ready for the trip to Bangkok tomorrow. All they had to do now was sleep.

18

One Day In Bangkok

At seven thirty on Saturday morning, they sat at a table in the Deimos Diner three doors down from The Silver Touch. Their table was at the back of the restaurant, so The Panther wouldn't see them when he passed by.

Sure enough, at ten minutes to eight, Pantheros Pavlos came walking down Mu Way and entered Morpheus's shop. Like they'd planned, they waited in the restaurant until a few minutes after eight and then walked to the shop. As expected, the door was locked; however, Gary had managed to obtain a single hair from Morpheus during the past week. Using the Chemistry lab back at school, he'd created a thin glove for Andy to wear containing Morpheus's DNA sequence. Andy placed his hand on the access panel, and the door slid open.

"Awesome," Andy said. "I'm sure glad someone's good at science."

Gary smiled. "Glad I could help."

"Just think what trouble we could get in to if we had samples of all of our teachers' DNA," Andy said. His eyes got a far away look as if he was dreaming of the possibilities.

"I'm afraid to think of that," Iva said. She hadn't wanted to clone the DNA signature, but couldn't come up with any better way to get into the locked shop.

They entered and quickly shut and locked the door. The teleporter was in the back of the store, the pad still glowing. Typing in the access code Heidi had obtained, the teleporter came out of standby, Benjamin, Gary, and Iva stepped forward, and then disappeared.

In light speed, they stood in an empty, back alley next to a large apartment building. Televisions could be heard from the high windows. A baby cried. A dog barked. Though they had only been in Lemuria a matter of weeks, Benjamin couldn't believe how strange it felt to be back in what he'd considered to be the normal world for so many years.

Teleporter protocol dictated that upon arriving at public teleporter locations in non-Lemurian destinations, the arrivers quickly vacate the area. The teleporters themselves were designed to only allow arrivals and departures when humans were not around, scanning constantly for body heat and DNA, and shifting locations if needed.

Benjamin, Gary, and Iva hurried from the alley and walked about a half a block before stopping to look around. Benjamin pulled out the paper map of the city of Bangkok he'd printed before they left. He looked up, looked around, and then pointed to the map.

"Based on our surroundings and the position of the sun in the sky, I think we are...here." He pointed about one mile southeast of the arena, circled in red, where the Bangkok Chess Open was being held. "We need to go here." He pointed due west about one and a half miles. "Gary, do you have your map?" Benjamin asked.

Gary nodded. "I'll let you know when I get to the Open, and I'll keep you posted on the progress of the chess matches. Morpheus mentioned he was scheduled to play in one of the first ones," Gary said.

"Let us know if anything goes wrong," Iva said. She and Benjamin set off to the west; Gary started walking northwest. Within a block, they could no longer see each other.

Benjamin and Iva saw the Grand Palace long before they actually arrived. Large golden spires rose up in the air, higher than any of the surrounding buildings. They quickened their pace and soon reached the main gate where they entered the grounds of the Grand Palace.

"*Okay, we're here,*" Benjamin thought to Gary. He looked at his watch. It was eight forty.

"*Yeah, I'm here too. The tournament's gonna get started soon, and Morpheus is in the first group of players, so he'll be starting right at nine. But since he'll never lose, he'll probably play all day,*" Gary replied.

Iva directed her thoughts to both of them. "*I can already sense the key somewhere close by. It's a really strong telemagnifier. I don't think finding it'll be a problem.*"

"*Oh, wow, you guys won't believe who just got here,*" Gary thought, and even across the distance Benjamin sensed Gary's excitement through the Alliance bond.

"*Asia Philippa,*" Benjamin guessed.

"*No. It's Alexander Chervenka, the chess champion from last year's tournament. He's fantastic. I watched him win last year on TV. I hope I get to see him play this year,*" Gary thought.

"*Okay, well have fun, and let us know what's going on with Morpheus,*" Benjamin replied.

"*Oh, yeah, I will,*" Gary thought, distraction already evident in his response.

Benjamin and Iva walked as normally as they possible could, but went straight to the Temple of the Emerald Buddha. Located just off the left as they entered, it was drawing more tourists than any other destination in the entire palace complex. Two large demon statues stood guard over the temple area.

"You think they were from Atlantis?" Benjamin said to Iva, gesturing to the large, frightening figures.

"Maybe Lemuria," she joked back. "Aren't they supposedly guarding this place?"

"Well, even if they are good guys, I wouldn't want to run into them in a dark alley," Benjamin said.

The temple of the Emerald Buddha looked like it had been dipped in gold and then decorated with gems. Benjamin wasn't positive the first key of Shambhala was located inside the actual temple, but he figured it was as good a place as any to start.

"*Hey, how's it going there?*" Heidi's voice said in his head. It took him by surprise.

"*Oh, pretty good,*" he thought back. "*We just reached the temple, and Morpheus should be starting to play any minute now.*"

"I just thought I'd check in. No activity here," she thought back. *"Morpheus has some pretty cool new things though. Andy found some telekinesis practice set that he won't stop using. He keeps talking about his need to beat you and Ryan Jordan. You guys are so competitive. Well, let me know when you get the key."*

Like the rest of the tourists, they took off their shoes outside, and entered the temple. Set deep inside, high up on display, was the green statue of Buddha. Iva stopped and stared. "It's breathtaking," she said to no one in particular.

Benjamin wasn't nearly so awestruck. "Come on," he said, nudging her. "Can you tell where the key is?" he whispered. "We need to hurry."

Iva stared for another moment and then shook herself out of her stupor. "It's somewhere very close by. I'm almost certain it's in this building." She looked around.

Benjamin followed her gaze as she looked around. Most of the tourists were watching them.

"I think we'd better follow the crowd and kneel down to pray," she said. "We're already standing out."

Benjamin grumbled, but dropped to his knees beside her. Iva bowed her head low to the ground, and Benjamin did his best to mimic her. "I don't know how to pray to Buddha," he said.

"Well, you don't really have to," Iva said. "Just make it look like you're trying. People are starting to stare at us."

They remained in the prostrate position for a minute before Iva spoke. "I can sense someone of great power placing the key somewhere in here to hide it. I can almost see it happening." She grasped her Ammolite pendant and closed her eyes, trying to keep her head toward the ground.

Just then, Gary's voice came quickly into Benjamin's mind. *"Benjamin, I don't know what happened, but Morpheus lost, and they're leaving. He lost! I don't know how it could have happened."*

"He lost? They're leaving? Now? Are you sure?" Benjamin asked.

"Positive. He sat down to play, but in no time at all, his opponent had him cornered. After the checkmate, he looked really upset. Worried. He talked to The Panther, and the two of them left and headed to the teleporter." Gary sounded panicked, even through telepathy. *"I don't think we can make it back before them."*

"No, we can't," Benjamin said. *"We don't even have the key yet."* Quietly he said to Iva, "Do you know where it is yet?"

"Don't hurry me," she hissed. "You're making me lose my focus."

"Okay," Benjamin thought to Gary, *"since we already missed our window, I'll talk to Heidi and let her know they need to get out of the shop. We'll just have to see if they can distract Morpheus and The Panther when we're ready to return."*

"So, what should I do?" Gary asked.

"Well, I guess just stay and watch the tournament for a while," Benjamin told him. *"I'll let you know when we get it."*

Benjamin looked over to get an update from Iva, but decided against it when she grabbed her pendant again and re-closed her eyes. So instead he connected to Heidi.

"*Heidi!*" he thought.

"*Hey, Benjamin. How's it going?*" she replied without missing a beat.

"*You guys have to get out of the shop. They're heading back.*"

"*Already?*" she asked.

"*Yeah, already. I'll explain it later. Just get Andy, and get out of the shop.*"

Benjamin severed the link with Heidi and looked back over at Iva; she hadn't moved. He did his best not to get impatient, but what was taking her so long? His knees were starting to hurt—badly. Wasn't she supposed to be good at this telegnosis stuff? Of course, he had no idea where the key was. It could be three inches from his nose for all he knew.

"Do you want the good news or the bad news first?" Iva said at last.

"How about the good news," Benjamin said.

"Well, I know where the key is," she said.

"It's about time," he said.

She glared at him.

"So, where is it?" Benjamin asked, ignoring her glare.

"Well, that's the bad news," Iva said.

Benjamin looked at her and raised an eyebrow.

"It's in a secret compartment hidden directly under the Emerald Buddha," Iva said.

"Under the Buddha?" Benjamin asked. "Are you sure?"

"Yes, I'm sure," Iva said. "Of course I'm sure."

"Okay, fine," Benjamin said. "So how do we get it out?"

"Well, I thought you could figure that out," Iva said.

"Do you think anyone would stop me if I climbed up onto the platform and lifted the statue up?" Benjamin asked Iva.

"Probably only the entire palace guard," Iva replied.

"Yeah, I thought so," Benjamin said. "I guess we need a different plan, right?"

"Right," Iva said.

They continued kneeling while Benjamin tried to devise some way to get to the secret compartment without being seen. It was probably only the discomfort of kneeling for so long which made Benjamin think of a brilliant idea.

"I think I have it," he said.

"I'm listening," Iva said.

"How good do you think you are at telekinesis?" Benjamin asked her.

Iva groaned.

"I mean, I know you're better than Heidi and Gary, that's for sure."

"You don't expect me to lift that thing, do you?" Iva asked.

"No," Benjamin said. "I'll lift it up, and, while everyone is watching the Buddha, you open the secret compartment underneath and get the key out. Then, I'll set the Buddha down, we'll leave, and no one will even know anything is missing."

"Won't people wonder why the Buddha is levitating?" Iva asked.

"They can attribute it to a religious miracle, or good karma, or dogma, or something," Benjamin said.

"But, do you think we're really supposed to do something

like that?" Iva asked. "I mean, it seems to go against everything we're being taught. Using our gifts blatantly. Misleading humans."

"Yeah, well, we're not even supposed to be here in the first place," Benjamin said. "So, even if someone did find out, they wouldn't be able to trace it back to us."

Iva sighed. "Okay, when I get the key out, where should I put it?" she asked.

"Just put it somewhere out of sight where we can easily retrieve it by hand," Benjamin answered. "Are you ready?"

Iva nodded.

"Here goes nothing," Benjamin said. He put his head to the ground, but angled it slightly, so he could see the brilliant Emerald Buddha.

The room was quiet—most of the tourists praying to the icon. Suddenly, magically, the Buddha lifted up in the air. A gasp escaped from the crowd. The Buddha rose up higher, now almost six inches off the pedestal on which it had rested. Benjamin continued to lift it higher. The crowd stared at the statue, then in unison, dropped their heads to the ground in humility. Benjamin heard excited whispers, but had no idea what anyone was saying in the unfamiliar language.

The Buddha was heavy—actually much heavier than he would have thought. Silently, he found himself wishing Andy were here. Benjamin hated to admit it, but sometimes he actually did think Andy was better at telekinesis. Of course if Andy were here, he'd probably be twirling the Buddha right now.

"*I think it's high enough*," he said silently to Iva. "*Get the key out. I'll keep it up here."*

Iva concentrated on the pedestal. Nothing happened. Benjamin didn't want to focus too much on the area, instead trying to keep his attention on the large Buddha. He didn't want to be responsible for dropping and smashing Thailand's most precious artifact.

"What's taking so long," he thought to Iva.

"I can't seem to get the compartment open," she said. *"I know it's there. It just won't open."*

New tourists kept entering the room. Quickly, it was getting more and more crowded. *"Just hurry,"* Benjamin said.

Another twenty seconds passed, but Iva had no luck. *"I just can't open it,"* she said. *"You're going to have to try."*

"I can't do that and hold this thing," Benjamin said.

"Oh, sure you can," Iva said encouragingly.

"No," Benjamin said. *"You're going to have to take it."*

"I don't think that's a good idea," Iva said. *"What if I drop it?"*

"You won't drop it," Benjamin said. *"But, I'll back you up, just in case."*

"Promise?" Iva asked.

"Yes, I promise," Benjamin replied. *"Now, just slowly take over holding the Buddha in the air. It's kind of heavy, so take your time."*

Iva started to hold the Buddha with her mind. Benjamin began to let up on his control of the statue. So far, so good. *"You almost have the whole thing,"* Benjamin said. *"Here's the last bit."* He let go of the Buddha completely. It dropped six inches, wobbled violently, then held steady. The crowd gasped. Apparently everyone was watching, though their heads were bowed to the ground. The Buddha held firm. Iva didn't attempt to lift it back up to its previous position.

Benjamin started concentrating on the pedestal. He easily found the compartment and slid open the lid. With his mind, he found exactly what he wanted inside. He lifted the key out of the secret area, closing the lid behind it. He moved the key behind the pedestal, and within ten seconds, lifted the Buddha from Iva's mind.

"*You have it?*" she asked.

"*Yes, I have it,*" Benjamin replied. "*I'm gonna set the Buddha back on the pedestal.*"

He gently but promptly placed the Buddha back down without even a sound. The timing couldn't have been more perfect. Three palace guards entered the chamber just as the statue settled. First one of them spoke something in the same language Benjamin couldn't understand. Everyone stood up, whispers turned to wild talk. The guard followed by repeating the message in English.

"Everyone must leave the temple," the guard said. "The Temple of the Emerald Buddha is now closed and will remain so indefinitely. Exit the way you came in."

Benjamin stood up and tried to put on his best I-wonder-what's-going-on look. Iva tried to do the same but didn't look nearly convincing enough to Benjamin. "*Where is the key?*" she hissed in his mind.

Benjamin didn't answer her question. "Let's go get our shoes on," he said. "It's time to go."

"*But where did you put it?*" she persisted.

The guard who had spoken looked at them and narrowed his eyes.

"I agree, Iva," Benjamin said is his normal voice. "That was the most amazing thing I've ever seen. I can't wait to tell mom and dad about it." He silently added, "*Play along.*"

Iva paused for only a moment, hardly missing a beat. "I wonder if anything like that has ever happened before?" she asked.

The guard overheard the question. "No, nothing like this has ever happened before. We must investigate the matter fully," he replied with a thick accent. "Now please proceed to the exit and do not forget to retrieve your shoes before leaving."

"Thank you for the reminder," Benjamin said. They exited through the main entrance, and walked over to the racks holding their shoes. Benjamin handed Iva her shoes, then picked his up off the rack. He reached into his right shoe, pulled out a small green neatly carved stone, winked at Iva, and placed the stone in his pocket.

"Clever, Benjamin," she said. "Very, very clever."

An Agent from the Other Side

Benjamin had to use every bit of self control he had to not run off the palace grounds. So instead he and Iva walked—quickly, heading for the teleporter. Benjamin talked to Gary, and they arranged to meet him at the same intersection where they'd parted ways. Benjamin also let Heidi know they were on their way back.

"*Okay, but let me know right before you guys teleport back so I can try to distract Morpheus. The Panther already left, so it's just Morpheus in the store. We're outside sitting on a bench,*" she explained.

Benjamin and Iva hurried as fast as they could without drawing too much attention to themselves. He didn't know if the Palace Guard was searching for anyone regarding the Emerald Buddha levitation, but he had no plans to wait around to find out. Within twenty minutes, they arrived at the intersection where they were supposed to meet Gary. Gary was absent.

"He should've been here before us," Benjamin said.

"I hope he's not in trouble," Iva replied.

"*Where are you?*" Benjamin asked Gary. "*We're waiting for you.*"

"*I'll be there in about three minutes,*" Gary replied. True to his word, in just under three minutes, Gary rounded the corner and crossed the street.

"What took you so long?" Benjamin said.

"I got caught up watching the match between Alexander Chervenka and the guy who beat Morpheus," Gary replied.

"You were watching a game?" Iva asked. Benjamin didn't think it would take the Alliance bond for Gary to feel her annoyance.

"I'm sorry, but I think it was actually important," Gary said.

"What's so important about a silly game?" Iva asked.

"Well, for starters, it's not just a silly game; it's the Bangkok Chess Open. Secondly, this guy who beat Morpheus has never been in the Bangkok Chess Open before. In fact, he's never competed in any kind of formal chess competition. So, everyone thought for sure he wouldn't make it past the first round."

Benjamin and Iva stared at Gary. "And?"

"And, once this guy beat Morpheus, he and the Panther hightailed it out of there. Which means they didn't stick around to see this guy play Alexander Chervenka. But they should've. This new guy was wiping the floor with Alexander—the world chess champion." Gary shook his head. "I'm not great at mind reading, but this guy was hiding something."

"Yeah, you'll probably have the chance to discuss it with Morpheus," Benjamin said.

Gary looked at him. "We're gonna get caught, aren't we?"

Benjamin shrugged. "Heidi says Morpheus is back and in his store. The Panther's gone, but I don't see how we can return without letting Morpheus know we used his teleporter."

"So we will get in trouble," Iva said.

"What choice do we have?" Benjamin shrugged.

"We could wait until he's left the store," Gary suggested, his eyes getting wide again. "We could go back and watch the chess tournament some more."

"It's only eleven o'clock in the morning," Benjamin said. "No way I'm waiting around. Morpheus'll be there all day, and we have research to do."

Gary sighed. "That's true. Not to mention the practice hours we need to log for the week," he said. "I'm way behind because of all the 'research' we've been doing."

"Yeah," Iva added. "We better just get back and deal with Morpheus as best we can."

"But what do we tell him?" Gary persisted.

"We tell him we came to watch him play in the chess tournament," Benjamin answered. "That way you can ask him about the guy who beat him."

Benjamin communicated the plan to Heidi, and asked her and Andy to meet them inside the store. He, Gary, and Iva walked to the alley where the teleporter was located. The palm pad lit up on the side of the building, Benjamin slapped his hand onto the pad, and into a pinprick of light, they vanished.

When they arrived in the back of the store, Benjamin could make out Heidi's voice coming from the front room.

"Are you sure the Moonstone is a more powerful telemagnifier than the Rainbow Boji stones?" she asked.

"Oh, much more powerful," Morpheus replied. "Have you tested your telepathic abilities in the chambers yet?" There were no other customers in the store.

"Yes, I have, and the moonstone really does seem to stretch my telepathic range," Heidi said.

Benjamin, Gary, and Iva tried to sneak from the back room into the front of the store. Morpheus turned around and looked directly at them, though they hadn't made a sound.

"What are you three doing?" he asked. "Did you just arrive on my teleporter?"

"Oh, um, ah, actually, ah, yes we did," Benjamin answered. He had still been holding out a slight hope that Morpheus wouldn't notice their return.

"Oh," Morpheus said, returning to his normal unconcerned voice. "Where from?" he asked.

"Bangkok," Benjamin replied.

"Oh," Morpheus said. "Bangkok. Well, I guess that's okay."

"What—you aren't upset?" Gary asked.

"No, not really," Morpheus replied. "Actually, that's pretty much what I figured when I noticed Heidi and Andy sitting outside my store for the last hour. So what were you doing there? Playing chess?"

"No, just watching," Gary replied. "We really wanted to see you play in the Open."

Morpheus flushed. "Not too much of a match, was it?"

"Well, don't feel too bad. After you, he played Alexander

Chervenka, and you'll never believe who won," Gary said.

"Alexander?" Morpheus replied.

"No—the other guy," Gary said. "The guy who beat you. Alexander didn't even put on a good show."

"You're kidding," Morpheus said as his mouth fell open. "He beat Alexander? Are you sure?"

Gary nodded. "Why did you leave so quickly?" he asked. "I would have thought you'd have stuck around to watch some more."

Morpheus answered a little bit too fast. "Oh, I had to get back to mind the store."

"I don't think so," Gary said. "You looked worried. Who was that guy? I think he's a telegen."

Morpheus leaned close and lowered his voice. "I think you're right; but I don't think he's on our side."

"You mean he's from Atlantis?" Heidi asked.

"Shhhh!" Morpheus hissed. "That's probably a good guess. Atlantis does have their own agents you know. And I've never seen him before, and never even heard his name mentioned in the chess world."

"That's because he's never played professionally before," Gary said. "I read his bio while I was watching him play. Alexander was furious about losing to him."

"Well, The Panther is going to ask around about him," Morpheus said. "But I don't think you guys should mention to him that you went to Bangkok after he told you not to."

"So you aren't going to tell on us?" Iva asked Morpheus.

"Not a chance," he answered. "You know, I was young not

too long ago, believe it or not. I may have left the city once or twice when I wasn't supposed to."

"Thanks, Morpheus," Benjamin said, a feeling of relief washing over him. He didn't want to have to stop searching for the keys. Thinking of them, he felt for the one in his pocket. It was safe, there next to the toy police car Derrick and Douglas had given him.

"Not tell about what?"

They all turned in the direction of the voice. Somehow, none of them had heard the door open. Benjamin immediately recognized Helios Deimos, one of the ruling twins. Benjamin wasn't sure what to say, and specifically did not want to answer the question.

"Ah, Helios," Morpheus said, immediately shifting his attention to his new, famous patron. "How wonderful of you to grace my humble store with your business."

"Always a pleasure to see you again, Morpheus Midas," Helios replied.

It then dawned on Benjamin that something was different about Helios Deimos. He was alone. "Where's you sister?" he mustered up the courage to ask, hoping to distract Helios.

"Selene had business outside of Lemuria she needed to attend to." Helios laughed. "You know, we don't do everything together."

"You don't?" Andy asked.

"If we did, what would be the point in having two rulers?" Helios replied.

"So you guys can leave Lemuria?" Benjamin asked.

"When it is required," Helios replied. "But you never answered my original question. What secret is Morpheus keeping?"

So much for distraction. Benjamin sealed his lips, hoping a plausible answer would miraculously spring into his mind. But none did except apparently the truth.

"Sneaking outside Lemuria?" Helios asked. "Now let me see. Morpheus, isn't there some miscellaneous school rule about Year One Denarians not being able to leave the capital city?"

"Absolutely," Morpheus replied with a smile.

Benjamin felt his heart start beating again when he sensed the humor.

"So you're not going to tell our teachers about it?" Gary asked.

"Trust me, Gary Goodweather," Helios said, "both Selene and I have much more important matters to deal with than which students are leaving the city to watch chess tournaments."

The Teachers Play With a Toy

Like every day, Proteus Ajax walked around HR0713 Monday morning watching the students practice. And like most days, Benjamin, Andy, and Gary sat at a round table in the back. But today, Benjamin had his Kinetic Orb on the table in front of him when Proteus walked over.

"So, what do we have here?" Proteus asked. He looked at the table. "Ah, a Kinetic Orb. Designed by Erno Rubik if I am correct."

"Rubik designed The Orb?" Benjamin asked.

"Of course," Proteus replied. "Erno Rubik was a telegen."

Benjamin, Andy, and Gary stared at Proteus.

"Kinetic Orbs were all the craze ages ago in Lemuria," Proteus said. "When Rubik became an agent assigned to Hungary, he was allowed to introduce a simplified child's version, the Rubik's Cube, to humans."

"So do you know how to solve it with your eyes closed?" Andy asked. "We've been trying to figure it out."

"Eyes closed? Let's see," Proteus said. "First you have to

learn how to solve it with your eyes open. If you can't solve it with your eyes open, you can't solve it with your eyes closed."

"So, how do we do that?" Andy asked.

"Practice, of course," Proteus replied.

Andy groaned. "Of course."

"If you've mastered the algorithms, I can think of two ways off the top of my head to solve it with your eyes closed. One—memorize it in its unsolved state, and then as you solve it in your mind, simply turn the Orb to match."

"Okay," Benjamin said. "And the second?"

"Use telepathy. See the colors in your mind, feel the colors through the tendrils of telekinesis." Proteus levitated the now solved sphere back onto the table. "Remember, you have to be many steps ahead of the Orb. Know the route to your destination before you get there."

In Telepathy, Benjamin decided to ask Mrs. Zen if she could explain how telepathy could be used to solve the Orb unseen. She closed her eyes and had Benjamin completely scramble it before handing it to her. She didn't look at it, but solved it in under three minutes. When she tried to explain the process, she confused Benjamin more than before he'd asked.

"You just have to speak to the Orb," she said.

"How do I speak to an Orb?" Benjamin asked.

"It will speak to you, if only you know how to listen," Mrs. Zen replied.

"But it's not alive," Benjamin argued.

"And what does that have to do with anything?" Mrs. Zen

asked. "One truly gifted at telepathy can sense the vibes from anything, animate or inanimate." She looked to Heidi. "I'm sure your friend, Ms. Dylan, could sense the color arrangement of the Orb without looking." Mrs. Zen levitated it back to Benjamin. "Here, scramble it," she said.

He did so.

"Now, Ms. Dylan, please close your eyes," Mrs. Zen said.

"But I don't know how to solve it," Heidi protested.

"I'm not asking you to solve it," Mrs. Zen said. "I just want you to tell us what the colors are. Now, please, close your eyes." Heidi did so.

Benjamin levitated the now scrambled Orb over to Heidi.

"Please tell us the color order for the first phase, Ms. Dylan," Mrs. Zen instructed.

Heidi didn't say anything. She didn't even reach out for the Orb.

"I don't think I can do it," she said to Mrs. Zen, not opening her eyes.

"Well, you most certainly cannot if you don't think you can," Mrs. Zen snapped. "I happen to know that you can do it. With your talents, it would be completely impossible for you not to be able to sense the colors on this silly little toy. Now, try again," she commanded.

Heidi began to concentrate again. It took almost a minute, but then she started. "Blue," she said.

"Right," Benjamin replied.

"Don't tell her if she is right or wrong," Mrs. Zen said. "Just let her read the whole phase, and then she can open her eyes and see."

Heidi began again, starting at the upper right and moving downward. "Blue. Green. Blue again." She began to pick up speed. "Gold." Her hands moved as if they were holding the Orb, though it still levitated in front of her.

Benjamin wasn't sure what was more surprising to him—that Heidi was getting the colors right, or that she was actually levitating the Orb for so long.

"Gold. Silver. Green. Red. Gold. White. Silver. Green. Silver. Red. Green. Blue." Her eyes snapped opened. "Was I right?" she asked, looking down.

"Completely right," Benjamin said.

"Totally right," Andy echoed.

"See, I told you that you could do it," Mrs. Zen said. "Now, let's put this toy away and get on with the class."

The Kinetic Orb became a fun release for Benjamin, Andy, and Gary, and quickly gained popularity with many of the other Year One Denarians. Iva didn't take too much of an interest in it, not understanding the fascination, and Heidi was only really interested in quickening her ability for feeling the colors. But for Benjamin, the Orb was the perfect way for him to get his mind off the search for other two keys of Shambhala.

Since returning from Bangkok, Benjamin had thought of little besides where the second key might be hidden. He tried watching the Geodine again, hoping that locating the second key would be as easy the first, but had no success. The first key had just been so simple. Almost too simple.

Another lecture rolled around, and Benjamin still had to force himself to go. Mr. Hermes began by talking about the history of the conflict between Lemuria and Atlantis. He showed a timeline for the continents and gave some background into the initial conflicts between the two peoples. Benjamin only partially listened, not wanting to be there, still thinking about the second key. Midway through the lecture, Mr. Hermes changed the lecture's direction just a little, catching Benjamin's attention.

"I'm sure many of you have heard of famous people in history whom you may suspect are from Lemuria or Atlantis. We talked about a few previously—Orion, Apollo, Artemis, and many of the other gods and goddesses. Would anyone else like to guess a few?" Mr. Hermes asked.

Gary said, "Erno Rubik."

"Yes, yes. I've heard about the Orb craze going around now," Mr. Hermes said. "I must say, I even dusted off my old Teleportation Orb for fun. Okay, who else?"

"Einstein?" Benjamin guessed.

"Yes, very good," Mr. Hermes said. "Einstein is a perfect example of a telegen who was raised in an agent family much like yourselves. He too was encouraged to not excel at school. The stories of how he received D's in many of his classes are famous. Some more please."

"Hitler?" Jonathan Sheehan guessed.

"No, not Hitler," Mr. Hermes replied. "Hitler was just a very evil human. There have unfortunately been many evil people like Hitler throughout history."

Benjamin raised his hand.

"Yes, Benjamin Holt?" Mr. Hermes asked.

Benjamin cleared his throat. "Are all the people from Atlantis evil?" he asked.

"Oh, no, no, no," Mr. Hermes replied. "That's a common misconception, and one that the Deimos twins do their best to dispel. The average telegen of Atlantis leads much the same life as the average telegen of Lemuria. In fact, not even all the rulers of Atlantis are evil. There have been many times in our history when the ruling bodies of Lemuria and Atlantis attempted to come to some sort of reconciliation. But inevitably, there are radicals and those in the ruling councils of the two nations who are opposed to the terms of the agreement, and it's called off."

"So, are agents from Atlantis sent out into the world?" Iva asked.

Benjamin's mind immediately flew to the guy from the chess tournament. Was he really an agent from Atlantis? And why did he happen to be in Bangkok at the exact same time they were there retrieving the first key of Shambhala?

"Yes, Atlantis has many agents. Some we're aware of, but not all to be sure," Mr. Hermes answered. "Yet as many infamous people throughout history have shown, Atlantians cause much of the disruption among humans. One starts a problem. Another comes along and solves it, giving humans guidance when it's needed the most. Soon, the humans come to depend upon the guidance, and they can't back away. We've had to interfere many times to remove the bonds of this slavery. Due to the barrier around Atlantis, telegens aren't able to escape in any great numbers. However, with the weakening of the barrier, more and more are entering the human world."

"So if most of the people of Atlantis aren't bad, then is it right to keep them locked within the barrier?" Benjamin asked. He felt Heidi and Iva's shock in his mind, and even sensed a little bit of surprise from Gary and Andy. But he didn't care. He wanted to know what was really at stake. What would it really mean to keep the barrier shield in place? "I mean, doesn't that sound a little bit like captivity to you?" he added.

Mr. Hermes looked at him and nodded. "I won't pretend that question has never been asked. I won't even pretend I haven't asked that very question. But I'm not the one who makes the decisions. I would guess that's the kind of question Helios and Selene Deimos face every day."

"*I can't believe you asked that,*" Heidi said.

"*Why?*" Jack replied, awake now from his nap. "*It's true isn't it?*"

"*You think so?*" Benjamin silently asked the Nogical.

"*Well, of course,*" Jack replied. "*Millions of people are encased in a giant dome against their will. All because of a few bad apples.*"

"*But those bad apples could cause world destruction,*" Heidi thought back. "*You heard how it was in the past. The humans were slaves. What's to say it would be any different now?*"

"*Nothing,*" Benjamin replied. "*It just makes me think. That's all.*"

Mr. Hermes decided to go into detail on the history before the barrier was put in place around Atlantis. Benjamin figured maybe it was to enforce in their minds the importance of keeping any sort of domination from occurring. It made him think about how best the humans and the telegens could coexist, if at all. With one race so much stronger mentally than the other, would domination always be the end result?

As he thought about world domination, Benjamin's mind began to drift. He'd always had special skills—or at least known about them—even when he was only as old as Derrick and Douglas. And to be truthful, he'd kind of always taken them for granted. What would it be like to be totally ungifted—like humans? Beyond all else, Benjamin figured it would probably just be really boring. No secret conversations, no levitating frogs, no teleporting …well…teleporting anything.

But aside from the boring factor, it would take away everything that had ever been special about Benjamin. He'd always had skills none of the other kids had—except Andy of course. Of course, now that he was at summer school, pretty much every bit of specialness was being taken away anyway. Heidi was better than him at telepathy. Iva was better than him at telegnosis. Nobody could even compete with Gary when it came to science. And if Benjamin didn't watch it, Andy would be better than him at telekinesis—if he already wasn't.

Heidi Drags Them to a Museum

The first weekend after their trip to Bangkok, Iva attained the ultimate achievement for a Year One Denarian—a field trip outside the capital city of Mu. So far during the summer, no one from their homeroom had legally been away.

Kyri, their telegnosis teacher, had asked Iva—and Jonathan Sheehan—to visit Fortune City, also known as the City of the Oracles. She'd lectured about the city all week. Nearly every one of the oracles was female; only one percent weren't.

Since starting telegnosis nearly a month ago, Iva insisted she wanted to be a telegnostic. She constantly asked her friends to hide objects around the school so she could find them. Benjamin thought if he had to hide one more pair of socks he would scream. Kyri said that Iva's knack for being able to find objects was due to her having a special ability to sense the vibes which the objects gave off. When people touched objects, they left a trace of themselves, and a gifted telegnostic could pick up on these traces.

Iva left early on Saturday, before breakfast. Heidi arrived

in the dining hall well before Benjamin, Andy, and Gary. Just as they rounded the corner, Benjamin heard her voice loud and clear in his head. *"It's about time you guys showed up,"* she thought. *"I've been waiting here for over an hour."*

"Well, Andy wouldn't wake up," Benjamin thought back. "We finally had to dump water over his head," he said audibly to her as they approached the table.

"Yeah, and I'm not gonna forget it," Andy said.

"So, what have you been doing for the last hour?" Benjamin asked.

"After I planned out our day, I talked to Leena for a while, and then decided to practice mind reading a little," Heidi replied.

"Who would you want to practice on in here?" Gary asked, looking around at their fellow Year One Denarians.

"Oh, no one in here," Heidi laughed. "Give me a break. I've been trying to mentally locate some of our teachers around the school and see if I can tell what they're doing and what they're thinking."

"Any luck?" Benjamin asked.

"Well, the only thing I was able to pick up on was Proteus and Asia, talking in the teacher's lounge again," Heidi replied.

Andy smirked. "Man, those two have it bad for each other. I mean, don't you think she could do better than Proteus Ajax?"

"I think Proteus is cool," Gary replied.

"But to date?" Andy asked.

"Well, he is kind of cute," Heidi said.

"Cute!" Benjamin replied, looking at her.

Heidi flushed. "Iva thinks so too."

"She does?" Andy asked with disbelief. "He's a total geek. Give me a break!"

"So, what'd you plan for us today?" Benjamin asked Heidi, changing the subject. All he could think about was how lucky Proteus was to be dating someone as pretty as Asia, and he didn't want Heidi to pick that thought out of his mind.

"Oh, I'm glad you asked," Heidi said, pulling out her thought cache and her sheaf. "Here's the itinerary for our weekend." She pointed to the thought cache, showing a list of about ten activities. "I thought we'd start in the Natural History Museum."

"That sounds great!" Gary said.

"A museum?" Andy asked. "Seriously. There's got to be something better that a museum."

"Trust me. You'll love it," Heidi answered. "They have exhibits that actually teleport you to other places."

"What about looking for the other two keys?" Benjamin asked. "We need to get on with that."

"*Shhhh!*" Heidi's response was telepathic rather than verbal. "*Didn't you notice Ryan?*" She nodded her head a few tables back. "*He and Jonathan are constantly trying to spy on us. They know something's going on, but I don't think they know what. Anyway, I haven't heard you making any brilliant suggestions on how to find the next two keys, so today we're going to the museum.*"

The museum itself took up two city blocks, with an invisible walkway bridging the expanse, complete with pedestrians walking on air between the two halves.

Since it was early and the museum wasn't crowded yet, they decided to head to the teleporter exhibits first. There were holograms along the line depicting the various destinations the teleporters were programmed to send people. Benjamin and Andy went first—to the summit of Mount Everest. Packed into thermal suits, in a flash they were suddenly twenty-nine thousand feet above sea level. The trip lasted fifteen seconds, and then they returned, breathing the oxygen rich air back in the museum. Gary and Heidi quickly followed.

A teleporter trip to a hidden base on Mercury was next, followed by a trip to the rainforest, a space station, the center of the Earth, and finally, the North Pole. As thrilling as the teleporter adventures were, Benjamin felt like taking a nap once they were over.

But instead, Heidi dragged them to a gem exhibit on the third floor, where, in addition to some of the most valuable gems in the entire known universe, were the more recent stones Benjamin had learned about—Ammolite, Moonstone, and even Moldavite. There was an entire cavern of sparkling, colored crystals, large enough for all four of them to walk abreast. According to the built-in museum guide, the crystals had been growing in place for millennia.

The first floor served as the main atrium for the whole museum. In the center was the largest globe Benjamin had ever seen. They walked over to read the plaque in front of it, and Benjamin was surprised to learn that it was in fact a type of Geodine.

"How does it work?" Gary asked, looking up at the Geodine twenty feet in diameter.

"*The Geodine shows all teleportations currently happening on the home planet of Earth,*" a voice in his head said.

"Did you hear that?" Gary asked.

Benjamin nodded, studying the activity on the large globe. Unlike his smaller Geodine, this large model showed details much smaller in scope, He could see airplanes flying about the world, boats on the oceans, and satellites orbiting the planet. The Geodine slowly turned. Before long, the continent of Lemuria was directly in front of them. Benjamin noticed small flashes of light all over the continent.

"*What are the flashes of light?*" he asked in his mind.

"*Those are the teleportations,*" a voice replied.

"*Why are some of them blue and some of them red?*" Gary asked.

"*Blue flashes are natural teleportations,*" the voice replied. "*Red flashes are machine teleportations.*"

Suddenly Benjamin had an idea. Could the second key of Shambhala have been teleported outside of the city to its current resting place? "*Can you show me the past?*" he asked the large Geodine.

"*I am only programmed to show the present,*" the Geodine replied and slowly kept spinning.

"*So how do I find out about teleportations that already happened?*" Benjamin asked.

"*All teleportations are recorded here and transmitted for storage,*" the Geodine replied.

"*And where are they transmitted?*" he asked.

"*The information you are requesting is stored in the records department in the Ruling Hall,*" the Geodine said.

Heidi kept them at the museum until they were kicked out and the doors locked behind them. Benjamin didn't share his idea of looking for some sort of historical teleportation until they were back at school in the dining hall.

"I'm thinking maybe the second key was teleported out of Shambhala," he said, "and if it was, we should be able to find a record of it in the Ruling Hall. Maybe we can find it that way," he said to Gary, Andy, and Heidi. Iva hadn't gotten back yet from her field trip.

"Don't you think that would be kind of hard?" Andy asked. "Like looking for a needle in a haystack?"

"Maybe not if we all look," Benjamin replied.

"I guess it's worth a try," Heidi said.

Just then, Iva hurried over to join them. She looked out of breath and hardly looked at the menu before ordering.

"It's about time you showed up," Andy said.

"Yeah, we'd just about given up on you for dinner," Gary said.

"I wasn't sure I was gonna make it either," Iva replied.

"So, how was your date with Jonathan?" Andy asked.

Iva rolled her eyes so far back in her head, Benjamin thought she might fall off her chair. "Good heavens, Andy. I did not go on a date with Jonathan Sheehan."

"Well you guys were gone all day," Andy said. "I just figured that maybe it was a date."

Iva chose not to respond.

"Really, though, how was it?" Heidi asked.

"You guys wouldn't believe Fortune City," Iva said. "It's amazing. Once we're allowed to leave the city, we'll definitely have to go."

"So, do you still want to be an oracle?" Andy asked.

"Well, their jobs are really cool, but most of them aren't married and don't have kids," Iva replied.

"Why?" Heidi asked.

"I asked Kyri," Iva replied, "and she said it was because they couldn't stand to live with some of the futures they might see for their loved ones."

"What do you mean, some of the futures?" Andy asked. "Isn't there only one future?"

"Oh, not at all," Iva replied. "When an oracle sees the future, it's only the most likely future to occur given the circumstances at the current time. There's no guarantee that it'll come to be. Anyway, the job itself is great. The oracles get visited by every type of person you can imagine. Everyone wants a glimpse at their future, no matter who they are." Iva went on to describe in detail some of the other basic aspects of the city— the size, location, appearance. Nobody thought to ask her if she'd visited an oracle herself.

She asked about the museum, and Benjamin described the large Geodine to her, and presented his idea of looking for a teleporter signature in the Ruling Hall.

Iva thought it was a great idea. "I think we should start on it first thing in the morning," she said.

Benjamin sighed inwardly with relief. Finally. Someone else besides him wanted to find the keys too.

"What's the urgency?" Andy asked. "It's not like there's a time limit."

Iva sighed. "Well, actually, they is. There's something else I need to tell you about Fortune City. I didn't just observe other people consulting with the oracles."

"You didn't?" Gary asked.

"No, it wasn't long after we entered the city gates that a messenger came and told me one of the oracles wanted to see me. Kyri was really excited and said it was quite an honor. So, Kyri, Jonathan, and I went to the complex where the messenger led us. The messenger told Kyri and Jonathan that they weren't allowed to come with me, so I went alone."

Iva took the time to give a brief smile. "Jonathan was really mad he wasn't invited to see one of the oracles, but you know the telegnostic world is really a woman's world. Anyway, even with all his arguing, he still had to stay behind with Kyri. The messenger led me to the very top floor where I entered the only room up there. A woman sat in the center of the room on large pillows. She motioned for me to join her on the cushions. She wasn't old—much younger, in fact, than I would have expected. She didn't tell me her name, but she knew mine."

"So, what did she say to you, this oracle?" Andy asked.

"Well, I didn't know it until the end, but this oracle was not just any oracle. She was The High Oracle, the strongest Telegnostic in all of Lemuria," Iva replied.

"You talked to the High Oracle?" Gary asked, his jaw dropping open. In class, even Kyri spoke of the High Oracle with awe.

"Actually she did most of the talking, and what she did say was rather brief," Iva said.

"Which was?" Benjamin said, very interested in what Iva had to say.

"Which was that finding the keys was critical to the survival of Lemuria. And she told me that we weren't the only ones looking for the keys. 'There are those who would take the three keys of Shambhala and use them for evil purposes,' she said. 'You must not let this happen, Iva Marinina. You have been selected as an ally to Benjamin Holt for your telegnostic abilities. The Alliance must find the keys before the guardian does.' I asked her who the guardian was, but she said she couldn't tell me, only that the guardian was in our midst and actively looking for the keys and would stop at nothing to possess them and their power."

"So that's not bad news," Andy said. "Maybe this guardian person knows where the keys are hidden. Maybe we can just wait around for him to get the keys."

"Actually, after Bangkok, I don't think anyone but Benjamin can access them," Iva replied.

Benjamin looked at her and cocked his head.

"Remember how I couldn't get the compartment open," Iva said.

"You probably just didn't know how," Benjamin replied.

"No, I don't think so," Iva said. "I think somehow, only you can retrieve them."

"Maybe his DNA has been coded into the keys," Gary said.

"How could my DNA have been put anywhere?" Benjamin asked. "They were hidden hundreds if not thousands of years ago."

"So who would the Guardian be?" Heidi asked.

"How about Hexer," Andy suggested. "Remember? He was the guardian of the Emerald Tablet."

"I doubt it," Benjamin said. "I don't think he ever leaves that room."

"Yeah, I don't think it's Hexer either," Iva replied. "I can tell he's above suspicion."

"That's exactly why he should be a suspect," Andy said.

"You know, now that I think about it, I felt someone— not Hexer—following us around the whole time we were in Fortune City," Iva said. "I thought I got a quick look at his face once, and then sensed his presence the rest of the time."

"Had you ever seen him before?" Heidi asked.

"No," Iva replied. "And after I saw him, he made sure to stay out of sight. But I've sensed his presence before; I think when we were in Bangkok. There was definitely something familiar about it."

The Records Department Is
Really Boring

Benjamin, Gary, and Andy got up early, but still didn't manage to beat Iva and Heidi to the dining hall. The girls were engaged in a deep conversation with Leena Teasag. She walked away once they approached.

"You know, I hope you're not telling her anything," Benjamin said. "She could be the Guardian for all we know."

"Leena Teasag is not looking for the keys of Shambhala," Heidi said definitively.

"How do you know?" Andy asked.

"You haven't said anything to her have you?" Benjamin asked Heidi.

"No, Benjamin," Heidi said. "I haven't said anything to her."

"So what were you just talking about then?" Benjamin asked.

"None of your business," Iva replied.

"What do you mean—none of my business?" Benjamin

asked. "Here we are trying to find the keys, and you're telling secrets to the cleaning lady who could, for all we know, be after the same thing we are."

"You know what, Benjamin?" Heidi said. "Just drop it. Okay?"

"Just don't tell any more secrets to Leena Teasag," Benjamin replied. He was half joking and half not. Someone was following them around, and they had no idea who it was.

They'd agreed to meet at eight o'clock, but here it was only seven forty-five and Iva was impatient. "Just hurry up and eat. We need to get to the Ruling Hall," she said.

"Hey, mind if I come?" Jack asked, teleporting directly onto Benjamin's shoulder.

"Do you always teleport?" Heidi asked.

"Of course not," Jack replied.

"I've only ever seen you teleport," she said.

"It's convenient," Jack said.

"And addictive, apparently," Andy added.

"So we're heading back to the Ruling Hall?" Jack asked as they started walking down Mu Way.

"Yeah. Do you know anything about the records department?" Benjamin asked.

Jack shuddered. "We're not really going there are we?"

"Well, yeah, actually we are," Benjamin answered. "Why? What's wrong with the records department?"

Jack shuddered again. "Think about it. What do they store there?"

"Records," Andy said. "So what?"

"Right," Jack replied. "Records. Billions and gazillions of records."

"We need to look up the teleportation records," Benjamin said.

"That'll be like looking for a needle in a haystack," Jack said.

"No, I actually researched it a little bit last night," Gary said. "If we cross reference the approximate date the first key was moved and factor in the telemagnifier strength of the key, we should be able to narrow it down to only a few hours searching."

"When did you have time to do research?" Andy asked.

"After I finished the science experiments I was working on for Mr. Hermes," Gary replied.

Benjamin wasn't sure exactly what he expected when they walked into the Teleportations Records Department, but after Jack's reaction, it most certainly wasn't this. The Teleportations Records Department was nothing but a big empty room. The door automatically closed behind them as they entered, and Benjamin walked to the center, with Jack still on his shoulder.

Jack shuddered again. "See? What'd I tell you?"

"It's empty," Andy said.

"Empty?" Jack asked. "Have you not noticed the walls?"

Benjamin looked to the walls and saw that they were in fact flashing light, just like the Geodine at the museum had been doing. Yet if the museum teleporter Geodine had been recording current teleportations, Benjamin wasn't sure what these lights meant. The walls were a constant stream of flashing lights upon lights upon lights. Red, Blue, Green, Purple. Every color imaginable flashed on the four walls and the ceiling. Benjamin looked down and even saw flashes below his feet.

"You know, as much fun as you guys are gonna have and all, I probably still should be going," Jack said. Benjamin grabbed at his shoulder but wasn't fast enough. The Nogical had vanished.

"So how are we supposed to get information?" Benjamin asked.

"There should be an access terminal around here somewhere," Gary said, walking the outer boundary of the room. He stopped in a corner. "Here it is." he punched a few keys on the holographic control panel. "Now check with your Geodine and tell me the date the first key was taken from Shambhala."

Benjamin got out his Geodine and activated it. Quickly he found the spot where the key moved from Tibet down the River Ping. "It was about four thousand years ago," Benjamin said.

"Great," Gary said. "Now what power rating do you think each key has?"

"I have no idea," Benjamin said. "I didn't know it had a power rating."

"Weren't you listening in homeroom when Proteus talked about power ratings for telemagnifiers?" Iva asked.

"When was that?" Benjamin asked.

Iva rolled her eyes. "My necklace is a three, Gary, so, to be safe, let's just input a ten for the key. I'm willing to bet it's actually higher than that, but ten isn't very common."

Gary finished entering the information. "Great. So we're looking for a level ten telemagnifier being teleported about four thousand years ago. Anything else?"

Benjamin shook his head.

"Don't forget to put in the teleportation source location," Iva said.

"Right, got it," Gary said, adding the information. "I'll just make it all of Tibet to be safe." He pushed a final button on the keypad. "Okay, here goes nothing."

Gary wasn't kidding. Nothing happened and nothing changed. Benjamin looked around the flashing room. "So what happens next?" he asked.

"I'm not really sure," Gary said. "Except I think we just watch the flashes and wait."

For the better part of an hour they waited. Benjamin sat on the floor, leaning up against one of the flashing walls. Jack had been right. Could this be any more boring?

"Don't fall asleep," Iva said. "And you're blocking one of the walls that way."

"I'm wide awake."

"Liar," Heidi replied. "I can read your mind."

"How much longer is this gonna take?" Andy asked.

"I would have thought based on the search criteria, we would have seen something by now," Gary said. "Wait! What was that? Did you guys see it?"

"See what?" Benjamin asked, propping his eyes open.

"The cyan flash! That's what I programmed our positive

search result to look like."

"A cyan flash?" Andy asked.

"Cool color," Heidi said.

Gary hurried over to the pad. "I'll repeat the last minute of search results."

Just as Gary had said, a bright cyan flash lit up the room. He hurried over to the place on the floor where the flash had come from. Sitting down, he pressed the spot and enlarged the record which caused the flash. "Here it is," he said. "We can zoom in on it and watch the source flash and the destination flash."

The spot enlarged until a large map was displayed on the floor. "This is a teleporter record up close," Gary said.

"It looks just as boring as I thought it would," Jack said, reappearing.

"You certainly pop in at the most opportune moments," Andy said.

"And why shouldn't I?" Jack asked. "You didn't expect me to sit around here waiting with you guys did you?"

"No," Andy sighed. "I just wish I could have come with you."

"The telemagnifier gets teleported here," Gary said, pointing to another area in Tibet, just north of Nepal, at the head of a river.

"It's in the Himalayas," Benjamin said. "That's the Himalayas."

"In the mountains?" Andy asked. "In Tibet? You mean it never left Tibet?"

"But where in Tibet?" Heidi asked. "What's there?"

"Narration on," Benjamin said, as he pulled his Geodine out of his pocket. "What's right here?" he asked, pointing to the spot on his Geodine where the flash had occurred.

"That is classified information which I am not programmed to divulge," the Geodine answered.

"What do you mean, not programmed to divulge?" Benjamin asked. "You're mine, aren't you?"

"It is not a question of ownership," the Geodine said. "My programming does not allow me to discuss the location to which you pointed."

"Well, how do we find out where the second key of Shambhala went then?" Heidi asked.

"Maybe we go to the library," Gary suggested.

It was noon, and everyone was hungry. Using the public teleporters to save time, they headed to the dining hall.

While they ate, Iva brought up the subject of the first key. "Now, where did you say you put the key?"

"I have it hidden away," Benjamin replied.

"Hidden where?" she asked.

"Away," he said. "Why does it matter?" he asked.

"But you have it somewhere safe?" she pressed.

"Yes," he replied emphatically. "I put it where no one will find it."

"Not even me?" she asked. "Is it hidden well enough that I couldn't even find it?"

The food levitating to Benjamin's mouth dropped to the table. "Well, I hadn't thought of that. I forgot about how good you are at finding things."

"Yeah, and if the guardian is as gifted as Iva at telegnosis, he'd be sure to find it," Heidi said.

"He or she you mean," Andy corrected.

"Yes," Heidi sighed with annoyance. "He or she would be sure to find it."

"I think we should check on it," Iva suggested, shoving her chair out without waiting for a reply.

"I thought we were going to the library?" Gary said.

"After we check on the key," Iva replied.

Once they finished eating, they headed to the boy's dormitories. Heidi and Iva had never seen the boys' room and didn't even try to mask their amusement.

"Look how small your room is," Heidi said. "You guys have four beds to a room here?"

"Well, yeah, don't you?" Andy asked, sitting down on Benjamin's lower bunk bed.

"Are you kidding?" Heidi replied. "Iva and I have a room twice this size, and our bathroom is easily four times as large as yours."

"So you don't sleep in bunk beds?" Benjamin asked.

"No way," Heidi said. "We each have a queen sized bed, with a canopy."

"Yeah, well I'm glad I don't have a canopy bed," Andy said. "Talk about girly. Bunk beds are cool." He stood up and promptly bumped his head on the upper bunk. "Ow!" he said, rubbing his forehead.

"They do seem pretty cool," Iva said. "So, where's the key?

No, don't tell me. Let's see if I can find it." She walked directly over to the wardrobe, opened the bottom drawer, and lifted out a small box. "It's in here," she said.

"Yes it is," Benjamin said, "but you can't open the box I bet. It's DNA coded for only me to open."

"But couldn't I just walk out with the entire box and worry about opening it later?" Iva asked.

Benjamin's face fell. "Oh, I hadn't thought of that," he said. "Well, I suppose, but the guardian doesn't even know we have the first key yet."

"You don't know that at all," Iva said. "In fact, I think we need to assume the Guardian does know we have it. And you need to keep the key with you at all times. That's the only way we can make sure no one steals it."

"I guess that's not a bad idea," Benjamin agreed. He opened the box, took out the key, and placed it in his pocket, immediately aware of the extra weight. It sat next to the toy car Derrick and Douglas had given him before he left. Thinking about the car reminded him of the telekinetic car chase his brothers had been having at home before he left. He smiled at the memory, and instantly missed his family.

"Now, can we go on to the library?" Gary asked.

The Universal Travel Agent

Gary had memorized the location of every library in Mu and, thus, didn't even need to check his sheaf. He claimed one of the small offshoots connected to the Ruling Hall library had the largest selection of maps in all of Lemuria. It seemed like a good starting point to Benjamin, so he didn't even think about disagreeing. When it came to libraries, no one disagreed with Gary. Leaving the school, they headed back down Mu Way toward the Ruling Hall.

Once they reached the third floor, it took a while, but they finally found the narrow, empty hallway leading to the dimly lit map room. Benjamin walked in and stopped. His eyes bugged out and started to loose focus as he stared around the room at probably a gazillion maps. Seriously. Some were made of paper, some looked like computer screens or holograms, shifting and changing. One map was encased behind glass, the paper old and cracking. Benjamin and Heidi walked over to get a closer look.

"Look," Heidi said pointing to the map. "This must be the

oldest map here. It shows Lemuria and Atlantis before they sank."

"How do you know?" Benjamin asked her.

"There's no Ring of Fire," she replied, motioning to where the ring of volcanoes would normally be. Andy, Gary, and Iva walked over to join them.

A couple of the maps gave off a faint light. Benjamin walked over to one such holographic map, a green glow emanating from it.

"Look at this," he said. Heidi joined him. Benjamin reached his right hand up to the map, and pointed at Australia. It lit up. He then dragged his finger to the northwest, into Asia. The entire map rotated, and Asia lit up as Australia dimmed again. The map looked like an early predecessor of a Geodine. By pointing to a timeline along the top of the map, the locations of the continents began to drift.

"Pretty cool," Heidi said.

"So, how do we go about finding the second key's destination?" Andy asked.

"I think we should split up and start searching," Gary suggested. "I can start over here," he motioned to a long aisle on the right. The aisle was packed from floor to ceiling with thick hardbound books.

"Thank God," Andy said. "Look at all those dusty books. They're all the same color too." He groaned in disgust. Gary didn't even hear him as he began walking toward the aisle of books. Well, actually, given Gary's hearing, he probably did hear Andy and just decided to ignore him.

"Heidi and I can check this way," Benjamin suggested, pointing to an aisle that seemed to contain some of the older maps in the library. "And, Andy, why don't you and Iva search over there." Benjamin fought to keep the smile off his face and noticed Heidi did the same.

"Great," Iva said, "You ready, Andy?"

Andy perked up. "Definitely."

They split off and began searching. Benjamin and Heidi started down the wide aisle, which was lined with tables down the center where the maps could be spread out and studied. Their aisle contained shelves and shelves of scrolls—large scrolls, small scrolls, burned scrolls, scrolls that hung on hooks.

"Any suggestions on how we should tackle this?" Benjamin asked her.

"Not really," Heidi replied. "I guess I'll start on the right and you start on the left."

Benjamin pulled a map off a shelf and spread it out in the table, trying to be a careful as possible. He didn't want to be responsible for destroying a map which was probably older than modern man. But after checking it over, he decided it didn't look anywhere near old enough, and shoved it back on the shelf.

"So why do you always pair Andy and Iva up?" Heidi asked.

Benjamin laughed. "Because I think it's funny. I've known Andy for thirteen years, and I've never seen him act like this."

"You know Ryan still thinks there's a chance he and Iva might get together," Heidi said.

"Ryan Jordan?" Benjamin asked.

"Yeah. I think that's part of why he's always trying to butt in on us," Heidi said. "But I also think he and Jonathan are nosy. They know something's going on, and they can't stand not knowing what it is."

"As long as they don't know anything about the Alliance or the Emerald Tablet, I'm happy," Benjamin replied. "The fewer people that know, the better."

Before he knew it, an hour had passed. Benjamin could tell by the growling of his stomach.

"I'm starting to think we may never find anything," Benjamin said.

"I think we need to find where they keep the oldest maps, the ones that wouldn't just be rolled up and shoved on a shelf," Heidi said. They continued down the aisle until they came to a room labeled 'Special Collections.'

"This may be exactly what we're looking for," Benjamin said, entering the room. He squinted to see until dim lights flashed on. Heidi stepped in behind him, and the door to the room closed.

The dust in the large, empty room was at least an inch thick. As Benjamin walked, he looked down at the tracks his feet were leaving.

"I guess this isn't the most popular place to hang out," he said.

"Yeah, and why do they keep it so dark?" Heidi asked.

"To protect the maps?" Benjamin suggested, nodding to the walls as his eyes began to adjust.

"Check this out," Heidi said, pointing to an old, brittle map behind some kind of force field. "Doesn't that look like pictures you've seen of Pangaea? But it looks like it has more land mass than I've seen on other maps."

"That's because of Lemuria and Atlantis," Benjamin said. "Remember the map Proteus showed us. They're both huge."

Though Benjamin was sure his interest couldn't have compared to Gary's, the maps still fascinated him, and as they walked around the room, he couldn't help but stop and look at each one. Most of these maps predated recorded history on Earth—at least Earth as they had known it.

When they reached the back wall, they both stopped, and Benjamin felt the blood drain out of his face. They'd found the map of all maps. Its borders lit up red when they stepped in front of it, and the inch-thick protective glass disappeared. Words flashed at the top of the map: 'The Universal Travel Agent'.

"'The Universal Travel Agent?'" Heidi said. "What do you suppose that means?"

"Maybe it's like a travel brochure," Benjamin said. "Look at Lemuria." The continent of Lemuria had several small red stars decorating it with names listed by them. Benjamin didn't recognize any of the names, and the capital city, marked with a larger star, wasn't even anywhere close to Mu.

"And look—Atlantis," Heidi said. "This map must be from when the two continents were both still above water. Telegens probably still traveled back and forth then."

Benjamin shifted his gaze over to Tibet. He saw Shambhala,

and then his eyes moved southwest to a red star. "Hey, look," he said to Heidi. "I think we found it."

Heidi looked over to where Benjamin was pointing, just in time to see him reach up and touch the star on the map. "See. Xanadu."

24

Xanadu Is Not Just in a Poem

The star lit up green, and, in an instant, Benjamin found himself being sucked into a bright vortex. It felt nothing like the teleportation he'd almost become accustomed to. He looked around and relaxed just a little when he saw Heidi next to him.

"What's happening?" She shouted to be heard above the swirling sound of the vortex.

"I don't know," Benjamin yelled back. "The travel agent seems to be taking us somewhere."

Heidi grabbed his hand, and Benjamin didn't mind at all; he felt about as uneasy as she looked. The vortex whipped and whirled and then was gone.

Benjamin glanced down at his feet just to make sure the vortex had really disappeared; they were planted firmly in green grass. He could hear the sound of birds chirping in the nearby trees. He looked down at his left hand just as Heidi looked at her right; she quickly released his hand and moved a couple inches away.

"Where do you think we are?" Heidi asked.

Benjamin again looked around. They stood at the bottom of a green slope, next to the bank of a running river. In the distance, at the top of the hill was a fortress of some sort, with a large crystal dome at the center, glimmering in the sun. Benjamin could just barely make out the sound of music drifting from the top of the hill.

"Xanadu, I'm willing to bet," Benjamin replied.

"Xanadu?" Heidi asked. "I've never even heard of it."

"Haven't you ever read *Kubla Khan* by Samuel Taylor Coleridge?" he asked.

"Coleridge," she said. "Didn't he write a poem called *The Rime of the Ancient Mariner*?"

"Yeah. I memorized it last year to impress some girl. He also wrote one called *Kubla Khan* about a mythical place called Xanadu. Nobody believed the place really existed, and everyone just blamed the poem on the ravings of a lunatic," Benjamin said.

"You were trying to impress some girl," Heidi laughed. "Did it work?"

"No, not really," Benjamin said. "Actually not at all. She fell asleep while I was reciting it. But my teacher was impressed. She started crying."

"Well, wherever we are, it's beautiful," Heidi said. "Can we look around?"

"I think we should stay on the main path and head up to the fortress," Benjamin said. "If the second key really is here, it's a pretty good guess that it's up there." He nodded to the top of the hill.

As they started up the hill, Benjamin could only think of one word to describe the place. Paradise. Xanadu looked like it had come off the pages of the world's most desirable places. He inhaled the scent of the cedar trees combined with the exotic flowers lining the path and the river. They had to stop once to allow a peacock to cross the path. A forest stretched off to the left, vast and dark, and, for some reason he didn't understand, Benjamin felt relieved it was so far away.

Suddenly, the smallest monkey Benjamin had ever seen jumped onto the path in front of them, shrieked, and started waving a stick at them. They both jumped, and Heidi let out a small scream.

"What is that thing?" she asked.

"Sort of monkey," Benjamin said.

"Yeah, well, little monkey," Heidi snapped, "next time don't sneak up on us like that."

The monkey stared back and began chewing on the stick. The sounds of the music got louder, and the monkey cocked its head to listen. It began to jump up and down, again waving the stick at Benjamin and Heidi.

"I wonder what it wants," Benjamin said.

"It wants us to follow it," Heidi replied, motioning down the path where the monkey stood.

"What, can you read monkeys' minds now?" Benjamin asked.

Heidi ignored him and leaned toward the small monkey. "Do you want us to follow you?" she asked.

At hearing this, the monkey shrieked again, this time it seemed in acknowledgement, and began to scamper toward the music.

"Well, I guess we could follow it," Benjamin said. "It does seem to be going in the right direction."

They set out after it. Every so often, the monkey, who was much faster than Benjamin and Heidi, scampered backward, making sure they were still in tow. Finally, they reached the main entrance to the large city.

As he stepped through the gates, Benjamin realized immediately that outside paled in comparison to inside the city walls. The sun shimmered, reflecting and refracting light off the crystal dome, casting rainbows everywhere, painting the grass and water. Lining the grassy walkway leading to the dome stood imposing statues clearly marking the path to follow. The monkey scampered down the walkway, and Benjamin and Heidi followed, sticking close together. Benjamin felt compelled to reach out and take Heidi's hand again, but he resisted and quickly shook the thought from his mind before Heidi heard it.

The grass pathway ended at the large crystal dome. The monkey, still holding the stick, sauntered between two columns into the open area beneath the crystal rotunda. Benjamin and Heidi followed.

"Welcome, Benjamin Holt and Heidi Dylan," a musical female voice said. "We've been expecting you."

Perhaps it was the last few weeks rubbing off on him, but the fact that Benjamin had just traveled to some mythical city and the people there knew his name didn't even surprise him. He looked in the direction of the voice. On a large pillow sat a beautiful Indian woman with hair so long, it reached the bottom of her back. She wore a bright red sari with large amounts of gold and colored thread embroidered into it. Her hands and arms had detailed designs dyed on them. A jeweled dot sat in the middle of her forehead. Beside her sat a golden man who seemed to glow. His curly, blond hair told Benjamin the man wasn't Indian, and the ornate clothes heightened his regal appearance. The woman smiled and motioned for them to approach.

Benjamin and Heidi walked over to the pillows. "Please sit," she said, and waved her hand. More pillows appeared, and they sat; it seemed like the polite thing to do.

"I am Ananya, keeper of this place," she said.

"What is this place?" Heidi asked.

"You already know that," Ananya replied. The small monkey, stick in hand, jumped up onto her lap, and she began stroking its head. Ananya laughed. "Oh, Chaos," she said to the animal, "you are so silly." She looked again at Benjamin and Heidi, "This is Xanadu, as you have guessed. I'm sure you have many questions, and also something to gather. But first, we shall dine."

"You know why we're here? You know about the key?" Benjamin asked, throwing caution to the wind.

"Of course I know, but we shall talk as we dine," Ananya said. "Please go and change clothes. Heidi, you may change in there." She pointed off to the left to a small enclosed room.

"And Benjamin, you may find new clothes there." She pointed to the right.

Benjamin looked at Heidi, shrugged, and then headed off to the right. He wasn't sure what was wrong with the t-shirt and jeans he wore, but figured maybe it was best not to argue about it. Entering the room, he almost laughed aloud when he found the clothes he was supposed to wear. The top was olive green with gold embroidery and gold buttons, and the pants were baggy and white. Green shoes with curved up toes were set out neatly along with a green embroidered scarf with tassels on the end. As he dressed, all he could think about was how happy he was Andy wasn't here to see him in this.

Once dressed, Benjamin went back out under the large crystal dome. He'd made sure to transfer the first key of Shambhala and the toy car to his new pants. The room was now empty except for a large table which had been placed in the center. The man who had been sitting next to Ananya entered the area and walked over to Benjamin. For whatever reason, the Indian clothes didn't look ridiculous on him.

"We're pleased to have you with us, Benjamin Holt," the golden-haired man said. "Xanadu does not get outside visitors much anymore, and we've been expecting you for some time."

"How could you have been expecting me?" Benjamin asked.

"You are the champion. Xanadu has been awaiting your arrival for thousands of years," the man said, flashing a smile showing perfectly white teeth.

"Thousands of years?" Benjamin asked. "How could that

be? I'm only thirteen."

"Things are not always as they seem, Benjamin Holt," the man said.

At that moment, both Ananya and Heidi entered the domed area. Without even thinking about it, Benjamin stood up; he noticed the golden-haired man did the same. Benjamin smiled when he saw Ananya, and then nearly passed out when he saw Heidi. He'd never thought of her as beautiful before. Cute maybe, but not beautiful. He couldn't find the right words to describe her transformation. But nonetheless, he decided to make a pathetic attempt.

"Wow, Heidi, you look...um....I mean you look a lot better than you ever look at school. Not that you don't look nice at school or anything. I mean, that's a pretty outfit," he said. She wore a blue, gold and red sari, with a green silk shirt underneath. It had so many colors, it reminded Benjamin of Iva's Ammolite necklace. Heidi had changed her hair to dark brown, and an ornate golden necklace had been woven into it.

"Oh, thanks," Heidi said, blushing and looked down at her sari. Thankfully, she must've decided not to give Benjamin a hard time about his pitiful compliment. "It was really complicated to put on. But luckily I had help."

"Please," Ananya said, "let us sit. We do not want the hour to get too late." She sat at the large table, and gestured Benjamin and Heidi to do the same. The golden-haired man cast her a perfect smile and sat to her right.

Benjamin's hunger returned when he saw the food, and they ate for a while in silence. He wasn't sure how to bring up the second key again, thinking it might be rude to just ask for it and then leave. Luckily, Ananya gave him the opening he needed.

"Now, I suppose you have some questions that you would like answered," Ananya said. "Where shall we start?"

Benjamin decided to be blunt. "What is Xanadu, how did you know we were coming, and do you have the second key of Shambhala here?"

"Well, I guess that should get us started," Ananya laughed. The monkey she had called Chaos jumped up on the table beside her plate. It turned to Benjamin and screeched at him. Ananya stroked it gently.

She took a long sip of her drink and began talking. "Xanadu is an ancient city from times before the sinking of the great continents—times when all was at peace between Lemuria and Atlantis. It was founded by two citizens of Atlantis, Sophus and Reva. Xanadu thrived as a growing city, hidden from the outside world. But it wasn't long before the true nature of Sophus and Reva began to show. Cruel and wicked, they were corrupted by power and greed, their unnatural lives extended by whatever means possible. A rebellion formed in Xanadu, and Sophus was thought to be killed, though his body was never found. Reva was kept alive but imprisoned here in Xanadu, in the depths of the caverns. A new government was set up, fair and democratic."

"It was said Reva was cursed, and it soon became apparent that her unnaturally long life was continuing. New generations were born, but the expelled female ruler didn't age. Fear of the

189

curse finally caused the citizens of Xanadu to seal off the part of the caves where she was kept. And as time passed, she became nothing more than a faint legend, told to children over firelight. She can still be heard wailing in the night, perhaps mourning the loss of her husband, her power, or her life."

Benjamin shuddered at the spooky tale. He looked at Heidi and saw that her eyes were wide with alarm. Again, he got the strange urge to reach out and grab her hand. But he didn't. Why did he keep thinking that? Using the biggest mental eraser he could, he banished the thought from his mind and looked back to Ananya who smiled at him.

"Xanadu became a popular retreat for artists of all kinds. Musicians, painters, sculptors—all would come to Xanadu for much needed rest and instruction. I believe you arrived by the same means many of them did—an old travel agent map, if I am correct."

Benjamin and Heidi nodded.

"These travel agent maps were the perfect means of transportation, as the precise location of Xanadu was always kept secret. Standard means of communication and travel were eliminated for Xanadu."

"So why were we able to arrive with the Universal Travel Agent?" Heidi asked.

"It appears that someone enabled the device," Ananya replied. "Though who, I cannot be certain."

"So can our friends use it also?" Benjamin asked. "Will they be here soon?"

"I think not," Ananya replied. "For only you and Heidi were

destined to visit this time."

"How do you know that?" Benjamin asked. "How did you know we were coming?"

"We have been awaiting your arrival for many years. Since far before you were born, we have known it would be you who would come for the second key of Shambhala," Ananya said.

"But how could you know that?" Benjamin persisted.

"Ages ago, an oracle at Delphi told me. We have been awaiting your birth ever since. At long last, thirteen years ago, we were visited by the High Oracle personally to deliver the news of your birth. The key has resided here in Xanadu for thousands of years, but now, I believe the time has come for it to move on."

"Do you know why I was chosen to have the keys?" Benjamin asked.

"Do not be mistaken, Benjamin Holt," Ananya said. "The keys are owned by no one. You have been chosen to be the guardian of the keys, nothing more. When your purpose with them is complete, they will be passed on. They own themselves."

Benjamin felt his face flush.

"Do not be embarrassed," she said. "It is a common mistake for people to make. Ownership comes so easily for so many things, that sometimes it is hard to know when to draw the line."

The golden-haired man discreetly cleared his throat.

"My companion reminds me that the hour is getting late. It is time for you to retrieve the key and depart," Ananya said.

"So, where is it?" Benjamin asked. "Where do you keep it?"

"It is kept where it was placed, and it has never been moved," Ananya said. She and the man stood up and began to walk out of the dome. Heidi and Benjamin got up and followed them. Chaos scampered at her feet. She headed toward a large fountain located near the entrance to the crystal dome. Upon reaching the fountain, she stopped.

"It is here, amid the waters of the fountain," Ananya said, pointing at the cascading water.

Inside the Fountain

Benjamin looked but saw nothing. "I don't see it."

"And you will not be able to until you are ready," Ananya replied. She waved her hand in front of the fountain, and the water stopped, frozen in midair. Benjamin looked down and was surprised to see a large stone staircase spiraling downward into the darkness below. Water drained down the steps.

"It's a secret passageway," Heidi said, leaning over to get a closer look. "Where does it go?"

"The fountain stems from the sacred river Alph and travels deep into the caverns. The water contains the power of truth and the power of healing. It is down there that you will find what you seek," Ananya said.

"When will I be ready to get the key?" Benjamin asked.

"When you have faced what it is you fear the most," Ananya replied.

"But what's that?" Benjamin asked.

"Only you know what it is you fear. Only you can control your feelings. And only within you is the knowledge necessary to retrieve the key from its resting place," Ananya explained.

Heidi stepped forward. "Well, I guess we better go down there and look, Benjamin."

The golden-haired man placed his arm gently in front of Heidi, barring her way. "This task is for Benjamin to face alone, Heidi. You will have to wait here with us."

"But what if he needs help?" Heidi persisted. "He shouldn't go down there alone. What about that story you just told us about Reva? It could be dangerous."

"It'll be okay, Heidi," Benjamin said. "I'll be fine. I can't think of anything I'm afraid of anyway." He smiled at her and began to walk forward.

"Just be careful," Heidi said.

Benjamin noticed her face was knotted with concern. Why was she worried? She should be able to sense that there wasn't any fear in his mind, and he was doing his best to mask the small feeling of doubt which was not normally there.

"Okay," Benjamin replied.

He started down the circular stone stairway. It was wet and dark, and after only two turns, he could no longer see the light from above. The fountain began flowing again, and the sound of the running water filled the air around him. The water flowed gently over the side of the stairs, cascading down the center of the spiral. There was no handrail to hold on to, so Benjamin chose his steps carefully, settling both feet on each step before moving on to the next.

His eyes adjusted to the dark in no time. The walls around him were barren, the stone steps simple and smooth. Benjamin continued walking downward, completing fifty turns of the staircase before reaching the bottom. The ground sloped downward, allowing the running water to travel away from the stairs. A path ran alongside the flow of the water, and Benjamin began walking next to it. He looked around, but didn't see any sign of the second key of Shambhala. Maybe it was down the path.

As Benjamin walked, he heard nothing except the sound of the running water. The rushing sound increased as he proceeded farther into the depths of the Earth. Benjamin continued walking though the water began to pool up over the banks of the small river. It sloshed against his feet, soaking his shoes through. With each step he took, the level of the river rose.

"Can anybody hear me?" a voice called out amidst the pounding of the water. "Please! Is there anybody out there?"

Benjamin turned in the direction from which the voice came.

"Help, please, anybody!" the familiar voice called. Benjamin recognized the voice at the same time he saw where it was coming from.

Benjamin ran over to the cell carved into the side of the cavern. There, behind solid bars, was his mother. "Mom! What are you doing here?"

"Benjamin! Help! The water's starting to rise."

Benjamin looked at the ground in the cell. Already, it was covered with water up to his mom's ankles.

"Mom! I'll get you out of there." Even as he spoke, the water quickened its rising pace. It now reached his mother's knees.

He tried to use telekinesis to bend the bars of the cell, but his mind wasn't strong enough.

"No, Benjamin! Don't worry about me! Save the twins!" his mother screamed.

"Derrick and Douglas! Where are they? Mom, I can get you out!" he called back.

"No! Get the twins. She's taken them! Please, Benjamin, save my babies. Don't let them die! Please, Benjamin!" The water was now mid-thigh on his mother.

Behind him, he now heard the distinct cries of his younger brothers. "Benji! Benji! Help us!" Derrick called.

Benjamin whipped his head around to look. Perched on the opposite wall were two shelves, set apart from each other. Water was nearing the base of the shelves.

"Benjamin, hurry, please!" his mom called out. He turned back to her. The water was now at her waist. "Don't worry about me. Save the twins."

"Stay where you are," Benjamin called out to the twins, making his way to the opposite side of the large cavern.

"Benji, I'm scared," Douglas cried.

The water was so high Benjamin could no longer reach the bottom with his feet. He began to swim over toward the wall shelves.

"Benji, why can't Mommy get out of there? I want my mommy." Derrick started to cry so fiercely he could hardly talk. "I want my mommy!"

"I'm coming, Derrick. Just stay where you are." Benjamin started swimming toward the shelf where Derrick was now mid-knee in water.

"Benji, don't leave me here," Douglas cried out. "I don't re-member how to swim. Please, Benji, help me!"

"I'll be right over to get you Dougie," Benjamin yelled out. "Just stay close to the wall."

Benjamin had no idea if he'd be able to reach them both in time. Would he have to choose which of his brothers to save? He didn't think he could make such a choice; so instead, he put the thought totally out of his head. He would save them both. There was no other choice.

Benjamin used quick strokes and reached the shelf where Derrick was still standing. The water rose rapidly. He grabbed Derrick around the waist in a vice grip.

"I want Mommy." Derrick was inconsolable. Benjamin turned to look back to the cell holding his mom. It was under-water.

"Derrick," Benjamin said firmly. "You need to calm down. Mommy will be fine. We need to swim over to get Dougie, and we can't do that unless you calm down!"

"Mommy! Where's my mommy?" Derrick cried.

"Hurry, Benji! Hurry!" Douglas called out.

Benjamin turned to the other shelf and saw that Douglas was now up to his chest in water. It had to be now or never.

"I'm coming, Douglas. Just hold on," Benjamin called. He began to swim over, holding Derrick firmly in his left arm. He had to swim on his back in order to carry the awkward load. The thought entered his mind that he might not be able to get there in time, but he immediately pushed it out. He had to get there in time. That's all there was to it.

With every bit of speed and strength he could muster, Benjamin swam his way over to the wall shelf. Douglas was clawing desperately at the wall, trying to climb up the smooth side. The water rushed at them without mercy. Benjamin reached Douglas just before the water would have covered his head. Grabbing Douglas in his right arm, Benjamin arranged himself and the twins, all on their backs, in order to stay afloat.

Derrick was still crying for mommy, and soon Douglas was crying too. "*Settle Down!*" He screamed the thought in his mind. He didn't know if the twins could hear him, but he didn't have the energy to talk. There would be time later to think about his mom. Right now, the most important thing for Benjamin was to get the twins to safety.

Benjamin tried to crane his head around, looking for somewhere to escape from the river flood. Off to the left was a large upper cavern, which, in normal circumstances, would have overlooked the river far below. Kicking his legs with every bit of energy he had left, Benjamin made his way to the floor of the cavern. The water level was stabilizing, and, using his remaining strength, Benjamin maneuvered the twins, one at a time, up onto the floor. Finally, he pulled himself up behind them, and rolled onto his back.

Suddenly, the world shifted around Benjamin. He no longer lay on the floor of the large cavern. He lay at the base of the stairway, the same one he'd descended earlier. He quickly felt to his sides, searching for the twins.

"*You have done well, Benjamin Holt,*" the voice of Ananya

said in his head.

"Where are my brothers?" Benjamin demanded. "What have you done with them? Where is my mom?"

"Your brothers are home safely with your mother and father and sister," Ananya said.

"But what about the river? What about the cell my mom was trapped in? Who put them there?" Benjamin yelled his reply.

"It was only a test. Nothing more. You have passed, and you are ready for what lays ahead," Ananya said.

Benjamin stood up quickly, looking around for Derrick and Douglas. They were nowhere to be found, and the water running off the stairway had returned to a normal flow, gently meandering its way through the cavern.

"A test! What kind of test was that? That was the most awful thing I've ever been through in my life. My mother was dead, and my brothers nearly were too." Benjamin felt a lump well up in his throat. He fought back tears with his anger.

"That was the kind of test that will face you if you continue on as champion of the Emerald Tablet," Ananya replied.

"What do you mean 'continue on'? Do I have a choice in the matter?" Benjamin asked, his anger only just slightly subsiding as relief that the whole thing might not have been true reached his brain.

"There is always a choice in everything we do in life," Ananya said. *"It is for you, and only you, to decide if you are ready and willing to accept the challenge. You must decide if you are willing to put the good of the world above your own."*

"And if I'm not?" Benjamin asked.

"*Then you may simply walk away,*" Ananya said.

"*And if I am?*" Benjamin asked.

"*And if you are, then the key is waiting for you,*" Ananya replied.

In the center of the stairwell, on the floor, a bright green light began to glow, pulsating out from beneath the cascading water. Benjamin reached his hand toward the light, knowing what waited for him there. His hand closed around the smooth stone and he slowly picked it up. It was green and carved and beautiful, just like the first key.

Benjamin held it in his hand for a moment, studying its beauty. Was he the right person for the task set before him? Would he be able to bring peace to the people of Earth? Was he willing to accept such a large responsibility? Before now, Benjamin hadn't really thought about the seriousness of the situation. It had seemed more like a game, a treasure hunt. Now he realized it wasn't a game, but something far more serious than he could have ever imagined before. But if he didn't do it, then who would? Would Earth be doomed to disaster?

He looked at the key once more, and then slowly slipped it into his pocket. He would face what lay ahead. Without looking back, he began the long walk up the circular stairway.

The Forest Is Haunted

With her telepathy skills, Heidi would have needed to be unconscious to not sense Benjamin's emotions while he'd been below the fountain. She must not have been able to reach him with her thoughts—or maybe she hadn't tried. Whatever the reason, to Benjamin's relief, nobody mentioned it. He had to put it behind him, at least for the time being.

Once again outside the fountain, Benjamin pulled both keys out of his pockets. They pulsated with light when he brought them close together. "So, can you tell us where the third key is?" Benjamin asked Ananya, pushing thoughts of the cavern test far from his mind.

"No, that is not possible, for I do not know," Ananya replied. "I only became aware of the location of the first key when you removed it from its hiding place beneath the Emerald Buddha."

"Will it be hard to get?" Benjamin asked, looking down at his shoes. "I mean, will I have to face another test?"

"The first key was a test of strength, the second a test of courage. There is no doubt the third key will have a challenge you must overcome, though what it is, I do not know," Ananya replied.

Benjamin looked down at the keys, then back at her. "Thank you," he said.

"No, thank you, Benjamin Holt. Now, I believe it is time to part ways," Ananya said. "Do you remember the way to the Universal Travel Agent?"

Benjamin began to shake his head no, but saw Heidi nodding hers. "I'm pretty good with directions," she said. "I should be able to get us back there."

"Then I suppose we should take our leave," Ananya said. "Goodbye for now."

"For now?" Benjamin asked.

"Yes, for we shall meet again, Benjamin Holt and Heidi Dylan," Ananya replied. She put up her hand, stopping them from asking any questions. "I cannot tell you when, for I do not know exactly, but I am certain that this is not the last time we are to see each other." Ananya and the golden-haired man smiled and bowed. Benjamin, unsure what to do, bowed back, and noticed Heidi did the same. Chaos jumped up onto Ananya's shoulder and screeched his goodbye. He then rested his head gently into the crook of Ananya's neck, much like a baby ready to fall asleep on its mother. Ananya and the man turned and walked away, leaving the shelter of the crystal dome—no longer glittering, as the sun had long since set.

Benjamin and Heidi turned and began to walk the other way. "So, you're sure you know where we're going?" Benjamin asked, trying not to think about the fountain experience.

"Definitely," Heidi replied. "It's just down the grassy hill, by the river."

Thankfully, she didn't ask about what had happened. When he felt ready to talk about it, he would—if he ever felt ready.

They set off, soon leaving the city walls far behind. While it had been light inside the city, the moonless sky was dark, and the farther they were from the city, the darker it became. Heidi slowed her pace, walking closer to Benjamin. Without warning, she stopped.

"Did you hear that?" she asked.

"Hear what?" Benjamin said. "I didn't hear anything."

"Shhhh!" she hissed. She listened, not moving anything but her eyes. A quiet mournful cry began, growing louder as the wind picked up. Heidi and Benjamin both jumped at the sound.

"I heard it that time," Benjamin said.

"It's coming from the forest," Heidi whispered, nodding toward the pitch black far to their right.

"Do you think that's what Ananya was talking about? Do you think that's Reva?" He couldn't help but think about his experience in the cavern. His mom had said 'she' had taken the twins. Was Reva the 'she' his mom had been talking about? But, he told himself, the whole thing had been contrived directly from his mind, hadn't it? Or was Reva more powerful than anyone, even Ananya, could know?

"Shhhh!" Heidi said again. Again she stood, immobile. The wailing gradually faded away to nothing.

After waiting for a minute Benjamin finally spoke. "Can

you tell what it is?"

"It's something old and something evil. I can't make out any thoughts, but I can sense it. It's not going to harm us— at least not tonight, but it's the most concentrated source of evil I've ever sensed in my whole life." She suddenly shook her head, trying to break off the connection. "Let's get out of here."

They hurried down the hill to the river, where they found the emersion point for the Universal Travel Agent glowing. Stepping on, they entered the swirling vortex which would hopefully return them back to Lemuria.

The Owner of the Universal Travel Agent

Only the dim lights lit the map room when Benjamin and Heidi walked out of the Universal Travel Agent. Iva, Andy, and Gary were pointedly absent.

Benjamin looked down to find he and Heidi both still had on the fancy, formal clothes they'd worn for dinner in Xanadu. "I don't know about you, but I for one am glad I don't have to explain this outfit to Andy," he said, with a chuckle.

"Oh, I don't know, I kind of like this," Heidi said, twirling around.

Benjamin couldn't help but stare; she still looked beautiful.

"I wonder what Suneeta Manvar and Julie Macfarlane would think. I may start dressing like this more often," she said.

"Where to?" he asked, shaking himself out of his stupor. "The dining hall? I think you'd be a little out of place."

"Yeah, maybe so, but it sure is pretty." Heidi looked around. "We should probably head back to the school."

"Creepy wailing we heard back there," Benjamin said.

"Yeah, creepy." Heidi shuddered. "You know, it's okay to talk about what happened back there under the fountain."

"There's nothing to talk about," Benjamin snapped. "It was just a little test. That's all. Stop reading my mind."

Heidi bit her lip, and small tears crept into the corners of her eyes. "I wasn't reading you mind, Benjamin," she stated. "I would never read your mind unless you told me it was okay."

Immediately Benjamin regretted his accusation; he hadn't meant to hurt her. But he had. He could see it in her eyes, and he could feel it through the Alliance bond. He stopped and looked right at her. "Hey, I'm sorry. It's just that you're so good at telepathy, and sometimes I don't like the thought that you can listen to whatever I'm thinking."

"Just because I can listen to whatever you're thinking doesn't mean I do listen to whatever you're thinking," she replied. "Besides, you're getting a lot better at blocking your thoughts. With more practice, you may actually be able to keep me out if you try."

Benjamin started laughing at the thought. "I'm willing to bet it'll take a lot more practice before that happens. Anyway, there's nothing to talk about."

"If you say so, but I'll always be here to listen if you change your mind," Heidi said.

Benjamin gave a small smile. "Thanks. Let's just get back to the school."

"Yeah, okay," she replied.

Behind them the Universal Travel Agent again came to life.

Its borders glowed red, and Benjamin heard the swirling sound of the vortex. Benjamin felt like he should run and hide behind something, but the room was empty except for the maps on the wall. With no other choice, he and Heidi both turned to look.

Without delay, a man arrived in the room. He was unmistakable with his long, dark hair. Upon his arrival, all life snuffed out of the Universal Travel Agent.

He began walking but stopped as he saw them near the entrance to the room.

"You two are up a little late, aren't you?"

"Helios Deimos," Benjamin said. "What are you doing here?"

"I think it is I who should be asking that question," Helios replied. "The map library closed hours ago." Unlike the times they'd met him in the past, Helios's face was void of any smile.

"We were just in here looking at some of the old maps," Heidi said.

"Does looking at the old maps entail the unauthorized use of my personal Travel Agent?" Helios asked.

"Your personal Travel Agent?" Benjamin said. "So you turned it on?" Well, that cleared up who had enabled the device.

"Yes," Helios replied. "I use it from time to time when I have business outside of Lemuria to attend to."

"So where were you tonight?" Heidi asked.

"The whereabouts of a ruler of Lemuria are not the concerns of Year One Denarians," Helios answered. "And now, if there's nothing else, I must ask you to leave."

Benjamin and Heidi did nothing short of run out of the library. It wasn't until they reached the main level of the Ruling Hall that they finally spoke.

"Don't you think it's strange he didn't even ask us where we went on the Travel Agent?" Benjamin asked, catching his breath.

"Not if he already knew," Heidi replied.

"Did he?" Benjamin asked. Had Heidi been able to read Helios's mind?

She sighed. "I have no idea. I tried to break through his mind block, but it was pointless. He could have been in Xanadu at the same time as us for all I could tell."

"But what reason would he have for being in Xanadu unless he were following us?" Benjamin asked.

"You think one of the rulers of Lemuria would be following a couple Year One Denarians around?" Heidi asked.

"All I'm saying is that it's a little bit suspicious that we ran into him after visiting Bangkok and then again tonight," Benjamin said. "Both times we came back with a key of Shambhala."

"Do you think he's the guardian?" Heidi asked.

Benjamin shrugged but didn't reply. It was late, and, at this point, all his mind wanted to think about was sleep—not the three keys of Shambhala. He had two of the three anyway, which wasn't all bad.

Quickly, they walked down the hallway leading to the entrance.

"Does the Atlantis scale look even more off balance than it did when we were here last?" Benjamin asked as they walked past the two large barrier strength scales.

Heidi stopped and studied it. "Maybe a little. Isn't it still supposed to be okay for years? Do you think its failure rate is increasing?"

"I sure hope not. We still have one more key to find, and then we have to figure out how to use them to fix the barrier," Benjamin said. He rubbed his eyes. "What time is it anyway?"

Heidi glanced over to the wall where a large clock was inset. "It's almost midnight," she said. "No wonder I feel like I'm about to collapse."

They continued on and, using one of the public teleporters outside, were able to quickly get back to the school. Benjamin found that Andy and Gary were both still awake when he got back to the room.

"Where have you been?" Andy said.

"Did Heidi make it back with you?" Gary asked. "I heard you guys talking in the map room, and then, the next thing I knew, there was no sign of you."

"Yeah, we waited around until they kicked us out," Andy said.

"Did you guys try to use the Universal Travel Agent?" Benjamin asked.

"The what?" Andy replied.

"The big map on the wall with the glowing, red borders," Benjamin explained.

"We didn't see any glowing maps," Andy replied.

"It was right in the middle of the wall, in the special collections area," Benjamin said.

"Special Collections?" Andy asked.

Benjamin opened his mouth to speak, but shut it again. For whatever reason, his friends hadn't even been able to find the Universal Travel Agent.

"So, where have you been?" Gary asked.

"And what's up with the outfit?" Andy said. "You look like something out of Arabian Nights."

It figured Andy would mention the outfit. "It's a long story, and I'm beat," Benjamin said. "Can we talk about it tomorrow?"

"Are you kidding?" Gary asked.

"Yeah, are you kidding?" Andy echoed.

Benjamin chuckled. "Okay, I'll give you guys the short version and then I'm going to bed." He reached into his right pocket and grabbed the first key of Shambhala and placed it on his desk. He reached into his left pocket and pulled out the second key of Shambhala, putting it next to the first key. The two keys began to pulsate as they'd done before.

"You found it?" Gary asked amazed. "How in the world did you get it? How were you able to travel?"

Benjamin quickly relayed the story—the Universal Travel Agent, Xanadu, and the dinner with Ananya and the golden-haired man. He didn't mention the test in the cavern or the strange wailing they'd heard while leaving the place, or even that they ran into Helios Deimos. Some things would just have to wait for tomorrow.

"Man, you're the luckiest guy I know," Gary said. "You

manage to be in exactly the right place at the right time, find what you're looking for, and get a gourmet meal while doing it."

28

It's a Good Thing Benjamin Has the Keys

The summer was passing quickly, and, with it, so were Benjamin's hopes of finding the third key of Shambhala. The primary focus of all the Year One Denarians, including the members of the Alliance, had become the upcoming ability tests—tests designed to measure each student's abilities so more focused teaching could be given in summers to come.

As the summer passed, it was more evident which subjects students would test well in and which subjects would require more basic instruction. Heidi would no doubt test the highest in the class for telepathy, but her telekinesis skills had improved little over the course of the summer. Gary excelled at science, but had nearly as little telekinesis ability as Heidi.

"Well, at least we'll be in the same Telekinesis class next summer," Gary said to cheer Heidi up one day.

"Even you'll probably skip ahead of me, Gary. I think I've actually gotten worse," Heidi said, planting her chin in her hands.

"Oh, you have not," Iva said. "You're just imagining things. And, plus, just think about how good you are at telepathy."

Heidi smiled at her friend, though it didn't reach her eyes.

The members of the Alliance were like all the telegen students in one regard. Their entire lives they'd grown up being the smartest kids in the class, never having to work hard for a grade, never having to stay up late reading or doing homework. In short, school had been way too easy—too easy that is until they came to Lemuria. Now, for the first time in their lives, they were challenged. They didn't excel at everything they studied. Teachers knew their skills and pressed them to work harder. They were pitted against each other in trials continuously, and every time they lost one of these challenges they were forced to work all the harder.

Benjamin tried his best to split his little free time between practicing for the ability tests and searching for some sign of the third key of Shambhala. Heidi, Iva, Gary, and Andy helped him as much as they could, but they, too, were busy practicing. With summer's end fast approaching, Benjamin was running out of ideas. Gary'd even managed to find a backdoor, encrypted method for using their sheaves to access the human Internet; Benjamin had searched the whole thing for some clue, but, like everything else, it came up empty.

As if they weren't busy enough, taking up their free time two nights a week was lecture. The favorite lecture for everyone had been the night Genetic Engineering was discussed. Mr. Hermes had given a detailed history of Genetic Engineering, adding to what Proteus had mentioned the first day of class.

Jack the Nogical had attended the lecture with Benjamin, adding his own commentary as required.

After the initial crackdown to prevent genetically engineered humanoids and telegenoids, the practice of genetic engineering again became more common, though highly controlled. In today's world, there were scientists and science academies full of genetic engineering work. It was still taboo to engineer any type of human or telegen, though research was still done on the subject. Benjamin overheard rumors that the people of Atlantis had no restrictions in place regarding genetically engineered humans and telegens, and that the continent had become more genetically synthesized than natural. Mr. Hermes assured him this was strictly rumor, but it still made for an interesting topic of debate.

The week after the lecture on Genetic Engineering, the first guest lecturer appeared, and Benjamin and Andy couldn't have been more surprised when Mr. Burton, their science teacher from Virginia, walked into the lecture hall.

Mr. Hermes walked to the center of the room and began to speak. "I would like to introduce you to our lecturer for the evening, Mr. Kennias Burton, an agent for Lemuria who functions as a middle school science teacher in Virginia."

Mr. Burton smiled and replaced Mr. Hermes at the center of the room. "Hi, I'm Kennias Burton, as Mr. Hermes told you. I know a handful of you and have even had the opportunity to teach a couple of you back in Virginia. I'm here tonight to talk to you about what it's really like to be an agent."

"Now if I am correct, every single one of you has been an agent your entire life and had no idea. Is that right?" This elicited a small round of laughter from the students. "Well, I myself have been an agent for over ten years, and am considered one of the best in the business. In fact, Benjamin Holt and Andy Grow, whom I taught back in Virginia, had no idea I even had any telegen abilities. Right?"

Benjamin and Andy nodded.

"One of the most important skills to have as an agent is good telepathy. Being able to read a human's mind is important. If any thoughts are detected with strange suspicions about yourself, it's an automatic yellow light to be more cautious with your skills. Skills should never be demonstrated in public, especially not for fun." He looked pointedly at Benjamin and Andy.

Benjamin thought of the time they'd levitated a frog onto a classmate's head and smiled.

"If you find that your life is in danger, or the life of someone you are protecting is in danger, then the use of abilities at that point is sometimes required, but should never be flaunted. The humans on Earth would have to throw away everything they believed in if they were to find out that a race of superior beings existed. Instantly, everything they knew would be gone. Suspicions would be everywhere. It would be assumed that those in power, those successful, were telegens. Society as they know it would have to be completely restructured."

As Mr. Burton talked, Benjamin began to realize how much of what he said caused things he'd noticed his whole life to fall into place. Why were his dad and Joey Duncan so quiet about their work? Why did his parents insist on mind blocking all their interesting conversations? The life of being an agent was full of mystery, secrecy, danger, and intrigue. It was just like being a spy.

As interesting as the lecture was, Benjamin was thankful when it lasted only two hours. He was getting more exhausted every day, the still unfound third key of Shambhala weighing on his mind.

After the lecture, Benjamin, Gary, and Andy lagged behind as the other students filed out of the auditorium. They walked up to the center of the room.

"Hey, Mr. Burton!" Andy said. "Great to see you."

"Yeah," Benjamin said. "You should've told us you were gonna be the lecturer for tonight."

"I was hoping it would be a surprise," Mr. Burton answered, smiling at them. "It's good to see you all. How have things been since I saw you last? Have you been keeping busy?"

"Oh, more busy than you could ever imagine," Andy said. "As if getting ready for the ability tests isn't enough, Benjamin always seems to have some extra task for us to work on." He laughed.

"What kind of extra tasks?" Mr. Burton asked.

Benjamin felt his blood get hot. How dare Andy even suggest what they'd been working on? It was nobody's business but the members of the Alliance. "Oh, nothing," Benjamin said. "Just extra research on the history of Lemuria," he lied, hoping his face hadn't gotten red. "You know the history of Lemuria is actually fascinating. It's hard to believe it's really as old as they say it is."

"Yes, I remember when I found out about Lemuria being 900,000 years old. I thought my homeroom teacher was lying," Mr. Burton said, apparently not noticing Benjamin's lie.

"Did you grow up in Lemuria or were your parents agents like ours?" Benjamin asked, still trying to steer the subject away from their activities.

"I grew up in the US, just like you boys. However, when I was only a year or two older than you are now, my parents were killed by a common criminal," Mr. Burton said. "After that I came to live in Lemuria with my aunt and uncle who didn't have any children of their own."

"Wow, I'm sorry to hear that," Benjamin said.

"Yes, it was a real tragedy. It was death without purpose caused by someone not worthy to wipe the dirt off my shoes," Mr. Burton replied. "Oh, the common justice system put him in jail for some nominal time period, but by the time he got out, I was gone, living full time in Lemuria." He shook his head. "But enough about that. I'm sure you boys are tired and don't want to hear me ramble on about my past. You should really get back to your room for bed."

"Yeah, I guess you're right, but I am sorry about your parents," Benjamin said.

"Thank you," Mr. Burton said. "I appreciate that, Benjamin."

"And it's good to see you again," Andy said. "Even though summer school is way cool and all, I still miss home and seeing you reminds me of it."

"Yes, well just keep in mind I won't be cutting you two any slack next year in science class," Mr. Burton said. "I expect you to be both the best and the worst students. I'll be keeping a close watch on you."

By the time they reached the boy's dorms, Benjamin felt like the only reason his eyelids were still open was because he didn't have the energy to shut them. Gary entered their room first, ready to throw himself down on the bed. He walked into the room and stopped. "Uh oh," he said.

"Uh oh, what?" Andy asked.

"You guys need to take a look at this," Gary said. Benjamin and Andy walked in behind him, immediately stopping as Gary had done.

The entire room was trashed. Books were everywhere. Clothes were scattered about. The wardrobes had all been forced open and all the contents removed. Sheets had been torn off the beds, and their desks were upturned.

"Whoa, what happened in here?" Benjamin asked.

"Looks like someone broke in while we were at the lecture," Gary said.

"Iva's not gonna be happy about this," Andy said. "Is anything missing? Are they missing? Are you still keeping them with you?" he asked Benjamin.

Benjamin put his hands in his pockets, feeling the carved keys under his palms. "They're safe. I have them right here. You really think someone broke in looking for the keys?" he asked.

"Why else would someone ransack our whole room?" Andy replied.

"Not my books," Gary said, picking up the treasured books he'd brought with him. "Man, I hope they didn't tear any of the pages. Do you think we should tell someone?"

"Who would we tell?" Benjamin said. "Nobody knows what we're doing, and, anyway, who could we trust?"

"I don't know," Gary said. "Maybe Proteus Ajax. Or Mr. Burton. Or even Morpheus Midas or The Panther or someone. I mean, someone broke into our room and trashed it. What if it's that telegen from the chess tournament? Morpheus should know."

"No, I agree with Benjamin," Andy said. "We don't tell anyone except Heidi and Iva. We can't trust anyone. I mean, for all we know, Morpheus Midas could have been the one who broke in here while we were in lecture."

"I don't think Morpheus would do that," Gary said.

"Well, I don't either," Andy said, "but all I'm trying to say is that nobody is above suspicion."

"Nobody except us that is," Benjamin said.

"That's right," Andy agreed. "Nobody except us."

Benjamin Shows Off

The ability tests were unbiased—at least as unbiased as any test could be. In addition to a grader, a skill catcher was given to each student to measure skill levels inside the body while different tasks were performed. Benjamin had no idea how this was done, and even after Jack had tried to explain how electrical currents were measured or something, it still didn't make much sense.

To prevent cheating, no telemagnifiers of any type were allowed while testing was going on. Homeroom teachers collected all the telemagnifiers the students had acquired over the summer; it seemed like everyone had at least one. Heidi had given her moonstone ring over to Proteus Ajax, and Iva had also turned in her Ammolite pendant.

The collection of the telemagnifiers posed a problem for Benjamin. The first two keys of Shambhala were powerful telemagnifiers; that would have been obvious to a rock wall. He wasn't about to place them in some bin and hand them over to Proteus Ajax, so when Proteus had come around the room with a large basket asking for all telemagnifiers to be put inside it, Benjamin obviously didn't put the keys in.

This seemed like an easy enough solution until Jack had told him there would be telepathic screeners in place to ensure that no one snuck telemagnifiers into the rooms. If this were really true, Benjamin wouldn't be able to keep the keys in his pocket during his ability tests. After the dorm room ransacking a week earlier, leaving the keys in the room wasn't an option. The guardian knew he had them and was trying to get them. And having Gary, Andy, Heidi, or Iva hold them while he tested wasn't an option either. Their testing schedules didn't leave enough time for the keys to be exchanged.

Benjamin considered finding a good hiding place somewhere in the school and leaving the keys there, but Iva's words of doom canceled out this idea. She pointed out (validly of course) that if she were able to find objects hidden around the school, then someone else would be able to do the same. The more Benjamin thought about it, the more he figured he might just have to skip all his exams.

Finally, it was Jack, the Nogical, who came up with a solution. Besides the members of the Alliance, the only person Benjamin had come to know and trust above all others was the small green man—if he could be considered a person.

"Why don't you let me take care of the keys for you while you're in the tests?" Jack asked Benjamin the day before the exams were supposed to start.

"You?" Benjamin exclaimed. "Where would you keep them? I mean, they're as big as you are." This was of course a slight exaggeration, but the infeasibility of Jack walking around carrying the keys was still sound.

"I'll keep them in my mind, of course," Jack replied.

"In your mind? How?" Benjamin asked.

Jack threw up his arms. "You're hopeless. Haven't you learned anything in Teleportation? When we teleport an object, where does it go?"

"It goes where we want it to go," Benjamin answered.

"Yes, but remember, what route does it take?" Jack asked, waving his small arms at Benjamin.

Benjamin thought for a second, then replied. "It goes through our mind."

"Right," Jack said. "So, what happens if we just keep it around in our minds for a little bit?"

"We can do that?" Benjamin asked.

"Of course we can do that. If it's in your mind for a second, it can be in your mind for an hour. Or two. Or all day. Or for a year," Jack replied. "The mind is a great place for storing all sorts of things you might otherwise misplace."

"You mean, if I was able to teleport the keys myself, I could just hold them in my mind during the tests?" Benjamin asked.

"Theoretically yes," Jack replied. "But it might fill your mind and make you not do very well on your ability tests. You might have to end up repeating all your year one courses. Anyway, I'm not sure if they would get past the telepathic screeners." He scrunched up his little green face. "That would be an interesting experiment though. But, another time, I suppose."

And so it was decided. Jack would accompany Benjamin

to all his exams, keep the keys in his mind while he waited outside the room, and then give the keys back. The thought of leaving the keys for even this small time made Benjamin's stomach queasy, but, really, what alternative was there?

Monday morning came too soon and too early. Benjamin and Gary had morning exams, but Andy didn't. Benjamin slammed the wardrobe door and turned on the lights, hoping to wake Andy, but had no luck and so hurried to the dining hall instead.

Telepathy was Benjamin's first exam, and even though he ranked in the top ten people in the class, he still felt butterflies in his stomach. Heidi's telepathic abilities so completely over-shadowed the rest of theirs, he sometimes wondered why he bothered going.

Benjamin, Gary, and Iva ate breakfast in near total silence. The closer the exam got, the faster the butterflies in his stomach moved. Did anyone ever have to repeat a year? Would it be possible to be a Year Two Denarian in Year One classes?

Jack appeared on the breakfast table beside Benjamin's plate. *"I don't know what you're worrying about,"* Jack thought. *"You're really not bad at telepathy at all."*

"Yes, but tests make me nervous," Benjamin thought back. *"Especially since I'll probably be in the front of the room with the grader scrutinizing everything I do."*

"So, think of it as your special opportunity to show off for a change—you know, just like when you recited the poem," Jack said. Benjamin had told Jack his story of reciting *The Rime of*

the Ancient Mariner to impress a girl, causing the Nogical to howl with laughter.

Benjamin hadn't thought of it that way. It was true though. He'd always been told to talk with his mouth, lift with his hands, and see with his eyes—at least up until this summer. His parents had always cautioned him against being too good at anything for fear he would stand out from the other kids. He'd spent all his time in public doing as he should, and all his private time practicing his abilities. Yet, now, Benjamin was no longer confined by these strict rules, at least not here in Lemuria. Here he could do as much as he wanted to. He should do as much as he wanted to. That was his purpose for being here.

Benjamin's thoughts drifted back to the beginning of summer when they'd attended the Ability Trials. People had gotten up in front of the entire crowd to show off. The ability tests he was about to take were much like his own personal version of the Ability Trials, except that his crowd was only one person—the grader.

And then it was weird, because the butterflies in his stomach either settled down or disappeared; he shoved his chair out and stood up from the table. "You know what Jack? You're right." Benjamin started for the door. He looked back over his shoulder at Jack, Gary, and Iva. "Are you guys coming or what? The exams start soon."

After breezing through his telepathy exam, Benjamin realized he had nothing to worry about. If he'd done fine in telepathy, teleportation should be no problem. He was the best in his class. Whereas most of the students hadn't been able to move even the smallest marble, Benjamin could now accurately move marbles from one location to another. He teleported blocks, though the destinations remained erratic. This had become a constant source of taunting from Ryan and Jonathan, although neither of them could move a block at all.

After a quick lunch on Tuesday, Benjamin set off for the fifteen story climb to his teleportation exam. At the top of the stairs, he sat down on a bench to catch his breath. Jack appeared beside him.

"You really need to get more exercise," Jack said. "Look at you. You're totally winded. That was only fifteen flights of stairs. What happens next year when you visit Wondersky City?"

"I guess I'll hope they have elevators or something," Benjamin replied. He couldn't imagine people levitating themselves to the top of skyscrapers, and teleporting himself seemed years away.

"Well, let's go find the room," Jack said. They set off down the hall, checking room numbers until they came to room forty-eight. "Here we are."

"Okay, you can take..." Benjamin started, but stopped when he felt the weight of the keys disappear from his pockets. "I guess you just did."

"Good," Jack said. "You should be watching out for that. Unless you learn to better protect them, theoretically, anyone could come along and teleport the keys away."

"I never thought about that," Benjamin said.

"Well, now's not the time to start worrying," Jack replied.

There were actually times during the two hours teleportation test when Benjamin thought he might fall asleep. It was way more theoretical than he could have ever imagined. All the formulas Asia had been going over all summer were reviewed. What variables must be taken into account when picking a destination? How do you account for the rotation of the Earth while teleporting? What effect does the force of the Moon's gravity have on teleportation? How about the gravity of Venus? Of Jupiter? Benjamin began to think the entire exam would be nothing but written questions. It was only in the last ten minutes of the exam that the grader actually asked Benjamin to try to teleport anything. After marbles, he moved on to blocks, and to his pleasant surprise, he teleported the blocks to the designated destinations with no errors. He was so elated with his success he wasn't even fazed when the grader asked him to teleport a mouse. And so he did.

It took him so long to locate the mouse, Benjamin was afraid it would get lost in his mind. Yet finally it reappeared on the table, quickly scurrying under the grader's desk.

"Man, I did great in teleportation," Benjamin declared Tuesday night at dinner. "I teleported a mouse."

"You did not," Andy said. "A mouse?"

There was the hint of jealousy again in the Alliance bond. But Benjamin didn't care; teleporting a living animal—and keeping it alive—was a big deal.

"Yep, it's true," Benjamin replied. "I feel like I can teleport anything. Watch this." He looked directly at Julie Macfarlane's plate on the next table. Without saying a word, he teleported the pizza off her plate. It reappeared on Ryan Jordan's plate a few seats down from her.

"Ryan!" Julie exclaimed. "Did you steal my food?"

"What are you talking about?" Ryan asked.

"You just took my pizza," Julie said.

Ryan looked down at his plate, now containing two pieces of pizza. "I swear it wasn't me."

"That's actually pretty impressive, Benjamin," Heidi said.

Suneeta reached over and grabbed the pizza off the plate, putting it back on Julie's plate. Andy, Benjamin, and Gary busted out laughing.

"Did you do that, Benjamin?" Ryan called over, apparently noticing them laughing.

"What are you talking about?" Benjamin replied.

Ryan only responded with a dirty look which Jonathan mirrored.

"Those guys are so annoying," Iva said. "I saw Jonathan after my Telegnosis test. He was going in for his. You can't believe how rude he was to me."

"What did he say?" Andy asked quickly.

"He told me that I was no good at telegnosis, and the only reason I thought I was doing so well all summer is because I was the teacher's pet," Iva said. "He said that he was ten times the telegnostic that I am." She sniffed.

Andy started laughing. "Oh, I thought it might have been something serious. I mean come on—Jonathan's no where near as good as you."

Iva gave Andy an award-winning smile, and he beamed back. "You really think I'm better?" she asked.

"There's no doubt," Andy replied.

"Actually, if you factor in that Jonathan's a guy, it does make his telegnosis abilities pretty impressive," Gary said.

Iva glared at Gary. "Well, he's still a total jerk," she said. "I wonder how he did on his exam."

"How'd you do?" Andy asked.

"I think I did rather well," Iva replied. "The grader was highly impressed. In fact, she said that she would be checking in on my progress over the next few years."

Benjamin Breaks His Leg

It was already Wednesday and having Jack hold onto the keys of Shambhala had worked out well so far; it left Benjamin not having to worry about someone else finding them. Benjamin tried not to think too much about the location of the third key during the week. He figured he had enough to occupy his mind, what with tests every day and night. The problem was that on Sunday they would all be heading home and wouldn't be back in Lemuria until the following summer. Benjamin had no idea if he'd be able to continue looking for the third key once he'd left the sunken continent.

Benjamin and Jack found the telegnosis exam at the end of a long hallway. There wasn't much activity around, but then there never seemed to be on the telegnosis floors. Jack transferred the keys from Benjamin, and Benjamin was just about to walk into the open door, when he caught someone out of the corner of his eye. It was a man with dark hair and a full beard, and Benjamin had never seen him before. The man looked directly at Benjamin and then walked around the corner.

"Who was that?" Benjamin asked Jack.

"I didn't see anyone." Jack said. "Do you want me to go look?"

Benjamin didn't even need to think about it. "No, I want you to stay here and wait for me. Whoever it was is gone now."

Jack studied the corner of the hallway, but nobody reappeared. "Okay. Good luck on Telegnosis. Do you know how you did on it?"

"How would I know how I did on it?" Benjamin asked, still thinking about the man.

"Well, I just figured if you knew how you did on your Telegnosis test, then you would have done well, right?" Jack said.

Benjamin gave him a confused look, and Jack laughed. "You know, you'd be able to see into the future. Come on," Jack said snapping his small fingers in Benjamin's face. "Get with it. That was supposed to be a joke."

The Telegnosis exam passed, and the rest of the day progressed normally. Benjamin decided not to mention the man he'd seen in the hallway to his friends; he'd probably just been one of the graders. Andy would be sure to think he was just being paranoid.

Thursday morning Benjamin woke up bright and too early for his Science Ability Test. Iva had her Telepathy test also in the morning, so she and Benjamin ate a quick breakfast.

"I'm sure I'll do fine on my telepathy test," Iva said. "I mean, it's got to be similar to the telegnosis test, right?"

"I don't even think my telegnosis exam was a test," Benjamin replied. "All my grader did was talk to me. And she was really young."

"How old was she?" Iva asked, stopping mid-bite.

"If I had to guess, I'd say twenty five," Benjamin said. "But she acted older than that."

"The High Oracle looked young also," Iva said. "I think when women are really good at telegnosis they stay young and live a really long time."

"What about men?" Benjamin asked.

"I don't think there've been enough men good at it to make a study," Iva replied. "Anyway, we better get going."

Benjamin headed off to the second floor and Iva to the sixth. Jack joined Benjamin on the way up the stairs.

"So, what do you think I'll have to do?" Benjamin asked Jack. "Grow a new limb on a rat? Dissect a frog?"

"Maybe you'll have to grow a third eyeball in the center of your forehead," Jack said. "They say the third eye can see everything."

"Yeah, well, thank you very much, but I don't really want a third eye. Anyway, I didn't see Andy or Gary walking around with a new eyeball," Benjamin said. Jack transferred the keys, and Benjamin headed toward the room.

"Hey, break a leg," Jack called out to Benjamin.

Benjamin walked through the door and turned to close the door behind him. He turned back around and immediately fell into a large hole about four yards deep. The cry of pain he let out surprised even him.

Amidst his anguish, Benjamin heard the slow footsteps of someone approaching the pit. An old woman looked down at him.

"Oh, my, are you hurt, Benjamin Holt?" she asked.

Benjamin looked down at his right leg which was twisted at an odd angle. By now the pain had become so intense it was all Benjamin could think about. He didn't even care how he did on his Science Ability Test at this point. He just needed some medical attention.

"I...think...I...broke...my...leg," Benjamin managed to get out between grunts. There were small tears in the corners of his eyes, but he did his best not to cry. Benjamin had never before broken a bone in his body, and it really hurt.

"Oh, wonderful," the grader said. "A broken leg. Excellent."

"Wonderful? Excellent?" Benjamin nearly screamed back at her.

"Oh, yes," the grader replied. "The last student I tested only broke her arm."

"Oh ... is that all?" Benjamin growled in reply.

"Unfortunately, yes, that is all." The grader turned and began to walk away, back to the front of the room.

"Where are you going?" Benjamin said between gritted teeth.

"Why, back to the front desk of course," the grader replied.

"But what about me?" Benjamin asked, a hint of desperation creeping into his voice.

"Oh, yes, please heal your injuries and you will be free to

go," she said. She sat down, picked up a partially completed sweater and some knitting needles and began to knit.

Benjamin stared at her, unable to believe what he was seeing. Was she serious? Heal his injuries? Heal a broken leg, the tibia bone and possibly the fibula too? But though it took him the better part of the two hours, Benjamin proudly but angrily succeeded in doing just that.

After his Science Ability Test, the written lectures exam felt like a piece of cake. Benjamin walked out of the sixth floor classroom with Heidi, Iva, Andy, and Gary.

"Did you get the question about what solar system produced a famous meteorite that landed in Tibet?" Gary asked.

"Yeah, we all better have gotten that one," Andy said.

"I liked the question about what was the perfect genetically engineered species," Heidi said.

They joined Jack on the bench outside the classroom. "They really asked that?" Jack asked. "Did you get it right?"

"I didn't have either of those questions on my exam," Iva said.

"There must have been different tests given out," Andy said.

"Well, why did I have to get a harder one?" Iva asked. "I had to draw out the orbits of all the planets."

"What's so hard about that?" Gary asked. "That was on my test too."

Iva rolled her eyes in reply.

"So, tomorrow's the last day of Ability Tests," Heidi said. "I only have Science left, and I mean, how hard could that be?"

Benjamin's leg started hurting when she said it, but he decided to keep his mouth shut.

"I have science also," Iva said. "In the morning, so I'll be done by lunch." As it turned out, everyone except Benjamin had morning exams on Friday.

"We could go visit Morpheus Midas in the afternoon," Heidi suggested.

Benjamin glared at her.

"Well, why should we sit around doing nothing just because you have Telekinesis in the afternoon?" she asked.

"Because you should feel sorry for me, that's why," Benjamin said.

"We can all have dinner together," Iva suggested. "We should be back by six o'clock. What time do you get out of your test?"

Benjamin snarled. "Not until five," he said.

"Yeah, and telekinesis lasts the whole time," Andy said. "Don't expect to get out early."

"You're not making me feel any better," Benjamin said.

"Well, at least you get to sleep in," Heidi said. "I mean, my science test starts at nine o'clock."

"Yeah, well, break a leg," Benjamin replied.

Benjamin and Jack found room fifty five on the third floor. Just as Benjamin felt the weight of the keys leave his pocket, Ryan Jordan rounded the corner; he stopped when he saw Benjamin and the small Nogical sitting on the bench in the hallway.

"Hi." Ryan sneered it more than said it.

"Hi," Benjamin replied back.

"Did you bring your pet along to help you cheat," Ryan asked, nodding his head toward Jack.

"Unlike some people, I don't need to cheat," Benjamin replied. "Have you stolen any more pizza from Julie Macfarlane lately?" he asked.

"I know you did that," Ryan replied. "You think that just because you can teleport a marble it makes you special."

Benjamin remembered what Heidi had said about Ryan still liking Iva. "Iva seems to think it makes me special," he said.

Ryan frowned in reply. "I have no idea why she hangs out with you and your dorky friends. I've never seen such a pack of losers."

"If we're such losers, then why are you always losing to me and Andy in Kinesis Combat?" Benjamin asked.

"I could take on you and your buddy Andy together," Ryan bragged.

"You could take us on, but there's no way you could win," Benjamin said.

"That's because you always have the Nogical helping you cheat," Ryan said. He turned to room fifty-four and walked in. The door slammed behind him.

"He's still mad about Iva," Benjamin said.

"Yeah, but he also knows something else is going on," Jack said.

"You think so?" Benjamin asked.

"Absolutely," Jack replied.

"He and Jonathan always listen in on our conversations," Benjamin said. "Or at least they try."

"Just watch what you think," Jack said.

Benjamin shook his head, trying to clear it of any thoughts of Ryan Jordan, Iva Marinina, or the Alliance. "So you'll be waiting for me after the exam, right?"

"Of course. Haven't I waited during every exam?" Jack asked.

"Yeah, you have. I guess I'm just starting to get uneasy," Benjamin said. "I mean, Iva has me all paranoid about making sure we find the last key soon."

"Good. One of you guys should be paranoid," Jack said. "I'll keep my eyes and ears open."

Benjamin got up from the bench and headed for room fifty-five. He walked in, and, as with Ryan, the door slammed behind him.

The two hours were excruciatingly hard work. Every object in the room came flying randomly at Benjamin just when he would let his guard down. He had bruises on his arms and legs, and his hand was cut where some scissors had hit him. Scissors and telekinesis! What was this grader thinking?

Every five minutes, the grader challenged Benjamin to a telekinetic dual. Benjamin knew the grader wasn't using his entire strength each time; however, each duel became harder. Benjamin wasn't sure if this was a result of his mind being more sluggish with each challenge, or a result of the grader increasing the strength he used each time. Whatever it was, by the time the grader announced the exam over and disappeared, Benjamin hardly even cared.

He remained sitting for nearly five minutes, trying to regain some of his mental strength. He was beat. Yet as he sat there, he smiled. Two hours of telekinesis was nothing to scoff at. What would Derrick and Douglas think? Actually, how would they have done? Benjamin thought that the two of them together could easily have done as well as Benjamin himself.

Thinking of the twin boys made Benjamin realize how much he missed his family. He reached into his pocket and pulled out the small toy car they'd given him. In just a couple days, he'd be able to return it to his brothers. Since the fountain experience in Xanadu, he'd thought of his siblings constantly. He looked forward to returning to Virginia, to the comforts of his own home. He would miss Lemuria and his new friends terribly, but he would see them all again next summer.

He put the police car back into his pocket. Slowly, Benjamin got up and headed toward the door. Well, that was it. No more exams for this year. He opened the door, looked out at the bench, and stopped in his tracks. Jack was nowhere to be found.

Benjamin Loses the Keys

Benjamin stared in disbelief at the empty bench in front of him. He looked left. He looked right. He looked up. Benjamin even got down on all fours and looked under the bench. The Nogical was nowhere. The hallway was totally empty in fact. Benjamin's heart began to race as he thought of the precious keys the Nogical had stored inside his mind. Had Jack decided to take the keys? Had someone come and kidnapped him? Every thought possible went through his head. He tried communicating with Jack through telepathy, but got no reply.

Benjamin started pacing in the hallway, not sure what to do. Jack had to be around somewhere. Or else maybe he'd had to go run an errand or something. That was it. There's just no way Jack would have left without an excellent reason. Benjamin walked all the way to the end of the hallway. Just as he walked back to the bench, the door to room fifty-four opened, and Ryan stepped out. He stopped when he saw Benjamin.

"Man, what are you doing?" Ryan asked. "Isn't your exam over?" Ryan followed Benjamin's gaze down the empty hallway.

"Are you waiting for someone or something?"

"Uh, no," Benjamin replied. "I'm just resting for a minute."

"Was the exam a little too hard for you?" Ryan asked.

"Oh, no, it was actually pretty easy," Benjamin replied. Even with Jack missing, he didn't want to give Ryan an inch.

"Well, you probably had an easy grader," Ryan said. "I've heard that some of the graders are much harder than others. I had a really tough grader, but I still think I did great," Ryan boasted.

"Yeah, I'm sure you did," Benjamin said.

"Well, good then. You won't be too upset then when I skip a few years of telekinesis and you're only in year two of it. I'm sure your friends Gary and Heidi will probably have to repeat first year," Ryan said and walked off.

Benjamin didn't even bother responding. All he could think about were the missing Nogical and the missing keys. Where could Jack be? Benjamin thought about it a while longer, but then figured he might as well go down and meet the others for dinner. Jack would be sure to turn up in a few minutes, and he'd know to find Benjamin in the dining hall.

Benjamin took his time walking to the dining hall, hoping that Jack would suddenly appear and explain where he'd been. By the time he got there, a half hour had passed since the end of his exam, and Jack was still missing. Sweat broke out on Benjamin's forehead, but did his best to keep his worrying under control. Apparently, though, the Alliance bond had other ideas, betraying him almost immediately.

"Hey, what's wrong with you?" Andy asked after one look

at Benjamin.

"Oh, nothing," Benjamin said.

"No, really," Andy persisted. "I can tell something's bothering you."

Just then Heidi walked in with Iva, and they joined the three boys. Heidi stopped before even sitting down and looked directly at Benjamin. "No way," she said. "You lost them?"

"I didn't lose them," Benjamin said. "Jack has them."

"But where's Jack?" she asked. "You don't know."

He glared at her.

"Of course I can read your mind," Heidi said. "And no, I'm not eavesdropping. I mean, it's exploding with anxiety right now."

"You really don't know where the keys are?" Iva asked. "How could you be so careless?"

"Careless," Benjamin said. "I wasn't being careless. If anything, I was being very un-careless. I mean careful."

"So, why don't you have the keys then?" Iva asked.

"Well, Jack was supposed to be waiting for me at the end of the exam. He's waited after every one so far, but, when I got out of Telekinesis, I couldn't find him anywhere," Benjamin said. "I'm sure he just had to go somewhere for a minute or something."

"You're exam was over a half hour ago, wasn't it?" Iva asked. "So tell me, where is Jack now?"

"I don't know," Benjamin admitted, "but I'm sure he'll turn up."

Benjamin tried not to think too much about the missing

keys during dinner. He had faith that the little Nogical would reappear as soon as he could. Benjamin half-heartedly asked about the afternoon's visit to see Morpheus Midas.

Gary was on the edge of his seat as he told Benjamin the Ammolite chess set had been sold. "Morpheus didn't even know who was buying it," Gary said. "They guy who came in to the store was just an independent buyer, hired by the person making the purchase."

"Well, it must have been someone with a lot of money," Heidi said. "That thing wasn't cheap."

"You know, I wonder if the guy from the Bangkok Chess Open bought it," Gary said. "You know—the telegen who beat everyone."

Iva turned to Gary. "Think about his face again," she commanded.

"What?"

"The telegen from the chess tournament," Iva said. "I could kind of see it in your mind. Think about his face again."

Gary complied, and Benjamin immediately received an image of a man with a full beard and dark hair. It was the man he'd seen in the hallway a couple days before.

"That's the guy I saw in Fortune City," Iva replied. "I noticed him watching me just before I was called in to see the High Oracle."

"The telegen from the chess tournament was in Fortune City?" Gary asked.

"Right," Iva replied.

"And I saw him on Wednesday before one of my exams,"

Benjamin added. "He walked away once I noticed him."

"So you're telling me there's some telegen who just happens to be in Bangkok the same time we are and then just happens to be in Fortune City the same time Iva is," Gary said. "And that he's following Benjamin around the school."

"It doesn't stop there," Andy said. "I saw that same guy when we were leaving the map library the other night. You know, the night you and Heidi went on your date to Xanadu."

Benjamin reached out to hit Andy, but Andy moved out of the way.

"Do you think he could have been the one who trashed our room?" Gary asked. "Do you think he's the guardian Iva was warned about?"

"I'd say it has a high probability," Iva replied.

"Morpheus said he thought the guy was from Atlantis," Gary said. "Remember?"

Andy nodded. "I think we should go back and talk to Morpheus again."

"When?" Iva asked. "If you haven't noticed, we're running out of time this summer."

"Maybe tomorrow," Benjamin said. "It could just all be a coincidence. Anyway, I'm not leaving this school until Jack gets back." He pushed back his chair and got up from the table. "I'm going back to the room to take a nap. That way when Jack does show up, he'll know where to find me."

"Are you sure?" Andy asked. "We're going to go to the main lecture hall for the holocam they're showing tonight. A movie might take you're mind off the keys."

"No, I'm tired," Benjamin said. "You guys have fun."

"Well I'm going to the library to do some more research," Gary said.

"Really?" Andy asked. "You aren't going to the holocam either?"

"Great idea, Gary," Iva said. "I think I'll join you."

"You're going to the library?" Andy's mouth dropped open with disbelief even as he asked it.

"Count me in, also," Heidi added.

"But don't let that stop you from going, Andy," Iva said.

Andy looked torn for only a moment. "I won't then," he said. "It's supposed to be a really popular one."

They split off in three different directions—Iva, Heidi, and Gary to the library, Andy to the lecture hall, and Benjamin back to the dormitories.

When Benjamin lay down in his bed at seven o'clock, he fell into a deep, dreamless sleep. After five hours, his eyes popped open.

"Whoa," he exclaimed. Jack was directly in front of his face, grinning.

"Bet you thought I wasn't coming back, didn't ya?" Jack asked.

"Well, now that you mention it, I was starting to worry," Benjamin replied.

"You didn't look too worried here sleeping," Jack said. "Let's go out and talk."

Benjamin got up quietly, trying not to wake Andy and Gary, both of whom were snoring. He crept out of the dorm room, closing the door behind them.

"Okay, Jack, do you want to tell me where you've been?" Benjamin asked. "I mean you were supposed to be waiting for me on the bench, right? Or did I get confused? Was it supposed to be seven hours later in the dorms?"

Jack sat on the table in the room. "No, of course you're right. But I was waiting there for a long time. And then something happened, and I had to get out of there fast."

"What do you mean, 'something happened'?" Benjamin asked. "What could have happened?"

"I mean, someone was coming, someone was trying to get to the keys," Jack said.

"Who?" Benjamin asked.

"I don't know," Jack answered. "All I know is that it was someone evil. Someone was trying to get to the keys and take them, and I wasn't going to hang around waiting to find out who it was," Jack said, a definite defensive note creeping into his voice.

"No, I don't blame you," Benjamin said. "You did the right thing. In fact, we realized tonight that some guy has been following us around."

"Really?" Jack asked.

"Yeah, really. The guy who played in the Bangkok Chess Open. It's the same guy we saw in the hallway the other day." Benjamin filled Jack in on what they'd put together. "I thought he kidnapped you or something."

"Well, that would be pretty hard since I'm not a kid," Jack joked. "But that wasn't the same presence I picked up on tonight."

"It wasn't?" Benjamin asked. "Who else could it be?"

"I don't know," Jack said. "Just someone I don't remember running across before."

"So, why'd it take you so long to get back?" Benjamin asked.

"I waited in one of my secret hiding spots until I couldn't sense the evil presence any more," Jack answered.

"Your secret hiding spots?" Benjamin asked. "Where are they?"

"Well, if I told you, they wouldn't be secret anymore, now would they?" Jack replied. "Anyway, here you go." The two keys of Shambhala appeared on the table beside Jack. Benjamin quickly picked them up and looked at them, inspecting them.

"Yeah, they're the same stones," Jack said. "They never left my mind."

"Thanks for holding onto them," Benjamin said. "Again."

"It was no problem, but I better go," Jack said. "I'm so tired I plan to sleep all day tomorrow—or today, that is."

"Yeah, okay," Benjamin said, "but don't sleep too long. We leave on Sunday you know."

"I know," Jack said.

"Are you able to visit other places on Earth? You know, like Virginia?" Benjamin asked.

"I'll take that as an invitation," Jack replied, then vanished from the room.

Benjamin stared at the spot where the Nogical had been, then again looked at the keys in his hands. He turned them over and over, feeling their smoothness. Where could the third key be? They'd researched the teleportation records again, but found nothing. Could the records be wrong? Could the third key have been teleported out of Shambhala but no flash been recorded? Benjamin didn't think so; why show the teleportation of the second key but not the third?

How else could the key have been taken from the city? Could it have been tunneled out from below? No, the Geodine should have showed that kind of activity. Maybe someone had teleported the key into their mind and then walked out of the city. Even that should have registered some kind of visible activity.

As Benjamin thought, he realized that he was no longer tired, his mind too busy.

"Okay, let's think this through logically," he said to himself. "The key was not teleported out of Shambhala. The key was not walked out of Shambhala. They key was not tunneled out of Shambhala. So, where could the key be?"

And then a light went on in Benjamin's head. "How about in Shambhala?" he said. "Of course. The third key of Shambhala was never taken from Shambhala. It's still there. It's being hidden there. How could I not have realized that? It's so obvious."

As the realization dawned on Benjamin, so did the fact that he had no way of getting there. "It may as well be on the moon," he said. In fact, Benjamin thought, if it was on the moon, he could at least have tried using one of the special exhibit teleporters in the Natural History Museum to get there. But Shambhala! Aside from being the landing spot of the meteorite, he had no idea how to get there. Everything in the library they'd read about the hidden city suggested it may even be deep below ground.

He ran back into the dorm room and commanded the light to turn on. "Wake up you guys!" he called. "The third key's in Shambhala."

"Heidi! Iva! Wake up! I know where the third key is!" he thought.

"What are you talking about?" Heidi asked.

"The third key. You guys have to come here quick." he replied.

"Are you kidding, Benjamin?" Iva asked.

"Yeah, are you kidding, Benjamin?" Andy said, rolling out of bed. "They can't come here in the middle of the night."

"Yeah, that is so completely against the rules," Gary added.

"I don't care about the rules," Benjamin said. *"Use a teleporter and get here now."*

Iva and Heidi didn't waste any time. The urgency in Benjamin's request brought them in less than two minutes, still in their pajamas.

"Those are cute," Andy said, nodding his head toward Iva's pink, fluffy slippers.

"I don't want to hear another word about it," she replied. "It's one in the morning. Now tell me, what are we doing here in the middle of the night?"

"Yeah, but tell us quietly," Heidi added, nodding her head to the room next door. "I don't want Ryan and Jonathan waking up."

"I know where the third key of Shambhala is," Benjamin replied. "We need a plan for how we're going to get it."

"Tonight?" Andy asked.

"Look," Benjamin replied. "This is our last day in Lemuria. If we don't find it today, we may have to wait a whole year before we get another chance. So yes. Tonight."

"So where it is?" Iva asked.

"It's in Shambhala," Benjamin replied. "It never left the place. That's why we never saw it leave. Remember the poem we read?

> Shambhala is always near
> Though hidden beneath our sphere.
> The keys will there again appear
> And all the world will quake in fear.

"The keys were intended to be reunited in Shambhala," he finished.

"Of course," Iva replied. "What better place to hide the third key then not to hide it at all."

"But Shambhala?" Gary said. "How in the world are we going to get there?"

"Maybe the Geodine will have some idea." Benjamin quickly pulled out his Geodine. "Show me Shambhala," he commanded it. It lit up, and the spot in northern Tibet began to glow red. There it was. Shambhala. He could see the location clearly on the Geodine. Shambhala. There was no doubt about the location. Shambhala. He closed his eyes. The image of the glowing Geodine was firm in his mind. Reopening his eyes, the last thing he remembered seeing were his friends' faces, quickly changing from sleepy to concerned. And then suddenly, Benjamin felt as if he were being pulled from his chair toward the glowing spot on the Geodine.

32

Practicing the Orb Pays Off

Benjamin didn't have time to react. He turned to look, knowing he wasn't in the dorms anymore, but having no idea where else he could be. Looking around didn't help; the rocks and grass could have been anywhere. And then he remembered the Geodine—Shambhala glowing in Tibet. And he knew exactly where he was.

Benjamin didn't think about the impossibility of teleporting himself around the globe to Shambhala. Now that it had actually happened, it seemed completely and totally feasible. The ability had always been a part of him. And there was proof. He was here.

Benjamin looked around again. Where exactly was here, aside from the general location of Shambhala? There wasn't a civilized looking thing in sight. He stood at the base of a rocky hill—maybe even a small mountain from the looks of it. And even though the sun was close to dipping below the horizon, there was plenty of light to see by.

"Can you guys hear me?" he asked Heidi in his mind.

"*Yes!*" Her reply came back immediately. "*Where are you? What happened?*"

"*I'm near Shambhala,*" Benjamin answered her. "*And I think I teleported myself here.*"

"*Okay, stay where you are,*" she said. "*We're going to get in touch with Jack and send him out after you.*"

"*I'm fine,*" Benjamin replied. "*I'm just going to look around a little bit.*"

"*No! Stay where you are. I'll contact Jack and get back in touch with you.*"

He felt her connection break.

Benjamin started to walk, slowly, circling the hill in a counterclockwise direction. If it was true that the city was underground, there must be some sort of secret entrance or something. He'd just look around for the entrance and then wait for Jack or Heidi to get back in touch with him. He circled the entire hill, looking for a cave or any kind of opening, but found nothing. By the time he reached his starting point, the sun was even lower in the sky—and it was starting to get cold.

Maybe he'd missed something. He started around the hill again, focusing more closely this time. He'd made it about half way around when he noticed the sun reflecting in ripples off a smooth rock wall. Benjamin backed up a few steps and looked at the vertical, brown wall. Nothing strange about it now. So he advanced again, and the strange reflection came back. A couple more steps forward, and the reflection disappeared. He backed up again.

Benjamin walked over and placed both palms on the wall,

and, although it looked smooth, when he touched it, he could feel it was actually carved. Benjamin's heart began to race. He'd found something—something man made. He blinked a couple times, and the fog lifted, showing a sculpture so bright and gold, Benjamin had to squint from the shine.

This had to be the entrance to the hidden city of Shambhala, if only Benjamin could figure out how to open it. With no knobs or buttons, there didn't seem to be an obvious way to do so.

"Heidi? Are you still there?" he asked in his mind.

Nothing.

"Heidi? Can you hear me? I think I found the entrance. I'm just need to figure out how to open it."

Still nothing. Maybe she was busy talking with Jack.

Benjamin studied the now completely visible sculpture with all its strange and bizarre carvings. Some looked like masks he had seen in the Natural History Museum in Mu. Some looked like mutated animals. But one caught his eye in particular—three hearts intertwined; he'd seen the image somewhere before, but had no idea where.

At the top of the relief was a sphere, slowly rotating in place. The colors of the sphere changed, cycling through the rainbow, constantly moving. As the colors came into focus and changed, Benjamin realized what the sphere reminded him of. The Kinetic Orb. A spherical puzzle just like the one Joey Duncan had given him except larger.

Could this be a game—some sort of key mechanism which required the game to be solved to open the door? Benjamin thought of his own Orb as he watched the colors of the one on the door. His own Kinetic Orb contained only six phases, but this one seemed to cycle through sixteen. Not a problem. Each one could be solved in turn and then saved.

Benjamin began working the puzzle. As he did so, he realized that aside from the increased number of phases, this orb was exactly the same as his own. He would be able to solve it and open the door. He decided to use Gary's technique—solve each phase separately, rather than storing the center pieces of each. Quickly he finished the first phase, the red one, and was halfway through the blue phase, when the red phase dissipated, merging back into the other fifteen colors.

What had gone wrong? Benjamin figured he must have accidentally touched the red phase. Starting again, he quickly reworked the first phase, moving on to the second. Yet, exactly as before, the red phase dissipated when he was nearly complete with the blue.

The sun lowered in the sky, and Benjamin felt panic begin to rise. Why couldn't he solve the Orb? It was a simple puzzle. Simple for him at least. He'd mastered it this summer. Yet no matter what he tried, nothing seemed to work.

And then he understood. He remembered Joey Duncan's words. "The trick is not only to solve all the phases, but learn to do it with your eyes closed." He knew what he needed to do.

Okay, back to the beginning—again. He studied the Orb long and hard, then slowly closed his eyes. Benjamin began working the phases, starting with the red, then moving on to the blue. He could feel in his mind the completed phases remaining intact. He didn't open his eyes, instead working the puzzle inside his mind. His telekinetic pathways became a direct extension of his brain, leaving his eyes superfluous.

Benjamin worked steadily and confidently. He knew the finished phases were remaining where they should. He could feel it. He could also feel the unfinished pieces jumping around on the sphere, changing position randomly. In his mind he could see the color of the pieces without having to look. This must be like the way Heidi used telepathy to know the colors of the Orb.

Without a doubt in his mind, Benjamin completed the final phase, hearing an audible click as a golden piece completed the puzzle. Benjamin flicked his eyes open. The entire sphere expanded, causing Benjamin to jump back, before shrinking to almost nothing and sinking deep into the bas-relief. The massive sculpture slid to the left, and vanished into the surrounding rocks.

Benjamin looked around, though he wasn't sure why. Maybe it was just the fact that being in the middle of Tibet with no one else around felt a little vulnerable. And why hadn't Heidi gotten back in touch with him? Glancing around, nothing looked suspicious, so he shrugged and walked inside. As soon as he was through, the door closed behind him. He jumped, making sure he was out of its way. The Kinetic Orb scrambled and expanded back out through the bas-relief.

Benjamin found himself in a dimly lit tunnel carved out of the natural rock and lit with torches set into the walls. There was only one way to go—forward—so Benjamin set out walking.

After what felt like a mile, Benjamin came to the bottom of the sloped path. The tunnel continued on, but changed dramatically. Whereas the tunnel behind him had been roughly plowed through the rock, the tunnel in front of him was smooth, rounded, and detailed. Columns set against the walls were cut and elaborate. The ceiling was taller. Even the holders for the wall torches were now made of detailed metalwork. But weirdest of all, the whole place felt oddly familiar to Benjamin.

Benjamin covered the distance in little time, approaching two large arched doors, made of stone, with heavy hinges on either side. He pushed on the doors, testing their weight, and to his surprise, they swung open without making a sound. A circular room lay in front of Benjamin, its flat ceiling held up by a circle of columns. Benjamin walked into the room, and the doors swung shut. He didn't turn, but instead walked straight toward the center of the room where a rounded pedestal stood.

The top of the pedestal was flat except for two indentations matching the shapes of the first two keys of Shambhala. Benjamin reached into his pockets and emptied their contents. He set the toy police car on the edge of the pedestal and held the two keys, one in each hand. He placed the first key into the notch on the right. It fit perfectly, and immediately clicked into place. Benjamin felt his heart speed up; he knew he'd find the third key any minute now. He took the second key and placed it into the notch on the left. Again, it fit perfectly and clicked into place.

As soon as it clicked, the entire top of the pedestal started to move downward, including the keys. As the top sank down, a new area of the pedestal rose upward, directly in the center. The area had looked solid, but from the center rose a third key, matching the first two exactly in size and color. The pedestal clicked to a stop, all three keys now visible.

"Finally," a voice to the right of Benjamin said. "I have been waiting for thirteen years for you to get those keys together."

Benjamin turned in the direction of the voice. A familiar figure stepped out from behind one of the columns. "Mr. Burton? Is that you?" Benjamin asked. Why in the world was his science teacher in Shambhala?

Mr. Burton walked ever so slowly toward Benjamin. "Yes, it's me," he said.

"But what are you doing here?" Benjamin asked. "How did you get here?"

"Oh, getting here is no problem. Being an agent for Lemuria, I have many special teleporter access levels," Mr. Burton replied with a smile. "As for what I'm doing here, that's quite simple. My entire life has been devoted to keeping you safe."

"Devoted to keeping me safe?" Benjamin said. "Are you kidding?"

Mr. Burton laughed. "It does sound kind of far fetched, doesn't it? But, it's true. My entire purpose for being an agent of Lemuria is to protect you."

That didn't make any sense. Benjamin had never felt like he needed protection. "But why?" he asked.

"You're a very important person, Benjamin Holt," Mr. Burton said.

"I am?" Benjamin asked, looking down at himself. "Why?"

"Because you were destined to find these three keys and bring them together, and, with their power, raise the continents and bring down the power shields around Atlantis and Lemuria," Mr. Burton explained.

"Bring down the power shields!" Benjamin exclaimed. "And that's a good thing?"

"The age of the shields is behind us, Benjamin. It is time for the telegens to again live with the humans of Earth. It's time for a new age of mankind. I thought the Emerald Tablet explained that to you."

"How do you know about the Emerald Tablet?" Benjamin asked.

"I have my ways, Benjamin," Mr. Burton answered. "I take my role as your protector very seriously. You shouldn't be wandering around in the bowels of the Ruling Hall alone."

"I wasn't alone," Benjamin replied. "I was with my friends."

"Yes, your friends. The Alliance. That was something I hadn't counted on. Regardless, we must trust the Tablet. If the Tablet feels it is important an alliance be formed, then it must be. The main point is that the shields must come down. The Tablet has instructed it," Mr. Burton said.

"The Emerald Tablet told me to restore the balance of the Earth," Benjamin defended. "Not bring down the shields."

"Yes, but what better way to restore the balance of the Earth than with the removal of the barriers holding in the people of Atlantis?" Mr. Burton cried. "Is having barriers enslaving innocent people peace? Is that peace on Earth?"

"It's peace for the Lemurians and the humans," Benjamin replied. But even as he said it, he knew Mr. Burton was right. Benjamin himself had questioned the very same thing. Was holding millions of people against their will a good thing? "Besides, even if I was supposed to raise the continents and bring down the shields, I wouldn't know how. And wouldn't the Atlantians try to take over the Earth or something?"

"It will remain to be seen what happens," Mr. Burton said. "We must let nature take its course. If it is best to rule those weaker than ourselves, then so be it."

"But how can that be peace for all?" Benjamin asked.

Whether the shields should come down or not, something about bringing them down here and now just didn't sound right. True, he had only known about telegens and Lemuria and the power shields for eight weeks, and true, the people of Atlantis did seem to be behind the shield against their will, but who was he to let out the people of Atlantis into the world?

"I don't think I want to bring down the shields," Benjamin said. "I don't think that's right."

"Of course it's right," Mr. Burton said.

Benjamin thought he detected a bit of annoyance creeping into Mr. Burton's voice.

"Is it right for Lemuria to have enslaved Atlantis as was done when the shields were put into place? Tell me, is that right?"

"Well, the telegens of Atlantis were cruel to the humans," Benjamin replied, remembering his lecture on the subject. "Somebody had to stop them."

"Why did somebody have to stop them?" Mr. Burton asked. "The humans of Earth are weak. They need guidance. I would think you of all people would understand that. I mean, you've had to live with them for thirteen years. Sometimes I cannot stand to live among the ungifted," Mr. Burton spat. "They are so pathetic. And yet, as an agent, I must act inferior to them. It makes me sick when I think about it. Never being able to show my abilities. Never being able to show any intelligence. If not for you, I couldn't have tolerated it much longer."

Mr. Burton had begun to move closer to Benjamin. Instinctively, Benjamin backed up. It didn't take a genius to notice that something wasn't quite right here. Mr. Burton reached the pedestal, and Benjamin backed to the columns on the other side of the room. Mr. Burton delved his hands into the pedestal, trying to remove the keys.

"They won't budge," he said while struggling with they keys. "Only you can remove them."

"Well, I'm not going to take them out," Benjamin said. He was starting to worry, really worry. Here he was in a hidden chamber in the middle of the Himalayas with not another living soul around except for Mr. Burton who was acting crazy. The doors to the room were shut, and Benjamin didn't think he'd be able to teleport himself out of here if his life depended on it, which at this point, it probably did. The whole teleportation thing had probably been a fluke.

"Heidi! If you were going to get back in touch with me, now would be a good time," Benjamin thought quickly.

"She can't hear you, Benjamin. No one can hear you. I've

placed a strong enough barrier around this place to keep even the strongest telepathic thoughts from passing. And yes, you will take the keys out," Mr. Burton said. "You will take them out, and you will use their power to take down the shields, just as you were destined to do."

Benjamin looked at him. What in the world was Mr. Burton talking about?

"Yes, it is your destiny. Before you were born, the high oracle herself prophesied it. Now, get over here and take these keys out immediately," Mr. Burton commanded.

"No, I won't do it," Benjamin said, backing up even further, hoping he sounded braver than he felt.

Mr. Burton began to advance on him. "Well, then I'll help you do it," he said. "And nobody will be able to stop me."

"I will be able to stop you," a voice said.

Hair Standing on End

Both Benjamin and Mr. Burton wheeled around to look in the direction of the voice.

"Helios." Mr. Burton almost spat out the name. "Even you won't be able to stop me."

Benjamin recognized the figure even before Mr. Burton identified him by name. This was Helios Deimos, one of the twin rulers of Lemuria. Benjamin felt relief sweep through him.

Helios didn't look at Benjamin, but instead fixed his eyes on Mr. Burton. "I will be able to stop you, Kennias," he said. "Are you prepared to die for this cause?"

"I don't have to be prepared for that. I will overcome you, and it is Lemuria who will be short one of its puppet rulers. And when the shields come down, it will be Lemuria who will beg at the feet of Atlantis. For Atlantis has not been idle in its period of enslavement," he said. "Yes, enslavement. That is exactly what it has been. Just as Lemuria claimed Atlantis was enslaving Earth, so Lemuria has enslaved Atlantis. Justice must be served. After I have dealt with you, and this boy takes down the shields, Lemuria will be overcome. Your dear sister Selene I'm sure will not survive the takeover. I'll do my best to see that she has as swift a death as I am going to give you now."

Helios Deimos smiled though Benjamin could see it contained no humor. "Well, if it has come to this, then so be it."

Benjamin had no idea what would happen next, and wished he wasn't here to find out. Mr. Burton's attention was taken, so Benjamin slunk to the floor behind one of the columns. Maybe if Mr. Burton got distracted enough, Benjamin would be able to get in touch with Heidi.

A statue from the far wall flew toward Helios. He easily diverted it with his mind. Another statue followed the first. Again, Helios avoided it. Time and time again, every object not connected to the floor or wall began to catapult at top speed. Helios diverted each one in turn.

As Benjamin watched from his hidden position, he noticed Helios Deimos fought a defensive battle. Not once did an object fly toward Mr. Burton. Neither man took any notice of Benjamin as they fought their telekinetic duel, and it wasn't long before Benjamin mustered up enough courage to try to help, though he wasn't sure how much help he could really be. Benjamin dove into the mind of Mr. Burton, just as he readied to telekinetically throw another statue toward Helios. Sensing the action, Benjamin quickly reached out for the statue with his mind. Mr. Burton picked it up and flung it directly at Helios. Benjamin diverted the statue just slightly from its path; it crashed into the wall.

Mr. Burton glanced over at Benjamin. "Don't waste your energy, Benjamin," Mr. Burton said. "I'll soon be done with Helios here, and we'll be on our way. You'll need your mind intact to control the power of the keys."

"I'm glad you are so confident, Kennias," Helios said. "Your confidence will be your downfall."

"And your weakness will be yours," Mr. Burton spat back. "Look at you, you weak, pathetic sham. Deceiving every telegen in Lemuria into thinking the shields are a good thing. 'For the good of all on Earth.' I'll kill the next person who says that."

With a crack, lightning bolts flew out of Mr. Burton's fingertips straight for Helios Deimos. Helios instantly put out his hands, fingers first, and absorbed the lightning into his body. Mr. Burton stopped and stared at this apparently unexpected reaction. But then he sent the lightning again, stronger this time and twice as long; Helios continued to absorb it all. As Helios absorbed the lightning, Benjamin thought he could see it coming out of the floor where Helios' feet touched the cold stone. It was like he was channeling it through himself without being electrocuted.

"Benjamin," Mr. Burton called. "Can't you see why the shields should be destroyed? Can't you understand how Atlantis has suffered and paid for its crimes?" Even as he spoke, the storm of light continued.

"I think you're crazy, Mr. Burton. I think all you want is power over humans. I think you could care less about the people of Atlantis; they're just an excuse," Benjamin yelled his reply to be heard over the maelstrom.

"The boy is right, Kennias," Helios said. "The truth flows through your mind. You want the shields removed for all the wrong reasons. Power is your strongest desire. You want the people of Earth to worship you as a god. I have never trusted you. When we first met that fateful night so long ago, I had a strong premonition about you. I knew you would turn to evil. But sometimes we must let events play out as they will. Things happen for a reason, and your conversion to evil will have some purpose."

"Yes, its purpose is for this boy, Benjamin Holt, to bring down the barriers," Mr. Burton said, motioning to Benjamin.

"Benjamin Holt cannot bring down the barriers," Helios said.

"Of course he can," Mr. Burton said. "I know about the prophecy. I know he will bring down the barriers, and Atlantis will rule over the Earth once again."

"You know nothing, Kennias," Helios replied.

For a moment Mr. Burton halted his attack on Helios. In that moment, Helios struck back. Blue light surged out of Helios' fingers, impacting Mr. Burton directly in the chest. Kennias Burton was thrown backward, hitting the wall hard. He levitated to his feet. Helios struck again. This time the impact left Mr. Burton stunned for nearly half a minute.

"Benjamin, help me," Mr. Burton called out, reaching his arm outward to Benjamin. "I've protected you your entire life. I've loved you and taught you. I've watched you grow. You were like my own child, Benjamin. Please, help me now."

"You were just my science teacher," Benjamin replied.

"Nothing else."

"No, Benjamin. I held you in my arms when you were just an infant. I swore to protect you, and I will continue to keep that promise, if only you will help me now," Mr. Burton said.

Benjamin realized Helios had stopped his assault of lightning, and was listening. Benjamin suddenly had a flashback to weeks earlier, at the ability trials. The vision he'd experienced when Andreas Matthias performed the mind control act. The silhouetted figure had seemed familiar. And now he realized why. It had been Mr. Burton. But he never remembered any such meeting with Mr. Burton. Had it been a memory from when Benjamin was an infant?

Mr. Burton made an attempt to levitate himself off the ground, but fell back to the stone. Benjamin looked to Helios, then back to Mr. Burton. Was that true? Had Mr. Burton really been protecting him his entire life? Had he know Benjamin as an infant? Benjamin immediately thought of his family, and the strong responsibility of protection he felt for them. The experience in Xanadu had crystallized his love for his brothers and sister. He would always protect them and love them, no matter what, even if it cost him his life. Yet here Mr. Burton was, swearing to protect Benjamin on one hand, but on the other, vowing to bring down the shields around Atlantis and assert his power over humans. Did humans need dominance and control? Could Mr. Burton possibly be right?

"You can sense what is right, Benjamin," Mr. Burton called. "I can see it in your mind. You know it's only natural for the strong to control the weak. Civilization has always been that way. We can rule, side by side. With the power of the keys on our side, no one will be able to withstand us."

Benjamin thought of his life, growing up among the ungifted. How often he'd thought of being able to let his true power show. How often he'd dreamed of using his mind to control the thoughts of others. But always, he'd known it was wrong.

"Benjamin, it is not wrong to live life to your fullest. It is not wrong to achieve your dreams. Go to the keys. Take the keys out, and use them now. Let us destroy anyone who would get in our way," Mr. Burton cried.

And that's when Benjamin decided to walk toward the pedestal in the center of the room. Toward the keys. Mr. Burton remained on the floor, against the wall. Helios stood, not taking his eyes off Benjamin. Benjamin reached the pedestal and looked inward toward the three keys.

"Yes, that's right, Benjamin," Mr. Burton said. "Just reach your hands in, and use the power of the keys. With their strength, your powers will be magnified twenty fold."

Benjamin reached out, toward the three keys. His hand hovered above them, not yet touching their glowing beauty.

"Good, Benjamin, good. Use their power to help me now, and I will continue to protect you forever," Mr. Burton said.

Benjamin reached his hands downward and, with fingers outstretched, touched all three keys at one time. Lightning flew out from the pedestal, directly toward Mr. Burton.

"I'll never help you, Mr. Burton," Benjamin cried out. "What you want is wrong, and I will not help you."

The lightning flew straight into Mr. Burton, yet he did not

falter as Benjamin had hoped. Instead, he slowly got to his feet and laughed. "Ah, but don't you see, you already are helping me."

"Benjamin, stop," Helios called out, then flew backward as the lightning channeled from Benjamin, through Mr. Burton, and to Helios Deimos. "He is using your power. He is trying to drain both the power of your mind and of the keys. You must stop." Helios regained his footing and began, once again, to absorb the energy through his body.

Benjamin looked to Mr. Burton and saw the evil etched on his face. He tried to lift his hands from the keys, to stop the attack he had attempted to make on Mr. Burton, but found his hands wouldn't move. The power continued to flow out of the keys, though Benjamin.

"I can't stop," Benjamin cried, hearing the desperation in his own voice. "I can't raise my hands."

"You must, Benjamin," Helios called back. "I don't know how much longer I can hold out. The power of the keys is too great. You must find a way to stop."

"There is no way to stop, Helios. Your time is over," Mr. Burton said. "I have been waiting for this moment for a long time. You don't deserve to be the ruler of Lemuria. You have never deserved it."

Benjamin tried to stop the power escaping from his body, tried to discontinue the energy flow. Immediately, the lightning changed. Instead of the blue visible light, it became invisible energy. Static electricity flowed in the bizarre triangle from Benjamin Holt to Kennias Burton to Helios Deimos.

"Benjamin, you won't be able to stop it," Mr. Burton called out. "I know you entirely too well. I did not lie. I have known you your entire life, and we are bonded together. I know your mind as well as you know your own mind."

"Benjamin, this must not succeed. This is beyond my control. Only you can stop this from happening." Helios faltered as he said it.

Benjamin could feel the buildup of energy in the chamber. Kennias fixed his eyes on Helios, and the two remained motionless. The energy level was increasing. The room felt electric. Benjamin began to feel drained. His mind was being exhausted. He had to do something, anything, to make this stop.

What was it Mr. Burton had said? He had known Benjamin his entire life. He knew his mind better than he himself did. This may have been true, Benjamin realized, at one point. But that point ended with the forming of the Alliance and the experiences since. Benjamin was not the same person he'd been at the start of summer school. Mr. Burton did not know the depths of emotion Benjamin had felt in Xanadu, the bonds of friendship that had been formed in Lemuria. Mr. Burton would never understand the love Benjamin felt for his family. He could see Becca clearly in his mind, giggling in her little baby way. And the sincerity in the minds of the Derrick and Douglas when they'd wished Benjamin farewell. Benjamin couldn't have borne the thought of letting something happen to them. Ever.

Benjamin delved deep into the mind of Kennias Burton, and, in it, he found no love, no sense of duty or protection.

There was only greed and lust for power.

"Helios, you are weak, and you know it. I think I will rule Lemuria in addition to Atlantis and Earth. Maybe I'll force your sister to marry me, just for fun," Mr. Burton taunted. He seemed completely unaware of Benjamin in his mind, too consumed with his own feelings of success.

How well could Mr. Burton know Benjamin if his own mind held only greed? Mr. Burton knew about the Emerald Tablet and the Alliance, but knew nothing about the Emerald Tablet and the Alliance. He may have overheard what had been said, what had been charged, but he had not been a part of it. He couldn't understand. Would never understand.

Benjamin immediately thought of the writing carved in the brilliant green stone of the Emerald Tablet. The verse that was forever etched in his mind. "*Take always the path of love*" it had read. He looked down at the keys again, and when he did, his eye caught something he had forgotten about. The small toy police car sitting on the edge of the pedestal. His brothers had given it to him as a going away present. His brothers whom he loved and who loved him. Mr. Burton had never felt such love. Never in his whole life.

Benjamin could think of only one thing to do. If he could fill Mr. Burton's mind with only positive emotions and feelings, then maybe, just maybe, it would be enough to change him. There was nothing else for Benjamin to do. He sent out a deluge of feelings in the link he had inadvertently formed with Kennias Burton. Friendship. Duty. Family. Trust. Love. All went through the link with full force.

Slowly, the doubt crept onto Mr. Burton's face. He looked at Benjamin, and his doubt began to change to desperation. The flow of electricity started to change direction. Instead of flowing from Kennias to Helios, it reversed, flowing from Helios to Kennias. Benjamin continued his flow of both electricity and emotions, to Mr. Burton. His hands were still glued to the keys. The level of electricity rose. Benjamin felt his hair starting to rise. He saw Helios Deimos' long brown hair standing straight out. Mr. Burton's shorter hair was also standing on end, responding to the electrical charge in the room.

"What are you doing, Benjamin?" Mr. Burton cried. "What have you done?"

"He has done what he knows, Kennias," Helios responded for Benjamin. "It appears you do not know Benjamin Holt as well as you thought."

Beads of sweat started to appear on Mr. Burton's face. Helios had, by now, regained his complete composure and control. The electric field was building even more. Benjamin could feel the air sizzling around him. Mr. Burton was breaking down. The battle was coming to an end, and Mr. Burton was losing. Desperation was full on Mr. Burton's face. Suddenly, just when Benjamin thought they could take no more electricity, Mr. Burton collapsed to the floor in a heap. The electrical field vanished.

Helios remained in place for a moment, looking at Mr. Burton intently. Benjamin thought he could still sense small electrical pulses and sparks in the air. He looked down into the pedestal, and quickly lifted his hands away from the three keys.

Helios smoothed his long brown hair down with his hands, and turned to where Benjamin stood in the center of the room.

"Benjamin Holt," Helios said. "It is a pleasure to see you again."

Benjamin Faces the Truth

"Are you going to tell me what's going on?" Benjamin asked.

"To answer that question, we need to start from the beginning, but this is not a safe place to do so," Helios said.

Benjamin looked toward Mr. Burton's limp form on the floor. "Isn't he...um...dead?" he asked. He felt a pang of regret; a loss for what could have been. What should have been.

"Yes, Kennias Burton is dead, but he could have informed others as to his whereabouts. We had better move into the safety of the city walls," Helios answered. He motioned with his hand to the pedestal where Benjamin stood. "Congratulations on bringing the three keys together once again."

Benjamin looked down at the pedestal, across from Helios Deimos, unsure of whether he wanted to reach in and take the keys or turn around and run for the door. Was he ready for the task ahead of him?

"Do not doubt yourself, Benjamin. It was you who was selected by the Emerald Tablet, was it not? It was you who was chosen to be the champion. Your chance for a normal life is gone. Everything as you know it has changed. By bringing these keys together you have inextricably bonded yourself to them. They have been lying hidden, waiting for you for ages. And now they are reunited."

"But why have they been waiting for me? What's so special about me?" Benjamin asked.

"Let us retreat to the city walls. There I can answer your questions," Helios said, turning to leave.

"But what about they keys?" Benjamin asked. "Don't I need to bring them with me?"

"Go ahead, and try," Helios answered.

Benjamin reached into the sunken top of the pedestal. He placed his hands over the keys, touching all three at once. They lit up a brilliant green, shining enough that the entire chamber filled with the green light. He could feel these keys held his destiny. He knew these keys were a part of him. Should be with him. He would choose to take the keys with him. He enclosed his hand around the first of the keys, but found it wouldn't budge. He looked to Helios; Helios raised a single eyebrow. Benjamin reached for the second key, but it too wouldn't move. He grabbed hold of the third key and pulled with all his might.

"It will take more than muscle to remove those keys," Helios said.

"Like what?" Benjamin asked. "What will it take?" After all he'd been through to collect the keys, he deserved to have them with him.

"It will take another to help you. Another just like you,"

Helios replied.

"Like who?" Benjamin asked. "One of my friends?"

"Your question will soon be answered, but for now, the keys must remain here," Helios said. "They will be safe," he said before Benjamin could protest. "But quickly now, we must leave."

Benjamin cast one final look at the three keys. He'd spent so much time and effort searching for them, bringing them together. It didn't seem right to leave them here now, unguarded.

"I promise," Helios said. "The keys will wait."

Helios sat opposite Benjamin. "You've been told the history of Lemuria and Atlantis, I assume."

Benjamin nodded his head.

"Good," Helios said. "Your story begins when your mother became pregnant. When she conceived a child, she was elated, and, like many young women of Lemuria, she scheduled a visit to Fortune City. Most pregnant couples are scheduled with one of the lesser oracles, but when your parents arrived in the city, the High Oracle herself immediately sent for them and would allow no one else to meet them."

"It was early on in the pregnancy. Imagine your mother's surprise when she found out she carried three babies rather than just the one she'd imagined."

"You mean there are three of us?" Benjamin asked. "Where are the other two?"

Helios motioned him to be quiet. "In a moment. Let the story be told in the order it was meant to be told."

He continued. "Your mother's joy was quickly diminished. The High Oracle first swore your parents to secrecy. They were to tell no one what she was about to reveal to them. She told your mother that within her womb was the power to bring down the protective shields surrounding Atlantis and Lemuria. 'Of the three, two shall bring down the barriers, and only the combined power of all three shall be enough to defend against the consequences.'"

"So, Mr. Burton was right?" Benjamin asked. "I do have the power to bring down the barriers?"

"Yes, you do have the power," Helios answered. "The Emerald Tablet chose you to be the champion. You are the first of the siblings."

"So how come my parents never told me about their other two kids?" Benjamin asked, sure Helios was wrong. There's no way his parents would have kept anything that important from him.

Again Helios motioned for silence. "I am coming to that. When the High Oracle was finished prophesying the future for your parents, she sent them away. Neither my sister nor I were present at the telling of the prophecy, but immediately following your parents' departure, the High Oracle left Fortune City to visit us in Mu. She told us what she had foreseen, and told us something more. 'The father desires the barriers to be disintegrated. He will use the children for evil purposes,' she told us."

"My dad would never do that," Benjamin defended. Helios, Mr. Burton—they both must have him confused with someone else.

Helios put up his hand. "This will be hard to hear, but I ask you to remain silent while I continue. My sister Selene and I knew what had to be done. By the time we located your parents, some number of months had gone by. Your mother was nearing her delivery. Your father had been trying to hide her, keep her in seclusion. His evil had manifested, and your mother was scared—scared for the futures of her unborn children. Your father detected our purposes, and fled from us before we could stop him. We assume he resides now in Atlantis."

Benjamin opened his mouth to speak, but shut it after one look from Helios.

"You mother was taken to a secret place—a safe place. For each child a guardian was chosen. I did not choose these guardians; it was the doing of the High Oracle. As you now must have figured out, Kennias Burton was chosen as your guardian. The guardians were instructed to choose families for you to live with, to be raised by. The guardians themselves were not to raise you. Their main purpose was to protect you, to keep you from harm or evil. I do not think Kennias was evil when I first met him. I think he was young and foolish, impressionable."

"And so it was that I met you the moment you were born. You were the first of the three to come into this world. Immediately, I took you from your mother—a sad task—and delivered you to Kennias Burton. He was to tell no one as to your whereabouts, not even Selene and myself. As we now know, he placed you with the Holt family in Virginia. Andy Grow's family was placed alongside yours, so you would always have a friend."

"So, you're telling me that my parents, the mother and father I've always known, aren't really my parents?" Benjamin asked. His voice quivered as he spoke, though he tried to control it. How could this be true? Of course his parents were his parents. Helios had gotten something wrong.

"Well, that depends on your definition of a parent," Helios answered. "The parents you know have loved you and taken care of you your entire life. They have nurtured you, taught you, and encouraged you. I do not know what more a parent could be."

Without being able to stop it, Benjamin felt a tear slide down his face. He quickly wiped it away. If it was really possible that this story was true, then he needed to know all of it. "So … so where is my mother, my real mother?" he asked.

"She died immediately after giving birth to the third baby," Helios answered. "Everything she had lived for was gone. Her mind was twisted. The months with your father, unguarded, were not easy ones for her. She had become delusional. She was in horrible mental anguish. Her husband was gone—a traitor—and now her children were gone. Selene told me she gave up the desire to live."

More tears slid down Benjamin's face; he didn't even try to wipe them away. "So, wouldn't Mr. Burton have told others who I am and where to find me? Wouldn't he have looked for my brothers?" Benjamin asked.

"Mr. Burton was unable to tell anyone where you were. When you were handed over to him, a bond was developed.

Your mere existence provided a mind block, one which would not allow him to speak of your whereabouts or even your existence to anyone. And as for your siblings, each guardian was only told about one child. As far as Kennias knew, you were the only child delivered that fateful night," Helios explained.

Benjamin wiped the wetness off his face. "Well, at least I don't have to worry about someone else trying to find me and use me to bring down the barriers," he said.

"Unfortunately, that is where you are wrong," Helios said. "You are forgetting about your father—your biological father. If it is true that he is living in Atlantis, then we must assume he has passed along whatever information he has. He knows there were three children and the approximate date of birth. He knows what the High Oracle foresaw. We would have to assume that even as we speak, there are those who are searching for you and you siblings."

"So, who are my brothers?" Benjamin asked. "Do I know them?"

"As with Kennias, I too am under a mind block. I am not able to divulge any information. However, the Emerald Tablet chose you; that in itself gives me a feeling of high confidence. You will find the other two. You must find the other two. You asked who would help you remove the keys. It must be one of your siblings. At least two of the three are required to remove the keys, and only with the combined power of the keys will you be able to defend against the forces that would bring down the barriers. You are destined to be the keeper of the peace, the protector of our way of life," Helios said.

"But why me? I never asked for this. What kind of keeper of peace will I be?" Benjamin said. "I just want to go back to living my nice normal life—well kind of normal life. I want to go back to making dead frogs move. I want to go back to watching my younger brothers levitate cars around the room." Helios raised an eyebrow at that, and Benjamin pulled out the car from his pocket. "Toy cars. You know, like Matchbox."

Helios smiled. "There's nothing that says you can't still enjoy life. Just think of it as having a higher purpose, a goal to work toward. I wouldn't advise scaring human girls with dead frogs, but that's for your mother and father to decide. Your real mother and father. Now what else did you want to know?"

"How will I find my brothers if no one can tell me where they are?" Benjamin asked.

"Only you will know that," Helios said.

"And what about the keys?" Benjamin asked. "How do they fit into all this?"

"We must assume that once the prophecy was foretold, the Emerald Tablet determined you were to become the keeper of the keys. As you now know, they are powerful telemagnifiers. They will aid you when they are needed," Helios said.

"So the memory I had at the ability trials was real after all," Benjamin said. "Remember when Andreas Matthias performed at the end?"

"Andreas Matthias may not be performing for a few years," Helios replied. "Mind control is very serious. But yes, I would be willing to bet that whatever you saw at the trials was a true memory."

He smiled at Benjamin. "You are strong; that much is evident. Your parents love you, as do your brothers and sister."

Benjamin looked surprised.

"Are you so surprised that I would know anything about you, Benjamin Holt?" Helios asked.

"Well, yeah, kind of," Benjamin replied. "I mean, you are the ruler of Lemuria and all."

"One of the rulers," Helios said. "And you are the champion of the Emerald Tablet. That is no light task. And now, we must think about being on our way. The hour is late, and we will have been missed."

And as Always, Life Must Go On

Heidi, Iva, Gary, and Andy nearly fell out of their seats when Benjamin walked into homeroom Saturday morning.

"What happened?" Heidi asked, jumping up. "I lost contact with you."

"Yeah, and Jack couldn't find you either," Gary asked. "He tried to teleport to Shambhala but couldn't."

"We thought you might be dead," Iva added.

Through the Alliance bond, Benjamin felt the concern of his friends. His true friends. Feeling their thoughts made him happy, and a smile crept onto his face. Whatever lay ahead, he wasn't going to be alone.

Heidi gave Benjamin her telepathy look. "You found the third key, didn't you?" she asked. "But where is it? Where are they?"

"Are you reading my mind, Heidi?" But he wasn't angry; he was just trying to ignore the story Helios had told him, trying to block it out of his mind so she wouldn't be able to see it. He'd tell it when he was ready. He felt her touch his mind, but quickly back away, seemingly sensing his desire for privacy.

Iva could hardly contain her excitement, which was saying a lot for Iva. "You found it! You got the third key? Are you sure? You really have all three of them now?"

"Yes. Well, no. Well, kind of," Benjamin replied.

Benjamin looked over to the table where Ryan and Jonathan sat. They were staring opened-eyed at him.

"*I think we should lower our voices,*" Benjamin thought.

"So it was in Shambhala?" Iva asked.

"Exactly," Benjamin replied.

"And you actually teleported yourself there?" Andy asked. "Do you realize how cool that is?"

"Pretty cool," Benjamin replied. "I mean one minute I was sitting there thinking about it, and the next thing I knew I was there—well almost there. I still had to find the secret entrance."

"Secret entrance?" Gary said.

"And what do you mean, you kind of have the keys?" Heidi asked.

Benjamin explained about how he had been unable to remove the keys from the pedestal. How one of his brothers would have to be there also.

"What brothers?" Andy asked. "Derrick and Douglas?"

"Not quite," Benjamin replied.

Just then Proteus Ajax walked into the room and called the class to order.

"I'll fill you guys in on everything after class. All right?"

Benjamin said.

"Yeah," Andy said.

They walked to the front of the room and took their seats. With everything else which had happened, Benjamin found he really didn't care much about his ability test results. He'd been tested enough.

But the grades turned out okay. To his credit, the first thing Proteus did was deliver them. There were no real surprises. And nobody flunked. Not even Heidi or Gary in telekinesis. Of course, they only advanced one year, but both seemed thrilled with the results.

"I knew I did well on my Telekinesis exam," Gary said.

"You did?" Andy asked.

"Yeah. I had to move one thousand pieces of paper, one at a time," Gary explained.

"All you had to do was move paper for your exam?" Andy asked. "You deserve to flunk."

Gary smiled as if he'd been complimented, causing Andy to shake his head with frustration.

Nobody was surprised when Gary got placed in Year Four Science, Iva in Year Four Telegnosis, and Heidi in Year Four Telepathy. Benjamin felt Andy's pride when he found out he'd move ahead to Year Four Telekinesis, but it soon was replaced by jealousy when he found out Benjamin would be right there with him.

Though he wasn't the best in everything, Benjamin couldn't help being pleased with his results. Level Three for Science and Telepathy. Level Four for Teleportation and Telekinesis.

He couldn't have cared less about only moving to Level Two for Telegnosis.

"Are you any good at science?" Andy asked. "How come you moved to Year Three?"

"Well, I did heal two broken leg bones during the ability test," Benjamin answered.

"Broken leg bones," Heidi exclaimed. "What kind of test did you take? All I had to do was grow my hair red." She tossed her hair around, showing off her long red locks. She, too, had been placed in the Year Three Science class.

"All you had to do was grow your hair?" Benjamin said, raising his voice. "Some old hag knitted away on a sweater while I lay in a pit in horrible pain, trying to heal my leg that had gotten broken when I fell into the pit."

"Well, if it makes you feel any better, I had to grow back my fingernail on my left pinkie," Gary said.

"No, actually that doesn't make me feel any better, Gary," Benjamin said. "My leg is still sore from the break."

"Well, so is my fingernail," Gary said. "It's not fun having it pulled out you know."

"You had it pulled out?" Heidi asked.

"Well, no, the grader actually teleported it out, but it still hurt," Gary confessed.

With the results delivered, homeroom turned into chaos. Proteus cleared his throat multiple times, but it took him blackening the room before the students finally settled down.

"Before I can dismiss you for the day, there are just a few basics to go over," Proteus began once everyone was quiet.

Andy rolled his eyes. "What now?" Benjamin knew that Andy, like himself, was probably itching for homeroom to be done so they could enjoy the rest of their day.

"When you arrive at summer school next year, you may or may not have me as a homeroom teacher," Proteus said. "You'll also be required to take one elective. This does not include an additional recreational activity. Use your sheaves, which you are free to take home, to review the electives and activities offered over the next year."

"And also a word of caution. Please practice over the year. But only practice in the privacy of your own homes. The fact that you are now old enough to know about Lemuria only makes it more important for you to always keep your abilities secret."

With thinking about home and thinking about his family, Benjamin finally started to relax. He tried not to think about what Helios had told him. He had the whole year ahead to think about his parentage, to ask his parents about it. There would be plenty of time for that.

Sunday morning came around quickly. Benjamin hurried to pack his bag, excited to see his parents, Derrick and Douglas, and little Becca.

They had agreed to meet Iva and Heidi for breakfast before heading for the main atrium teleporters. Benjamin didn't eat much and noticed that his friends didn't either. Everyone was looking forward to going home.

Yesterday, Benjamin had explained to Andy, Gary, Iva,

Heidi, and Jack everything that had gone on during his trip to Shambhala. Andy couldn't believe Mr. Burton had turned out to be evil, trying to bring down the shields.

"Are you sure it was really Mr. Burton," Andy had asked.

"Yeah, it was him," Benjamin replied. "He said he'd been watching me my whole life."

"Sounds kind of creepy to me," Heidi said, shivering.

"Yeah, it was," Benjamin agreed. He was still trying not to think too much about everything. He knew what had to be done. All he had to do to keep the shields from coming down around Lemuria and Atlantis was find his two brothers. Shouldn't be too hard, should it? But even he had a hard time believing himself.

"So, where do you think your brothers are?" Gary asked.

"I don't know," Benjamin admitted. "You'd think I'd have some sort of idea or something."

"Maybe you should focus on practicing your telegnostic powers over the next year," Iva suggested. "It might help you to locate them."

"Maybe," Benjamin said, "but how do I practice?"

"Well, I'll see what I can do," Iva said. "We can talk on the telecom. Proteus did say we could use them."

Benjamin noticed that Andy looked up at the mention of Iva talking to Benjamin, but didn't say a word.

They finished eating and began the long walk toward the main atrium. Their bags had already been taken to the tele-porters via the luggage terminals.

"So, maybe we can all get together over Christmas break

or spring break or something," Heidi suggested.

"Yeah, that's a great idea," Gary said. "We should ask our parents right away so we can make plans."

"Cool," Andy said. "We could try to meet here."

They reached the main atrium and got into a line for one of the teleporters.

"Well, I guess it's goodbye then," Benjamin said when it was his turn to depart.

"Not really," Andy said, laughing, stepping back from the teleporter. Benjamin noticed that as Andy stepped away, he moved closer to Iva.

"You know, you can call any time you want," Heidi said.

"Yeah, let us know how you're doing," Gary agreed.

"I'll be waiting to hear from you," Iva said, "and, if I don't, you better have a pretty good reason for it."

"Hurry, hurry, hurry," the teleporter operator said to Benjamin. "We don't have all day, now do we?" Benjamin turned to look at the man. It was the same old man with the super-sized ears who'd greeted him when he first arrived in Lemuria eight weeks earlier. A lot had happened since then. Benjamin felt older, more responsible.

"Oh, sorry," Benjamin said. "I'm not trying to hold up the line. I'm just saying goodbye."

"Goodbye?" the man said. "But you'll be seeing your friends in no time at all."

"In no time at all?" Benjamin said. "I may not see them until next summer. That's forty-four weeks away."

"Sonny, when you get to be my age, forty-four weeks is no

time," the man said.

Benjamin stepped up onto the teleporter pad. His suitcase arrived just as he did. He reached down, picked it up, then turned back and smiled. He waved a final goodbye just as the teleporter operator punched in the code for his home.

Whatever lay ahead, Benjamin wasn't sure. But there was one thing he did feel sure about—he would have friends by his side. Friends who would support him and help him. Friends who would be there for him. Summer school may not have been what Benjamin had planned for the summer; but now, with all that had happened, he could hardly wait until next year.

Author Acknowledgements

To Riley for giving me the opportunity to write night after
night...
To Zachary and Lola for providing inspiration with every
word and action...
To Mom and Dad for giving me a love of the unknown and a
great education...
To Carla for listening to all my crazy writing ideas and offer-
ing helpful feedback...
And to Madeline for brilliant editing...
Thank you!